TROUBLE IN TAMPA

TROUBLE IN TAMPA

AN OLIVER REDCASTLE HISTORICAL MYSTERY

LOUISE TITCHENER

LOUISE TITCHENER

Redcastle

Published by Kindle Direct Publishing

ISBN 978-0-999-899-3-0-4

Typesetting services by BOOKOW.COM

ACKNOWLEDGMENTS

Cover Art by Carey Abbott

Epigraph

Dear Reader, if you enjoyed this story, please post a review on my Amazon page. Thanks in advance, Louise Titchener

CHAPTER ONE

1885: twenty miles from Tampa on the last leg of Henry Plant's newly constructed Jacksonville, Tampa & Key West railway.

The train screeched to a halt. Passengers thumped to the floor. A woman screamed as she tumbled off a bench, and her feathered hat slid down over her nose. Oliver Redcastle had been watching two boys toss apples at a gator on the riverbank. Caught off guard by the sudden stop, he jammed his shoulder into the back of the bench in front of him. Nursing his arm, and wondering whether he'd broken a bone, he pulled himself to his feet. Two men cradling shotguns crashed through the door into the car and stationed themselves at the head of the aisle.

"Settle down, folks. This ain't a robbery. We're lookin' for an escaped criminal. Be quiet, and we won't trouble you."

They were both in shirtsleeves and suspenders, their faces flushed and sweaty. The speaker, a short man with a wiry build, wore a broad felt hat pulled low over his forehead. His cohort, a muscular six-footer, stalked down the walkway. At intervals he steadied his gun on his forearm and stopped to look closely into the faces of passengers still scrambling for their benches.

He halted to stare at Oliver. Of a similar height and physique, the two men stood eye to eye. The intruder's pale blue gaze drilled into Oliver's steady gray one. "Why ain't you sitting down like you were told, Mister?"

"What's this about?"

"Sure as hell ain't about you, Yankee. So mind your business."

Before Oliver could get another word out, a hand came down hard onto his injured shoulder. As it dragged him back into his seat, he turned to find a stranger's face inches from his. The man's narrowed brown eyes sparked a warning.

A commotion burst out at the other end of the car. Both armed intruders galloped down the aisle. A woman screamed, and a male voice yelled for help. "I'm Innocent! Kidnapped!" The stranger pressing Oliver to his seat leaned closer. He hissed, "If you value your life stay put, and keep your mouth shut."

"What's going on?"

"Nothing worth getting your head blown off for."

The sounds of struggle at the back end of the car grew louder and more violent. Oliver tried to look, but the stranger tightened his hold. Oliver struck out and yanked himself free. When he got up and turned, he glimpsed a pair of sockless white ankles. They disappeared as the armed intruders dragged a man's kicking body off the train.

Oliver started toward the doors when once again the stranger slammed him into his seat. Furious, he confronted the man.

"Lay a hand on me again and I'll break it!"

"Is that so? Well now, is that any way to talk to a Good Samaritan?"

"Meaning what?"

"Only an ignorant fool Yankee wouldn't know. Railroad men rounding up work gang escapees ain't polite. Interfere with them, and they'll shoot you dead. You being a meddling northerner, they'd enjoy pulling the trigger."

Like a sleepy dragon jolting to life, the train began to creep forward. Oliver shot a rueful glance toward the back of the car. He judged it already too late to do anything about what had occurred. Nor was he sure that he should. After all, William

Walters hadn't sent him to the south to interfere with local law enforcement—if that's what he had seen.

The other passengers seemed to have no trouble putting the incident from their minds. A motherly woman in charge of three youngsters opened a picnic basket. Behind her an elderly gentleman adjusted his neck cloth as he carried on an animated conversation with his plump wife.

Oliver rubbed his sore arm and turned to the man who was now bending to rescue his crumpled hat from the floor.

"I still don't understand what happened."

The man rested the hat on his round belly with one hand and steadied himself on the swaying train with the other. "All I can tell you is that the fella' those two deputies drug away was either a convict or a debt peon."

"Debt peon?"

"Mister, you're in the south. Around these parts folks who don't pay their bills wind up on a work gang. How do you think Henry Plant put the railroad through this jungle? Not by throwing a tea party for the local darkies."

"The man who just got dragged away wasn't a negro."

"No, that's why I say he was a debtor, or a foreigner who answered the wrong call for employment. Either way, there's nothing you or I can do for him."

Oliver regarded the speaker. His gray handlebar moustache framed his small mouth. His fringe of gray hair brushed a sweat stained collar. He inclined his head. "Wendell C. Hartley at your service."

"Oliver Redcastle."

"Pleased to meet you, Redcastle. Guess I riled you just now. Believe you me, it was for your own good!"

"If you say so."

"Well, I do say so. I know what I'm talking about. You didn't even realize I was sitting behind, did you? Before this ruckus started you was a million miles away staring out the window."

Oliver shrugged. That was true.

Hartley nodded. "I been in the cab up front. It got so infernal hot I thought I'd see if I could catch a breeze back here. I'd just set myself down when those two fellas stopped the train."

They were both silent, eyeing each other. Hartley broke the awkwardness. "Going to Tampa on business or pleasure?"

"A little of both." That wasn't true. Oliver didn't expect to get any pleasure from this trip.

"Me, strictly business. I don't travel otherwise. Travel don't suit my constitution the way it did when I was young." He winked. "I sure detect from your accent you ain't from anywhere near here."

"Baltimore."

"Baltimore?" Hartley's eyebrows jumped up. "Now what kind of business would bring a Baltimore man to Tampa? Bet it has something to do with this new railroad of Plant's."

"Maybe."

Hartley chuckled. "Half the people on this train wouldn't be in Florida otherwise. Thanks to Henry Plant northerners can escape from snow and ice in comfort."

"If you call this comfort," Oliver said, raising his voice over the clack of the rails, "and if northerners want to come to Tampa."

"You ever been there?"

"Never."

"Thought not. Well it ain't much now. From what I hear, Plant reckons to turn what used to be a sleepy fishing village into paradise on earth. He even plans to build a grand hotel the likes of which will stun even a sophisticated fella' like yourself. Tampa's going to become a regular seventh heaven."

"How heavenly is it now? I'm going to be spending several days there."

Hartley shrugged. "Any place where it don't snow ought to be paradise for a northerner this time of year. As for myself, I don't plan to linger."

"But Tampa is the end of the line."

"For Henry Plant's train, not for me. Now, if you don't mind, I think I'll head back to the front car. It's no cooler here than it was up there. In fact, I'd say it's hot as hell back here."

CHAPTER TWO

WENDELL C. Hartley pushed through the car's vibrating door. When he was out of sight, Oliver glanced around. All the other passengers had settled back into the routine of travel. Three blond youngsters wolfed down sandwiches from their mother's picnic basket. Several other people had opened box lunches. An old woman wearing a pancake hat with a veil that covered her nose, dozed. Her head lolled back and forth like a mechanical doll's.

Oliver turned back to his own troubling thoughts. Could it be February? He gazed at the thick greenery streaming past his window. Blinding sun knifed through the encroaching tangle of trees and vines. It was as if the train and its passengers were being swallowed into an endless maw of tropical vegetation. He closed his eyes and breathed in the sticky, pine-scented air. He had sworn never to come back to this land. Yet here he was, captive on a train twisting into the bowels of the south.

He pictured the wintry dawn in Baltimore less than a week ago when all this had started. A messenger had knocked at Oliver's door. Stamping snow from his boots, he'd handed an envelope to Mrs. Milawney. "Note from Mr. William Walters to Mr. Oliver Redcastle. I'm to wait for a reply."

Duly impressed, for everyone knew that William Walters was one of the richest men on the East Coast, Mrs. Milawney had brought the letter to the kitchen. Oliver, who had been dozing over his breakfast, opened it. "To hell with him. I'm finished dancing to the tune of men stuffed with money!" He had dropped the communication on the floor.

"Oh sir, but you must!" Mrs. Milawney retrieved the message and smoothed it against her apron. "I'm only the housekeeper, and it ain't my place to tell my employer what to do. But, oh, think of that poor little mite upstairs struggling to catch a breath."

Sighing, Oliver pictured his nine-year-old daughter as he'd last seen her, unconscious with exhaustion. "How is Chloe doing now?"

"Still got her pretty eyes closed, thank the good Lord. Oh Sir, I know you're tired. We're both tired after spending the night boiling water for steam just to help her get a breath."

Sleep. Right now all he wanted was a decent night's sleep.

Mrs. Milawney patted his shoulder. "Think of what the doctor said. This ain't the climate for Chloe. She needs to go west where the air is dry and clean. She was breathing good last summer when she and I was in Arizona."

Oliver sighed again. He'd beggared himself borrowing money to pay for his daughter's summer out west. The doctor had been right about the dry desert climate. It had improved Chloe's health, and Mrs. Milawney had liked the open spaces. Since returning to Baltimore his housekeeper had harped on taking the child to Arizona permanently.

He said, "Moving will mean selling here and starting new. It won't be easy."

"It will take money. And don't I know that money is in short supply?" She handed the note back to Oliver, "I've got eyes, and I know for a fact you haven't had a good paying case in weeks. Go and hear what William Walters has to say. Maybe he wants to hire you. Maybe he'll pay you smart enough so you can do something for your little girl."

Oliver had swallowed his pride. He had pulled on his boots and slogged through the ice and snow to Walters' townhouse in fashionable Mount Vernon Square. That's why, a week later, he was on a train headed to Florida, the last place on earth he wanted to go.

CHAPTER THREE

THE sun was low when Oliver stepped off the train in Tampa. He looked around, taking a moment to appreciate the dreaming beauty of the Hillsborough river edging the tracks. No alligators in sight, though they might lurk beneath the surface.

Turning, he caught sight of Wendell C. Hartley hurrying off as if he had a vital appointment. Hartley disappeared behind the loading warehouse, and Oliver shrugged. Most likely, he'd never to see the man again. A few minutes later he approached a cart driver pulled up in the shade of a live oak draped with beards of gray Spanish moss. Both he and his bony horse appeared half asleep.

"Can you take me to the Palmetto Hotel?"

The driver, a handsome, dark skinned fellow, opened his eyes, shook himself awake, and agreed to the fare. After Oliver had climbed up beside him, he urged his sorry looking horse into a slow walk. He said, "That Palmetto is brand, spanking new and the fanciest hotel in town."

It was also the hotel where an employee of William Walters named Ruben Spooner had stayed. Walters, an investor in the PICO Investment Company which had financed Plant's newly completed Jacksonville, Tampa and Key West Railroad, had sent Spooner to Tampa. He was to look at the operation of the newly minted rail line and report back. But Spooner had never reported back.

Members of his family had traveled to Tampa searching for him. When they'd failed to find Spooner, they'd appealed to William Walters. He'd commissioned Oliver to track the missing man down, or find out what had happened.

As the cart rolled toward town, the driver introduced himself as Rigo Alvarez. Rigo began commenting on the passing scene. "You being a northerner, you might not know that tree over there to the right. Don't look like much, but it's key lime. They say the Spanish brought it here. It's hard peeling but great in pies. My woman loves it."

A cow meandered into the road, and Rigo reined in. Cursing at the animal which appeared to be settling in for a long stay, he jumped down and whipped it out of the way. When he returned to the cart, Oliver asked if cows wandering into the road were a common occurrence.

"Nobody fences in these parts. So long as you got your mark on an animal—cow, pig or chicken, it's yours no matter whose grass fills its belly."

"Some people might find that annoying."

Rigo picked at his teeth. "Some people do. Mostly nobody cares."

The Palmetto was an attractive structure with a two-story porch attached to a tall tower. A gingerbread mansard roof topped its widow's walk. It dominated the corners of Polk and Florida streets, two broad dirt lanes that appeared deserted. "Quiet part of town," Oliver commented as he alighted from the cart.

"Not for long," Rigo said. Another couple of years you northerners will be swarming our little town like bees in honey."

"Sounds as if you think that'll be good."

"Be mighty good for me. Man's gotta' feed his young'uns."

"How many children do you have?"

Holding the reins in one hand, Rigo started counting on the other, his expression bemused. "Eight last I looked."

Oliver raised his eyebrows. "Can't be easy, supporting such a large family on fares from this cart."

"My woman raises vegetables and sells lunchtime food. I preach. We get along."

Oliver glanced at Rigo's fine-looking profile. Despite his threadbare clothing and humble cart, he radiated the self-confidence of a man happy with himself and his life. "You're a preacher?"

"I am." Rigo chuckled. "And a mighty good one when the spirit moves me."

"I believe it. My father was a preacher. It's not an easy life. At least, it wasn't for him. Where's your church? I'd like to hear your message."

"Oh, I ain't got a church. When I get the itch to preach the word, I travel. You'd be surprised how many people hiding out in the piney woods around here need a good spirit talk."

Oliver would have liked to hear more about the people hiding in the woods and what they needed. But Rigo's horse, bitten by a particularly aggressive fly, had begun to stamp his feet. Oliver dug deep into his pocket and handed Rigo a large tip. "Buy your little ones a treat."

Rigo lifted his straw sombrero and grinned. "That's mighty fine. My little ones can use a treat. You ever need a favor, I'm your man. Remember that. I'm a man of my word. I ain't just talking."

Oliver watched Rigo drive away and wondered if he'd meant what he'd said. If things didn't go well down here, Oliver might need a favor.

Inside the hotel's lobby, he stood for a moment taking in the quiet, lazy warmth of the high-ceilinged room. He breathed in deeply, smelling the scent of flowers edged with a hint of mold. Shutters screened the tall windows from the late afternoon sun. Potted palms on either side of the doorway cast slatted shadows on the polished wood floor. A man with slicked hair and a dark moustache sat in an armchair smoking a cigar. He glanced up from his newspaper and tracked Oliver's progress to a mahogany reception desk. Behind it a clerk dozed with his arms folded over his belly. His eyes popped open when Oliver hit the bell.

"Staying long?" he asked when Oliver requested a room.

"No more than a week." At least, that's what he hoped.

"Long enough. You want to pay now?"

"I'll pay when I leave."

"You'd better. We don't take to debtors around here."

Shrugging, Oliver signed the register, then flipped it back two pages.

"Hey now, that's not allowed!"

Ignoring the clerk's protest, Oliver pointed to a signature. "I see a friend of mine, Ruben Spooner, stayed here a couple of months ago."

The clerk squinted at the signature and shrugged. "What of it?"

"Do you remember him?"

"If I remembered all the people who stayed here, I could join the circus."

Oliver held up a tintype Spooner's sister had given him. "Fortyish, medium height, dark hair. Came from Baltimore. Some of his folks were here looking for him a few weeks back."

The clerk squinted at the image. "Now I recall. They were mighty persistent. Asked a lot of questions. All I could tell them was he left without paying his bill. Seeing as he's your friend, maybe you'd like to pay it for him?"

Ignoring the suggestion, Oliver replied, "That doesn't sound like Ruben. I'm worried he might have met with an accident. Did he leave anything behind? Clothing? Personal items?"

"Like I told his folks, not so far as I know. Ask Rosella, here. She cleans the rooms. She'll show you to yours."

Oliver turned to find a dark-eyed young woman sauntering toward him. Her shapeless maid's uniform didn't disguise her lush figure and pretty face. She stopped a few feet away and smiled beguilingly, her shapely lips pink against velvety skin the color of milky coffee. "You like I take your bag?"

Oliver assured her that he could carry his own carpetbag. He spent an enjoyable few minutes admiring her as he followed her back across the lobby and up the staircase to the second floor. Despite the distraction of Rosella's gracefully swaying hips, he was aware of the curious gaze of the man in the armchair. At the top of the staircase he paused and looked down. The man took a cigar out of his mouth, tapped it against the armrest, and returned his attention to his paper.

"Who is the gentleman in the white linen suit?"

Rosella cocked her lovely head. "Oh, that's Senor Ybor."

"Cuban?"

"He's American now. He has a cigar factory in Key West. They're saying he might move his business here to Tampa."

"Who's saying that?"

"Oh, just people. You hear things when you work in a hotel."

"I bet you do." Oliver took a silver dollar out of his pocket and offered it to her. "Do you remember a man named Ruben Spooner. He was a guest here a couple of months back?"

Her hand was out for the coin. But when she heard the name Ruben Spooner, she snatched it back. The smile disappeared, and her eyes went blank. "I don't remember anyone by that name, sir. Here's your room." She unlocked a door, opened it, and stood back. "We serve breakfast at eight. Is there anything else I can help you with?"

Oliver shook his head and watched thoughtfully as she hurried away, her hips no longer swaying quite so seductively.

CHAPTER FOUR

THE next morning Oliver made his way to the docks. Unlike the sleepy lanes around his hotel, Tampa's waterfront bustled. Vessels crowded the wooden piers.

Four- masted schooners tied side by side vied for space with steamships and smaller sailing craft. Stevedores groaned and shouted as they unloaded cargo and carted it to a ramshackle warehouse area.

Pausing at the water's edge, Oliver inhaled humid air flavored with the scent of shellfish and rotting wood. A dead mullet caught in a web of seaweed sloshed against a piling. Pelicans wheeled overhead, disappearing into the glare of the morning sun.

Nearby a small steamer named *Gypsy Dancer* edged between several small craft loaded with pineapples, bananas and strings of fresh caught kingfish, grouper and tarpon. Oliver's eyes narrowed as he studied the rakish angle of Gypsy's twin smokestacks. She was a long, low, lead-colored vessel. He considered her convex forecastle deck extending aft, nearly as far aft as the waist—placed there to force through and not over heavy waves. Old memories stirred. He knew this ship.

She looked old because she was, he realized. These days she might be plying the waters of southern Florida carrying passengers from Key West. But she'd once been a blockade runner, famous for her speed. He knew because he'd been a sharpshooter on a Union vessel chasing her through the fog in hopes of drawing a bead on her daring captain. Where was that captain now, he wondered

Gypsy Dancer docked and a few minutes later began disgorging passengers. Women carrying parasols against the sun held small children by the hand. A man in a Panama hat and white linen suit pushed an elderly woman in a wheeled chair. As he steered her onto dry land she waved a fan and chattered at him in high-pitched tones.

Oliver wondered what their purpose in Tampa might be. Did they have relatives here? Were they planning to set up a business because of Plant's new railroad?

The crack of a bullet sent the gulls and pelicans into a panic. The old woman in the chair screamed, and one of the men stepping onto the dock from the ship slumped against a piling. Oliver caught sight of a puff of smoke at the side of a warehouse nearby and sprinted toward it.

As he rounded the building's corner, he spotted a man throwing his rifle into a cart. Oliver made a dash for the cart, but he wasn't fast enough. The man leapt into the seat and whipped his horse into a gallop. Seconds later the wagon vanished down a dusty lane.

A voice at Oliver's shoulder asked, "Who was he? Did you see?"

Oliver turned. A stocky young Negro in a rumpled suit stood with his broad chest heaving.

"I only caught a glimpse of the shooter, but I've seen him before."

"Where?"

"Yesterday, on the train. He told me his name was Wendell C. Hartley."

"Hartley?" The young man shook his head. "Means nothing."

"No and probably isn't his real name. I wonder why he took a pot shot at the gent leaving the steamer. How is the poor fellow? I hope he wasn't injured."

"I don't know. When I heard the shot and saw Jose Marti fall, I followed you to catch the villain. I wasn't quick enough. I'm no runner."

"Marti? You know the man who was attacked?"

"I'm here to fetch him from the boat. He's to be my guest."

"Then we'd better see what we can do for him."

As the two hurried back to the scene of the violence, the young man introduced himself as Ruperto Pedroso and gave his particulars. Oliver had already realized from his accent that he was not an American Negro. Pedroso had emigrated from Cuba. He told Oliver that he and his wife, Paulina, ran a boardinghouse on the corner of 8th Avenue and 13th Street.

"And Marti is Cuban also?"

"Oh yes, a patriot of rare courage. He's here to raise support for our cause."

"What cause is that?"

Pedroso looked surprised by the question. "Why, to win our freedom from the Spanish rule that oppresses us. We Cubans yearn for our freedom just as you *Norte Americanos* yearned for yours. Praise God, one day we'll be successful, too."

When they arrived at the scene of the shooting, they found Jose Marti on a bench. A handsome Negress was pressing a wet cloth to his forehead. She stepped back when Pedroso rushed up and asked Marti about his condition.

When Marti replied in Spanish, Pedroso translated for Oliver's benefit, "He says it's only a nick on his arm. The shooter missed his mark. He's shocked, but otherwise fine."

"He doesn't look fine to me." Nor did he sound fine. Marti waved his hands about and gabbled Spanish curses, clearly enraged by what had happened to him. Oliver muttered in Pedroso's ear, "He should see a doctor."

Marti refused this suggestion vehemently. He struggled to his feet with the help of the black woman. He was a small, slender man with a bush of dark hair. His moustache covered his upper lip and bracketed his mouth almost to his chin. Marti had removed his white jacket. A spot of blood stained the sleeve of his shirt.

Pedroso, muttering soothing words in Spanish, took his arm and directed the woman to secure their cart. After bidding Oliver a distracted farewell, he and Marti headed off.

Oliver watched them for several minutes. The oddity of his encounters with Wendell C. Hartley struck him. He had not taken the brash man on the train for an assassin. He had dismissed him as someone he would never see again. Now, that had changed. Now he had a gut feeling he and Hartley would meet—and that when they did he'd better be prepared.

Could Hartley have anything to do with the disappearance of Reuben Spooner? That seemed unlikely. But then so did what had just happened. He heard a splash and turned his head but saw only a faint ripple on the dark surface of the river.

CHAPTER FIVE

O LIVER spent another quarter of an hour exploring the waterfront and then walked into Plant's headquarters. The building sat close to the area where carpenters were hoisting beams and pounding nails into Plant's new waterfront hotel. Nearby, other workers were busy enlarging the piers and walkways, anticipating much greater traffic through Tampa to parts south.

Inside the headquarters, a young man, whose carroty hair gleamed with pomade, looked up from a telegraph key. "May I help you?"

"My name is Oliver Redcastle. I'm here to see Mr. Henry Haines."

"Mr. Haines is busy at the moment. Do you have an appointment?"

"I have a letter of introduction from one of your investors, Mr. William Walters. He contacted Mr. Haines to let him know I would be paying him a visit."

The redhead gazed at the signature on the letter for several seconds, then rose and disappeared behind a door to the rear of his desk. Oliver looked around the outer office. It was almost as hectic as the waterfront. Telegraph keys clacked. Men in shirtsleeves hurried in and out carrying rolls of what looked like architectural drawings. Clerks scribbled schedule changes on a blackboard. Minutes later they erased them and scribbled new numbers. The constant hum from all this activity sounded like bees in a hive.

Finally, the young gatekeeper emerged. "Mr. Haines will receive you now. Please come with me."

Inside the office Oliver saw two men, both in shirtsleeves rolled to the elbows and light colored pants held up by suspenders. The fair-haired younger of the two sprawled in a swivel chair, his booted feet crossed at the ankle. A wrinkled but expensive looking linen jacket hung from the back of his chair. He straightened when Oliver entered the room. The older man, dark haired and mustachioed, stood behind the large oak desk that dominated the office. He leaned over the desk with his hand outstretched and introduced himself as Henry Haines.

Oliver shook his hand. He had done his homework and knew that Henry Haines had supervised the building of Plant's railroad. It had been a formidable undertaking. He'd had to oversee the laying of over seventy miles of track through the sub-tropical forests and swamps of central Florida. And he'd had to do it in record time. Oliver also knew that Haines had been a colonel in the Confederate army. So at one time he and Haines had been mortal enemies.

The man in the chair was unknown to Oliver. Haines introduced him as Lawrence Thomas, a junior surveyor. He was boyishly handsome and obviously well aware of the fact. Tall and blessed with an athletic build, he lounged with the confidence of a sleepy Adonis

After Oliver explained his reason for coming to Tampa, Haines gazed back at him with a troubled expression. "I have to tell you the same thing I told Spooner's family when they made inquiries a few weeks back. He never came to the office. We never met the man." Walters had sent Spooner to check up on the Tampa operation incognito. But the cat was out of the bag now. Spooner's family had already come to Tampa and made a ruckus.

"Spooner checked into the Palmetto Hotel. I'm staying there myself. I saw his signature on the registry."

"In that case, talk to the people at the hotel. They must know more about him than we do."

"Unfortunately, they claim not to. They say he stayed only one night and disappeared the next day without paying his bill."

Haines scratched his ear and directed his gaze to Thomas. "You know anything about this, Larry?"

Larry smirked. "Not me. It's a mystery, ain't it? Man comes here in secret. Don't bother to tell us what he's up to and vanishes into thin air. Could be a lot of things. Maybe he swam in the wrong pond and met a hungry gator. Maybe he ran off with someone's wife. Hope you haven't come all the way from Baltimore on a fool's errand, Mr. Redcastle."

"Spooner couldn't have vanished into thin air," Oliver said. "William Walters sent him here to have a look at his railroad investment. Something happened to him, and I'm here to find out what."

"I have the greatest respect for Mr. Walters," Haines declared, shooting Thomas a frown. "We all do. I know for a fact that he and Henry Plant are good friends. Mr. Plant would want us to give you all the help we can. That is what we'll do.

"Meanwhile, since you're new to town, I'd like to invite you to a small shindig my wife and I are throwing. It's tonight at the Hillsborough Hotel. It'll be dinner and a little dramatic performance. If you can come you'll meet some of the town's important people. They might know something we don't. They might help you complete your assignment."

A few minutes later Oliver left the railroad office. He had accepted Haines' invitation, though he suspected the "shindig" would require more formal dress than he possessed.

He thought for a moment about the two men he'd just met. Young Larry, Haines' handsome underling, was a puzzle. He didn't have the southern drawl Oliver had been expecting. He spoke with an eastern twang. Where did the swagger and ill-disguised hostility that rolled off him come from? Haines seemed more straightforward—a competent engineer who knew how to get things done, and who had no need for swagger.

The sun was high in the sky. Already Oliver could feel sweat slicking the inside of his hatband. His black suit felt travel-weary and inappropriate to the weather. It wouldn't do for a fancy dinner party. Should he acquire some lighter weight clothing that could pass muster? Distracted by this question, he looked up and caught sight of a figure that made him snap to attention.

A woman in a dark blue skirt and white shirtwaist stood on the edge of the dock. As she gazed down at the water, she twirled a parasol. Her back was to him, but her trim figure, and light brown coil of hair, looked familiar. It couldn't be, could it?

CHAPTER SIX

O LIVER said, "Hannah?" The woman turned. He studied the familiar pointed chin shadowed by the wide brim of her untrimmed straw hat. "Hannah Kinchman, is it really you?"

"So far as I can tell." Her dry tone confirmed her identity.

Oliver said, "It's been almost two years since you left Baltimore. I never expected to see you in Florida."

"I could say the same." She cocked her head. "I was going to remark that you haven't changed, but I think I see a few flecks of gray at your handsome temples. Of course, on you it looks good. What are you doing in Tampa, Oliver? Or shouldn't I ask?"

"Ask away. I think we both have questions."

"You're right. Let's discuss our answers over lunch." Hannah took his arm and led him to a picnic area across the road. A young Negress with a half dozen children for helpers had set up a stand selling a midday meal. As the children doled out food to a crowd of dockworkers, Oliver smiled down at Hannah. "Is this a respectable place to entertain a delicate young woman?"

Hannah chuckled. "A humorous question, since you know I'm neither delicate nor respectable, nor even young." She spread her skirts and dropped onto a rough bench with a view of the river. An old live oak with wide-spread branches offered shade—a relief from the Florida sun aflame overhead.

Oliver snaked his way through the crowd at the food stand. He returned a few minutes later balancing two cups of lemonade and a twist of paper stuffed with fried chicken and hot biscuits.

"Smells delicious," Hannah exclaimed. She watched as he sat down next to her and distributed their lunch on a pair of napkins. "Maizie is a fantastic cook."

"You eat here often?"

"Whenever I get the chance."

"An odd place for a woman to eat alone—a spot for hungry dockworkers."

Hannah looked up from the drumstick she was about to sample and licked the juice from one of her fingers. "What makes you think I eat here alone?"

"Let's stop fencing. You've been in Tampa long enough to get to know the locals. I doubt you're here on holiday. You must be on assignment from Pinkerton."

"I might be in a theatrical production."

"Are you?"

"No." She took off her hat and laid it on the bench.

For the first time Oliver could see the whole of Hannah's face. She looked older. The years were not treating her kindly. The new lines around her fine eyes, and threads of gray in her hair, were not surprising considering the difficulties of her life. She'd lost her family. Her actor husband had deserted her. She'd had to make her own way. Despite her resourcefulness, it couldn't have been easy.

Oliver said, "It's good to see you, Hannah. Since you left Baltimore, I've thought of you often. I had hoped we could be partners. If Pinkerton hadn't snatched you out from under my nose, we might be working together. Are you still with the outfit?"

"I am. But I was hardly 'snatched,' as you put it. William Pinkerton offered me a salary. As you must remember, I gave you the chance to do likewise. You weren't able to manage it. You know very well I couldn't afford to turn him down."

Oliver sighed. She was right, of course. When he'd proposed that Hannah stay in Baltimore and help him establish an agency, he hadn't been in a position to pay her. Impressed with her skills as an investigator and—if he were honest—intrigued by her personally, he'd offered her a partnership. Realistically, it had been a partnership in nothing

He bit into a biscuit, which was not soft and flaky like those he'd savored in Baltimore, but crisp and every bit as delicious. He swallowed and then nodded at her. "You were smart to go with Pinkerton. Even now my agency is barely scraping by. In fact, for the sake of my daughter's lungs, I'm thinking of relocating out west."

"I'm sorry to hear that Chloe is still suffering breathing problems. But then why are you here? You must be on a case. Who's the client?"

"William Walters."

She lifted an eyebrow. "The oh-so-rich William Walters? The man who made a fortune out of the war while gallivanting about in Europe collecting art?"

"The same. He sent me here to find an agent of his who disappeared. Name of Reuben Spooner. Ever hear of him?"

Hannah shook her head. "No, but if I do, I'll let you know."

She said that a little too quickly. Oliver wondered if she was telling the truth. Hannah was capable of deceiving him if she chose. She was a talented actress, and he had good reason to know she could lie. He said, "I'll do what I can to help you. What are you working on?"

Hannah avoided his gaze. "I'm not free to discuss it."

"Then let me guess. Does it have something to do with a Cuban named Jose Marti?

Hannah set her lemonade down on the bench and pushed it to one side. "How do you know about Marti?"

"I was only a few feet away when he was shot this morning. I saw the man who fired the rifle. In fact, the same man was sitting next to me on the train yesterday."

She stared. "You astonish me. Who was he?"

"He called himself Wendell C. Hartley. I doubt that's what's written on his birth certificate."

"You're right. If it's the same shooter I've been looking for, it isn't."

"Short, pot belly, gray handlebar moustache—sound right?"

She hesitated, then raised her hand to shade her eyes. "Sounds like my man. His real name is Chester Glass. He has an interesting history. Before the war he captained a slave ship making the run from Cuba. During the war he was a blockade runner smuggling supplies to the south from Cuba."

"Now?"

"Now he makes a living as a wrecker in Key West, operates a salvage yard and takes the occasional odd job. Currently, the odd job he's taken comes from his connections in Cuba. They hired him to relieve them of an irritant."

"An irritant named Marti?"

"Exactly. Glass is good at that sort of thing, removing irritants—though he bungled the job this morning." Hannah explained that officials in Washington, worried about Cuban revolutionaries making trouble on American soil, had hired Pinkerton to look into the matter. The agency had learned that Marti was about to visit the Pedrosos to raise money for the revolutionary cause. A possible attempt on his life was also in the wind. They had dispatched Hannah to Tampa to keep an eye on developments.

Oliver gazed out at the river, slick and green and dancing with reflected light from the powerful noonday sun. "I wonder what Glass was doing on a train coming from the north."

"I wonder the same. I expected him to arrive in Tampa off one of the ships from Key West. I've been here two weeks, boarding with the Pedrosos and haunting the docks. I knew Marti was due to arrive this morning. Glass fooled me. I never considered he'd come in from the north."

"Would you have tried to save Marti from Glass's bullet if you'd been on the scene?"

"I'm not here to be a bodyguard. Just to keep an eye on developments and report."

"I see. Do you think Glass will try to get at Marti again?"

She stood and brushed off her skirt. "He will if he wants to earn his pay. Which means I must get back to the boarding house and earn mine. Thanks for lunch, Oliver. It was good seeing you. Good luck with finding this Spooner fellow."

"Thanks. Shall I see you home?"

"I'd rather you didn't. If we're spotted together it might raise questions."

He nodded. "Will we meet again?"

"I wouldn't be surprised." She pulled her straw hat down over her forehead and snapped open her parasol. "Actually, these days nothing surprises me very much. Be advised, if you stay in Tampa, I think you'll be in for more surprises yourself." With that cryptic remark, Hannah turned and walked away.

CHAPTER SEVEN

OLIVER finished his lunch, tossing a few bits of bread and meat to the gulls. As he watched them snatch at the crumbs, he mulled over his meeting with Hannah. He knew from experience that she was a chameleon—able to be pretty or plain, young or old. Now, she had chosen to look like a spinster schoolmarm. Seeing her in her shirtwaist and unadorned hat, one might think she was an uncomplicated woman. That would be a mistake.

Oliver had met her trying her damnedest to put a bullet into him. At the time she'd blamed him for the death of her outlaw brother and wanted vengeance. She had come close to achieving her goal. After they'd resolved that issue, Hannah's courage, audacity, acting skills and uncanny talent for disguise had helped him unravel his first case in Baltimore.

He had a great deal of admiration for Hannah Kinchman, but they'd never been more than colleagues. From the first he'd sensed she wouldn't be receptive to any advances he might make. That wasn't because she was a cold woman. Quite the contrary. She could be passionate and immoral. She could also be as calculating as a banker arranging an eviction.

Oliver knew that, despite her independent airs, Hannah had adored her runaway husband. His abandonment, and the loss of her family, had wounded her. Perhaps that was true of everyone who had lived through the war. It had torn the country apart.

It had wreaked the same havoc on people, on their families, their friendships, their bodies, and their minds. Oliver pictured the cripples who clustered at train stations begging for a handout. He recalled the forgotten veterans who lived in attics, unable to face the world. The whole nation will stumble through the rest of life injured, he thought. And that, he acknowledged, included himself.

Oliver swallowed the last of his lemonade and looked around for transportation. Finding none, he headed back to town on foot. This was a mistake. He tried to keep to the shade of the palms and live oaks edging the road. But the afternoon sun overpowered him. He removed his jacket and loosened his collar.

The black bowler he had worn down from Maryland did not offer enough protection. He would need to purchase a hat with a wider brim. There was the dinner party tonight. Sweat drenched his only clean shirt. At the least, he'd have to buy new linen and get his jacket and trousers brushed out.

The few shops he passed were closed for the afternoon. He did not find a haberdashery open until he neared his hotel on Florida Street. He paused outside and studied the articles in the window. Everything looked too dear for his pockets. He was beginning to regret the large tip he'd handed to Rigo Alvarez. He couldn't afford such grand gestures.

Oliver moved on to the next window. It displayed children's clothing. He saw a blue dress that he was sure would look well with Chloe's auburn hair. He liked to bring his daughter little gifts when he traveled for his work. But a dress such as this would not be a little gift. It looked every bit as costly as the items in the men's haberdashery.

"Blue isn't your color, old chap. Wouldn't look well with that undertaker's suit you're wearing," a plummy voice teased.

Oliver turned and stared.

The handsome man standing a few feet away twirled a silver headed cane between his manicured hands and favored him with a slow wicked smile. "I knew our paths would cross again, though I never imagined it would be here. Charmed to see you, Ollie."

"My God, Gentleman Jake Jaggard!" Oliver took in the scarlet camellia protruding from Jake's lapel, and the John Bull hat adorning his pomaded curls. In the two years since they'd last met he'd acquired a moustache and small pointed beard.

He leaned in close and murmured, "I'm going by the name Sir John Jaggard. I'd appreciate it if you kept that in mind. After all, I saved your bacon back in Baltimore. You owe me."

"I owe you a trip to jail for robbing a bank under my nose. Since when did you become British aristocracy?"

"I've always been creative about identity, wouldn't you agree? After all, you are what you make of yourself. Speaking of which, I'm no longer a bank robber."

"Or a con man with a fake British accent?"

"Olly, you do me an injustice. I'm an investor."

"In what?"

"The best possible currency—hopes and dreams." Jake winked.

The door to the shop opened, and a young woman emerged. A slim gentleman carrying a package tied up in pink ribbons walked behind her. "Oh Jake," she cried in a sultry southern drawl, "Sir Harvey just bought such a darling outfit for little Mandy!" She paused, looking from Jaggard to Oliver and back. "Oh, silly me! You're talking to a friend and I'm interrupting. Do forgive me, gentlemen."

"Nothing to forgive, my dear lady. Mrs. Letitia Thomas, let me present Oliver Redcastle. Oliver, behold the treasure of Tampa, the delightful Mrs. Letitia Thomas. She is accompanied by my fortunate friend, Sir Harvey Lexton."

Oliver shook the Englishman's fine-boned hand and tipped his hat to Mrs. Thomas. She nodded her pretty head in gracious acknowledgement. He wondered if this was Lawrence

Thomas's wife. If so, Lawrence was a lucky man. With her dark curls, classic profile, and sparkling brown eyes, she was an appealing woman. She wore a straw hat like Hannah Kinchman's. Unlike Hannah's, feathers and pink velvet ribbons adorned it. The ribbons on her hat matched the velvet cinch that emphasized the curve of her tiny waist.

She peeped up at him through her lashes, a little half smile tugging at the corners of her full lips. The moment didn't last more than two seconds, but it left him feeling hot under the collar. As Jake, Sir Harvey and the adorable Mrs. Thomas strolled off, Oliver stood looking after them with knitted eyebrows. There was more to Letitia Thomas than pink ribbons and a southern drawl. What an odd coincidence that Hannah Kinchman and Jake Jaggard should show up in Tampa within hours of each other.

They had both been in Baltimore when he'd set up his investigation agency. Had they known each other? He wasn't sure. Was it a coincidence that they were here? Or was something going on that he hadn't yet understood? Shrugging because he couldn't answer the question, Oliver threw caution to the winds. He entered the shop and purchased a wide-brimmed slouch hat, two new shirts and the blue dress for Chloe.

Back at his hotel, he paused in front of his door. He smelled cigar smoke. Someone was in his room. He drew his revolver from the holster hidden inside his jacket, unlocked the door and stepped back as he threw it open.

"Finally. Where have you been, Ollie? I've been waiting an age!" Jake lounged in a chair near the window, one foot propped up on the desk, looking as if he owned the place.

"How did you get in here? Or is that a silly question to ask a professional thief?"

"It's a very silly question." Jake removed his feet from the desk. "You can put that firecracker away. I took the key off the hook at the front desk while the manager was visiting the loo.

Nothing could have been easier. In fact, you should complain about the hotel's security."

"I'll add that to my long list of other complaints." Oliver replaced his gun and tossed his packages onto the bed.

"I do hope you've been shopping for a decent suit. In that threadbare black outfit of yours you look like an out-of-work preacher."

"We can't all equal your sartorial splendor."

"True, but at the very least you can present a decent appearance. Look here, we're of a size. I'll lend you one of my suits."

"No thank you," Oliver replied tightly.

Jake shrugged his graceful shoulders and flicked an ash from his cigar. "Well, you always were a little too high-minded for your own good."

"High mindedness has never been one of your character flaws. What do you want, Jake? You didn't break into my room to counsel me on fashion."

"I thought we should have a chat, Oliver."

"About what?"

"About why we're both here. About how we can avoid stepping on each other's toes."

"I'm here on business."

"As am I. Does our business intersect?"

"I shouldn't think so. William Walters hired me to track down an employee he sent to Tampa. His name is Reuben Spooner. He's gone missing."

Jake smiled, but not with his eyes. "If that's true, we have no problems. I've never heard of Mr. Spooner. I wish you luck in your quest." He picked his hat off the desk and sauntered toward the door.

Oliver said, "Now that I've told you my business, you should return the favor. What is your connection with Sir Harvey Lexton, and how do you know Letitia Thomas?"

Jake looked back from the open door. He took the cigar out of his mouth and flashed an amused grin. "You're the detective, Oliver. You shouldn't have any trouble ferreting out the answers to those questions. I'll give you a head start. I'm here for reasons like yours. I'm here to locate something that's gone missing."

CHAPTER EIGHT

OLIVER arrived at the Hillsborough Hotel a few minutes late. He'd had to wait while the staff at the Palmetto dealt with his suit. He'd hoped to get help from the lovely Rosella, but she was nowhere to be found. So he'd relied on the half-hearted efforts of an aged laundress with a moth-eaten brush and a bottle of homemade spot remover. The result left much to be desired. At least his jacket wasn't obviously travel stained.

The Hillsborough was a square, three-story brick building with an impressive portico. It occupied a corner lot and took up a good third of the block. Many private carriages and carts for hire were pulled up outside, including Rigo Alvarez's wagon. After returning Rigo's salute, Oliver went inside.

A servant took his hat and directed him to the lobby where he was the last in the dwindling reception line. Henry Haines and his wife greeted him with smiles that couldn't be real. Nobody could stand for an hour shaking hands in this humidity and feel cordial. Even so, they both kept their artificial beams in place. "Glad you could make it to our little shindig, Redcastle."

"Looks like a mighty fancy shindig to me." Both Haines and his wife were dressed for a night at the opera. Mrs. Haines, an agreeably plump woman, wore a rope of pearls, and a fashionable egret feathered headdress. She carried a large ostrich feather fan which she waved constantly.

Colonel Haines, resplendent in a tailcoat, double vested waistcoat, and striped trousers, patted Oliver's back. "How's the investigation going?"

"Not much progress yet."

"Maybe one of our guests has seen your missing person. We've got about all Tampa's movers and shakers."

Glancing over Haines shoulder, Oliver saw the lobby had been set up for a large party. Garlands made of palm fronds and tropical flowers festooned the balustrades. Floral wreaths hung from white silk ribbons which encircled corner columns. The sound of polite chatter bounced off the ceiling.

The group gathered around the punch bowl at the far end of the room was dressed to impress. The men were in formal attire. The ladies wore gowns decorated with a frou frou of lacy petticoats, gossamer tulles, flounces and glittering jewelry.

Who were they, Oliver wondered. Railroad people? Men and women attracted by the promise of an economic boom? Most of the locals were homesteaders, fisherman and farmers. This crowd looked to have far more grandiose ambitions. The fluttering fans of the overdressed women made Oliver think of a flock of flamingoes anticipating flight. In his black suit, he felt like a crow among tropical birds.

He said "I can see that you're entertaining a very select group."

"Bankers, merchants, government officials—the fella over there in the corner talking with the redheaded twins is Arnold Pepperwhite."

Haines indicated a well set up man in a pearl gray tailcoat adorned with gleaming silk lapels. A large diamond stick pin sparkled from the nest of his sky blue pouf tie. Sporting a comb of taffy colored hair and a waxed moustache, he looked to be in his late forties. Oblivious to Oliver's scrutiny, he was carrying on an animated conversation. A pair of young redheaded girls dressed in matching white muslin party gowns hung on his words. Each wore a spray of lavender orchids in her hair. Both were smiling sweetly up into his flushed countenance.

Haines declared, "A lot of ambitious new men coming into Tampa. Pepperwhite is only one of many entrepreneurs. Our railroad has been likened to a fire breathing dragon. But it's a good dragon, breathing vitality into this sleepy part of the world."

"I'm sure it is," Oliver replied. "A railroad opens up all kinds of possibilities, good and bad."

Haines frowned. "True, but Pepperwhite's a real asset to the community. He's an investor with creative ideas and get-go. He's followed the railroad here because he's smart enough to see the opportunities it's going to inspire. He has a scheme to put up houses along the waterfront. Fine houses that will attract fine people. Matter of fact, he's the benefactor responsible for bringing in some theater folk to perform for us tonight. Come along and let me introduce you."

Oliver followed Haines into the room. But after the introduction, it became obvious that Arnold Pepperwhite had no interest in talking to a gaunt Yankee wearing an inappropriate suit. He took each of the young redheads by the arm and left Oliver standing alone.

He wandered further into the room. Three string players sat behind a bank of greenery playing softly. Long tables dressed with starched white cloths and flowered centerpieces took up a third of the tile floor. Opposite the tables, a stage had been erected in anticipation of some kind of performance. A bed draped with white satin sat in the middle.

As Oliver took in the scene, someone seized his arm. Startled, he turned to see Letitia Thomas grinning mischievously up at him. She wore pink. Fresh pink roses decorated her coiffure of puffs and ringlets. A velvet ribbon sewn with seed pearls circled her white throat.

"Aren't I clever to corner the handsomest man in the room?"

"You flatter me, Mrs. Thomas. But I believe your husband deserves that tribute." Oliver nodded in the direction of the punch bowl where he had spotted Lawrence Thomas. He and Henry Haines were in earnest conversation.

Letitia winked. "Do call me Letty. Yes, my Larry is handsome, isn't he? But not in your style. Something about those gray eyes of yours makes me think you can be dangerous. Am I right?"

"Never dangerous to women. That I promise."

"Now why don't I believe you? I think men like you are always dangerous to us poor women!" She glanced back at her husband. "Larry is only dangerous when he's got an oar in his hand. He was on the rowing team at Princeton. That's where we met. I had been invited to a dance by a fella who'd courted me back home. Poor little me! When I saw Larry winning his race in that darling outfit they wear, I knew I had to make him mine. Do you row, Mr. Redcastle?"

"Only when I must."

She laughed. "Well, until recently that was the one good thing about Tampa—plenty of water so Larry could indulge his favorite exercise." Her heart-shaped lips pouted, and she fluttered her long, dark lashes. "I swear, I just about died when I realized we were going to be marooned here. None of the locals did anything but fish and swat mosquitoes."

"You're a southerner. That's a Georgia accent I detect, isn't it?"

"It is. But Savannah is a very different matter from this wild Florida territory. When Larry and I arrived in this place we practically had to camp out with the alligators."

"But now things are looking up," Jake interjected in his fake British accent. He had come up behind them carrying a glass of punch which he handed to Letitia.

After taking a sip, she gave him a playful slap. "Oh, you vain creature. You mean that things are looking up because you're here. Well, of course we're delighted to have such distinguished visitors from abroad as you and Sir Harvey. But there's more to be happy about. Thank heaven, Tampa is not doomed to remain a cultural wasteland. We are so pleased to have a new theater company setting up in town."

"Are they to perform for us tonight?" Oliver asked.

"They are indeed. Isn't that exciting?"

"I'm looking forward to it," Oliver agreed.

"Larry tells me you're here to find a man named Spooner," Letty said.

"Yes, have you heard of him?"

"No, but somebody else may have. I'll introduce you to a few of the other guests." Jake headed toward the punch bowl, and Letty guided Oliver further into the room. "I know what it's like to be a stranger in a strange place."

"Do you?"

"Oh yes. You'd be surprised." She gazed up at him with an oddly intent expression in her dark eyes. Again, Oliver felt a flush welling up under his collar.

A half hour later dinner was announced and Oliver found himself sitting across from Sir Harvey Lexton. He was a good looking young man with an Oxford accent and the confident air that went along with it. His sand-colored hair framed his high forehead in smooth, silky ribbons. Jake Jaggard was acting the part of an upper class Englishman. Sir Harvey was the real article.

The bony looking woman next to him, the widow of a dry goods merchant, worked her fan with one hand while she scooped up the first course of savory soup with the other. "I hope you don't mind," she said to Sir Harvey between spoons full. "But really, the heat is unbearable tonight."

"My dear lady," he replied, "I'm grateful for the ventilation. I never dreamed I should wish for my own fan at the height of the winter season. If I were home, I should be shivering beside a roaring fire."

"I'm surprised you left your fireside to cross the Atlantic for a small town in Florida," Oliver said. "I doubt Tampa is in the travel plans of many of your countrymen."

"This is my first visit to Florida," Sir Harvey agreed. "But I'm not a stranger to the American south. My father and I were frequent visitors to Charleston. Delightful town before the Union forces bombed it to rubble."

Next to him the lady with the fan exclaimed, "Charleston will rise again! Those damned pusillanimous Yankees haven't the power to destroy a jewel of the south!"

Lexton chuckled. "Bravo! I judge from your words, and charming accent, that you're not in sympathy with the north."

"Certainly not," she proclaimed . "Passel of shopkeeper thugs and Irish riff raff. It's criminal what they did to us during the war and after. But we'll have our own back, never fear!"

Sir Harvey smiled across the table at Oliver. "And you, sir? Where do your sympathies lie?"

"The war is over," Oliver said. "My sympathies lie with the whole country."

"Yankee," the woman with the fan declared. "Written all over him."

Oliver turned his attention to his soup, spiced with a tasty ingredient he didn't recognize. Listening quietly to the conversation around him, he speculated about the reasons why Sir Harvey might be visiting Tampa in the company of a scoundrel like Jake Jaggard. Many Brits had been southern sympathizers during the war. Wealthy Englishmen with vested interests in the cotton trade had financed blockade runners. If Lexton and his father had spent time in Charleston, they'd probably been among these. But why was he here now with Jaggard? Jake had said he was looking for something. What?

An elderly serving maid cleared away the soup. Afterward, a black servant placed a dish of roast turkey in front of the diners. Lexton and two other men at the table began singing the praises of their host, Colonel Haines.

"He got thousands of men working like clockwork to put this railroad through," an engineer named MacLew declared. "Crews of blacksmiths and wheelwrights worked twenty-four hours a day. Why, it took a thousand men just to clear a path through the Florida jungle."

"The rainy season didn't make it easier," another railroad official chimed in. "I'll never forget how rain would turn our worksite to mud just about every blessed afternoon. It's a wonder Haines managed to finish the job with a couple of days to spare."

Oliver buttered a dinner roll. He had no doubt Haines's organizational talents deserved credit. Putting a railroad line through to Tampa was a big achievement. But what about the men who'd cleared an alligator and mosquito infested jungle in the deluge? They'd done it for little pay and no recognition?

Once again the gray-haired waitress removed a side dish. Though Oliver hadn't really looked at her face, something about the curve of her hand on a plate of half-eaten stewed carrots struck him as familiar. He turned his head in time to see her walk away carrying a loaded tray.

He recognized that trim waist, the graceful curve of that hip. My god! Was that Hannah? Could that nest of gray hair be a wig? He wouldn't put it past her. But why would she be here in disguise? What would this party of Haines' have to do with her assignment from Pinkerton?

He wanted to follow the waitress into the kitchen to determine whether his suspicions were correct. There was no way he might leave the table without awkwardness. If Hannah Kinchman were here in disguise, she must have a good reason. Perhaps someone in this hotel was connected with the Cuban revolutionaries. It would be unprofessional to give her away.

He was mulling all this over between bites of cake and preserved fruit when Colonel Haines rose from the head table. He tapped his fork on a glass. The buzz of conversation subsided, and all heads turned toward him.

He gazed benevolently at his guests. "Welcome friends and colleagues, welcome newcomers. It's wonderful to see you all here together at a very exciting time in what I truly believe is going to be a very stimulating place. Tampa has finally come into the 19th century. She is destined to be a great hub of commerce on our country's southern border. She will be a mecca for winter-weary travelers seeking paradise. Tampa is reborn!"

Laughter, applause, and several spirited huzzahs greeted this remark. Beaming, Colonel Haines held up his hand for silence. "To celebrate that rebirth, let's all raise a glass to the new men, the men of courage and vision who've come here to realize Tampa's glorious future." He lifted his wine glass. Everyone else in the room, many of whom had already drained several glasses, did the same.

After taking a sip, Haines lifted his glass again. "And now, a special thanks to one of our illustrious newcomers, Arnold Pepperwhite. We are in for a treat tonight, owed entirely to Mr. Pepperwhite's kind offices. He has persuaded a thespian with an international reputation to grace our evening. He will perform the murder scene from William Shakespeare's renowned tragedy, *Othello*."

There was a murmur of interest, not all of it enthusiastic. The woman across from Oliver muttered, "I hate that dreadful play. A white woman married to a blackamoor. And what does she get for it—strangled in her bed. Disgraceful!"

"The role of Othello's beauteous wife, Desdemona, will be played by a young lady from our own Tampa, Miss Rosella Beauchamp."

Oliver raised an eyebrow. Rosella? It couldn't be the pretty mixed race maid from the hotel, could it? No, very unlikely. Though such casting might make an interesting twist on the story.

Haines was going on to praise the artiste who would take the role of Othello. "We are honored to have among us the acclaimed actor, the talented Mr. Gilbert Kinchman.

While the audience clapped politely, Oliver froze in his seat. Now he knew why Hannah was here in disguise. He had to stop her!

CHAPTER NINE

WHILE waiters placed chairs in front of the stage, the diners left their seats to stroll about the room. Oliver studied the perimeter of the hotel's lobby, assessing the situation. The room was rectangular, divided into two large sections by a grand staircase climbing to the private rooms.

He walked behind the staircase and peered into the hallway it screened. The serving staff had been bringing out food from this area. He surmised this corridor must lead to the kitchen. In fact, he could hear the clatter of dishes and detect the lingering odors of turkey and overcooked carrots.

On the left side of the passage he spotted three closed doors. They might be broom closets or other kinds of storage rooms. They might be offices. Or the actors about to take the stage might be using them for dressing rooms. If that were the case, and Hannah were still in the kitchen disguised as a serving maid, she'd have easy access to her wayward husband.

Oliver walked to the end of the corridor. He discovered an exit to the lane at the rear of the hotel. It made a likely escape route if you were planning something risky. To his right was the kitchen. When he stepped into it he saw a table piled high with dirty dishes. A young Negress swathed in an oversize apron was pushing scraps into a garbage bin. An older woman bent over the sink. There was no sign of Hannah.

When the Negress let out an exclamation of surprise, the woman at the sink turned around and stared at him. "Can I help you, sir?"

"I was looking for the actors' dressing rooms. I need to give them a prop for their performance."

"The theater folks are in the rooms at the top of the stairs."

"Thank you." Oliver walked quickly back through the hall. He stopped to gaze at the last door on his right. Where was Hannah hiding? Was he even correct about her being here in disguise? Was he about to make a fool of himself?

At that moment Haines rang a bell and summoned his guests to take their seats in front of the stage. Oliver listened to their shuffling feet and glanced from the staircase to the closed doors in the hall. If he'd guessed right about Hannah, she was either close by or lurking about somewhere on the second floor. Too late now to go upstairs and find her.

The lights in the makeshift theater area had been dimmed. He could see audience members turning their heads to the staircase in anticipation. So that's where the actors were about to make their entrance.

A swell of excitement rippled through the crowd. He heard whispered exclamations. Something on the staircase had captured everyone's interest. Oliver flattened himself on the wall next to the closed door and waited to see what would happen next.

He heard the measured tread of feet descending the staircase. Craning his neck to get a better view, he saw part of a shapely figure in a gauzy white nightdress pausing for effect at the curve of the flaring banister. And what an effect she was having. All he could see was part of her back, but the waist length fall of her black hair, and the rounded outlines of her hips were instantly recognizable. This could be no other than the lovely Rosella who worked at the hotel.

Now she was someone else as well. She lifted her candle so that it cast a circle of golden light around her. Head high, she began a stately walk toward the stage. The audience gawked. This was no longer a chamber maid. This was a beautiful princess walking fearlessly to her death.

As she climbed up onto the stage and arranged herself on the makeshift bed, amazed exclamations rippled from the audience. The performers had elected to reverse the casting of Shakespeare's play. Desdemona was to be black and Othello white. Such a thing was unheard of—most especially unheard of in the south. Who had arranged this, Oliver wondered. And why?

Another actor descended the stair and headed toward the stage. Oliver could see only his back. But that was impressive enough. Gilbert Kinchman was a tall, well-built man with a fine head of curly brown hair. After he climbed the stage he turned and presented his undeniably handsome visage to the audience. So this was the man who had deserted Hannah and broken her heart.

She was not a woman to take such a blow lightly. Had she known that her runaway husband would be here? Was she lurking somewhere in the building? If so, what did she have in mind?

A moment later the question was answered. Kinchman had started intoning Othello's famous speech. *"It is the cause, it is the cause, my soul. Let me not name it to you, you chaste stars! Yet I'll not shed her blood,"*

As he uttered the word *"blood,"* the door next to Oliver flew open. Hannah shot out of it, still disguised as a gray-haired waitress. Both of her hands wrapped the grip of a Colt revolver pointed at the stage. Oliver lunged. He knocked up her arm just as lead exploded from the barrel. The bullet ricocheted off a chandelier, raining broken crystal on the audience. Cursing, Oliver grabbed Hannah's wrist and shook it until she dropped the gun. He seized her by the waist.

As he dragged her down the hall toward the back exit, she screamed and kicked. "Let go of me! You have no right!"

Shifting his grasp, he put one hand over her mouth and used her squirming body to shove open the door to the alley.

She bit his finger, drawing blood, then screeched her rage when he swatted the back of her head, knocking her gray wig over her eyes.

"Ow! You have no right to interfere with me!" She shook her head, and the wig fell to the ground.

"Shut your damned mouth, you fool! Do you want to get us both hanged?" He squinted through the darkness. He could hear shouts and stamping feet inside the building. The sound made him think of angry hornets. In a matter of seconds a hive of men with blood in their eyes would swarm out here.

He hissed into Hannah's ear, "If you're not a total idiot, you've arranged some kind of get away for yourself. Where is it?"

"Damn you to hell!"

"Tell me where it is, or I'll leave you to the mercy of the crowd!"

"Drop dead, you interfering bastard!"

He loosed his grip and dumped her in the alley.

Cursing him, she scrambled to her feet. As she sprinted away she flung over her shoulder, "There's a cart waiting behind the bank."

CHAPTER TEN

OLIVER caught up with Hannah and yanked her into the shadow of the next building. The door of the hotel behind them crashed open. A half dozen male dinner guests spilled out shouting contrary orders at each other. Oliver recognized Arnold Pepperwhite, and Sir Harvey Lexton among the cluster. The men stood for a moment staring uncertainly into the darkness. Pepperwhite shouted "Head for the harbor, boys! That's where they'll go!" He took off at a run. After a second's hesitation, the others followed.

When they had disappeared into the night, Oliver pushed Hannah through the shadows toward the back of the bank. "Lucky us. If they'd looked our way we'd probably be swinging from a tree by now."

"That would be your fault for sticking your nose in," Hannah hissed.

"If I hadn't stuck my nose in, you'd be a murderess."

Hannah stamped her foot. "I'd be a happy murderess, and my worthless husband would have what he deserves."

"No man deserves a bullet through his brain."

She sneered, "That's rich coming from you. How many bullets did you deliver during the war? Besides, what do you know about what Gilbert deserves? A bullet would be too good for him. Anyway, I wasn't going to kill him. I was just going to spoil his pretty face."

"You're not that good a shot, Hannah. Shut up and take me to this cart."

They rounded the bank, and he saw the vehicle in question. A figure huddled on the seat of a buckboard wagon, obviously expecting to aid Hannah in her get away. As they drew closer, moonlight picked out the person in greater detail. Gathering the reins of a mule, she turned her face toward them.

"That's the Negro woman Pedroso employs. How in hell did you persuade her to risk her neck helping you? Or didn't she have a choice?"

"Oh, she had a choice. And her name is Callie. Callie Beauchamp."

Oliver stutter-stepped. Beauchamp? Wasn't that Rosella's last name?

Hannah lifted her skirts to scramble onto the buckboard's high seat. "Let's go, Callie!"

"Yes Ma'am. We takin' that man with us?"

"Yes."

"Well, he better hurry himself. I ain't waitin' on him."

Oliver managed to fling himself into the wagon bed as Callie whipped the mule into action, saying "Gee up, Flowerpot." Flowerpot trotted down the dirt alleyway. Oliver raised himself on his elbows and peered over the edge of the wagon skirt. He saw that burlap had been tied around the mule's hooves to muffle the sound. So some planning had gone into this ridiculous caper.

He looked over his shoulder, fearing that Pepperwhite might have realized his error and turned back. The lanes behind the jolting cart appeared dark and quiet. He guessed from the direction the mule was taking that they were headed toward the Pedroso boarding house.

He had injured himself jumping into the cart and was beginning to feel it. Groaning, he levered himself on bruised knees and tapped Hannah's shoulder. Even from that brief contact he could tell she was tight as a drawn bow. When her head fired around, he caught the glint of her barred teeth. "What?" she hissed.

"Why is Callie helping you?"

"Ask her yourself."

"She's busy driving, and we haven't been introduced."

Callie hunched further into the dark cloak swathing her and shot a glance at Hannah. "You want me to talk to the man?"

"Oh, go ahead. I don't care."

They rounded a corner lit only by the moon, and Callie flicked her whip over the mule's backside. It hardly seemed necessary. Despite the darkness the animal appeared to know exactly where they were going. The night wind had risen. It crackled through the dry palms which clattered overhead like chattering teeth. An insect slammed against Oliver's forehead, and he flicked it away.

Callie said, "Rosella Beauchamp is my child. I came to save her from being a fool in another white man's bed."

Oliver took a few seconds to absorb that. "What white man?"

Hannah glared at him. "She's talking about Arnold Pepperwhite. How do you think Rosella got cast as Desdemona?"

The buckboard jolted over a deep rut. Oliver clutched the side rail to right himself. "I thought you were there for your husband, Hannah. Did you plan putting a bullet in Pepperwhite as well?"

"If I got the chance."

"Good God, woman! You can't go about shooting every man who displeases you!"

"No. That would be impossible. There are so many."

"Are you imagining the fine citizens hereabouts are too chivalrous to hang a woman for murder? You're not such a fool. Like it or not, men rule the world."

"How well I know! But once upon a time so did big lizards. Well, there couldn't be anything uglier and stupider than a big lizard. If one came after me, or my daughter, I'd shoot him right between the eyes!"

Callie chuckled. "I like you attitude Mzz Kinchman."

CHAPTER ELEVEN

A half an hour later, Oliver stood in the shadow of a live oak across from the Pedroso boarding house. He eyed the lighted bedroom window where he supposed Hannah was composing herself for the night. What now?

Earlier, he'd had trouble concealing his gun under his freshly pressed coat. Foolishly, he'd left it behind in his hotel room. He wanted to go back and retrieve it. But that was not a good idea.

He put a hand on his belly, reassured to feel the slight padding of his money belt beneath his clothing. He could buy a ticket out of here. He could walk to the train station, wait until morning and board the first train north.

What would happen if he tried that? He might find a lynch mob waiting for him. For a few seconds he allowed himself the luxury of shaking his fist at Hannah's window. She had made a complete muddle of his assignment. When he'd left her and Callie at the Pedroso boarding house, she had insisted she was in no danger. She'd been confident that her disguise and acting abilities would keep her safe from discovery.

"Unfortunately, Ollie," she'd declared as she'd descended from the wagon seat, "that's not true for you. You weren't wearing a disguise."

"I had no reason to disguise myself. I wasn't planning to shoot anybody."

"True. But by now everybody else at that dinner party knows you were in the servants' hall when the shot was fired. They'll assume you were the one who pulled the trigger."

"Damn you, Hannah!"

"Don't you curse at me! It's your fault. If you'd stayed out of it, I'd be fine, and you wouldn't have a problem."

Now, as he was realizing in full, he had a big problem. How was he going to get out of this situation with a whole skin? Could he do it on his own? If he weren't in the bowels of the south with no safe means of transportation, maybe he could. But in this place, surrounded by human enemies and alligator-infested rivers? No, he needed help.

Once again he glanced at Hannah's window on the second floor of the Pedroso boarding house. Could he get help from her or from the Pedrosos? Unlikely. The Pedrosos had no reason to offer him aid. What's more, if he and Hannah were caught together, that would endanger both of them. He only hoped she was right about the value of her disguise.

Oliver frowned. What had happened to her wig? He remembered that during their flight from the hotel it had fallen off her head. He pictured it lying in the dirt like a bedraggled rat. In the morning it would be found. What if someone who remembered the gray-haired maid found it?

Twenty minutes later Oliver was behind the Hillsborough Hotel. As he slipped through the shadows, he scanned the moonlit alley for something that might be a fallen wig. Twice he had darted out into the dirt lane to retrieve what turned out to be lumps of rag and then the remains of a dead cat.

A few yards farther he spotted a shape that might be the wig. He was making sure it wasn't another decomposing animal before he picked it up when he heard a footfall at his back.

Oliver pivoted and ducked in time to receive only a glancing blow on the side of his head. A burly figure lunged at him. Still off balance, Oliver toppled over, rolled to one side and grabbed his attacker's foot. Cursing, the man fell backward. Struggling to hold on to his assailant's thrashing feet, Oliver tried to regain his balance. But the fallen man was not alone. Something hard came down on Oliver's head.

He woke up lying on the floor of Letitia Thomas's parlor. He was at the center of a circle of familiar faces, all looking down at him as if he were a fly in their soup.

Letty Thomas, fetchingly arrayed in a ruffled pink dressing gown, was the first to speak. "Oh look, the Yankee villain's opening his eyes. I never was so disappointed in a man. When I first laid eyes on him I thought he was a gentleman. I soon learned different. Not only is he a philanderer, now I find he's a cold-blooded assassin."

Henry Haines, who stood next to her, muttered, "Are you sure you saw him fire a shot at your husband?"

"I saw him clear as day. I saw him take aim at my husband and fire. Now poor Larry is lying in bed with a terrible bloody wound on his shoulder."

Oliver opened his mouth to protest. Letty kicked him with the sharp point of her pink satin slipper. While he lay gasping, Jake Jaggard said, "Why would Redcastle want to shoot your husband?"

"Why wouldn't he? The dreadful man has been trying to seduce me ever since he arrived in town. Why, I can show you a note he sent me—a terrible note suggesting dreadful, dreadful things! She pulled a crumpled bit of paper out of her pocket and passed it to Haines.

Oliver tried to sit up and defend himself. Haines put a foot on his chest to hold him in place. It knocked the wind out of his lungs, rendering him mute.

Haines scanned the note. His eyebrows shot up. "Good heavens! This is disgraceful."

"Oh, it's just horrid!" She wiped a tear from her eye with her knuckles and sniffed. "Like I told you, I was shocked to bits when I received it. You know very well I'm not the sort of woman who could ever think of betraying her husband! Of course I didn't reply." She sniffed again, and Haines handed her his handkerchief. "But that didn't stop Mr. Oliver Redcastle. I suppose he thought with Larry out of the way he had a clear field." She wiped her eyes with the handkerchief and returned her gaze to Oliver's astonished face. "Well now, Mr. Redcastle, you know I'm not that kind of woman. You know what kind of woman I really am."

CHAPTER TWELVE

Two weeks later Oliver lost his balance and fell against the prisoner at his elbow. He struggled to right himself. The jolting cart they were in, and the shackles binding them to each other, made this difficult. He muttered an apology. It was not well received.

"Stay offa' me if you doan want your throat cut open! Where we goin' accidents happen easy."

Oliver had heard enough about the turpentine camps to know this was true. A dozen men jammed the wagon, convicts packed together like canned oysters. The enforced closeness didn't generate friendly conversation. Oliver was the only white prisoner in the group. Except for the occasional curse, and the soft moans of one felon who appeared ill, all maintained a sullen silence.

They had left at dawn and made part of the journey by water. They'd huddled on a flat bottomed boat that offered no shelter from the ball of flame searing the sky. All morning, and most of the afternoon , the sun had threatened to cremate them alive. Now, they bumped along a narrow path scarred with ruts, rocks, and tree roots. It had been hacked through a stand of tall pines which seemed to stab at the clouds. The place was silent, pervaded by heat and the smell of pine needles carpeting the ground. An occasional scrawny squirrel darted out, peered at them nervously, then vanished. A Turkey buzzard circled high above the pine heads.

The prisoners stared into the passing screen of vegetation as if they were looking into the gates of hell. Oliver was doing the same thing, mulling over, half in disbelief, the nightmare of the last two weeks.

From the first his accusers had treated him more like a trapped animal than a person with rights. Try as he might to explain his innocence, nobody would listen. His demands to contact William Walters for a character reference were met with sneers. His pleas to inform his family were ignored. His money belt had disappeared during the scuffle in the street. He was unable to pay a lawyer, or even his bill at the hotel. He had found himself locked in jail with a five-year sentence for vagrancy, non-payment of debts, indecency, and attempted murder.

The only person who had made the slightest effort to help him—and that very slight indeed—had been Jake Jarggard. Two days earlier Jake had come to see him. Splendidly groomed, as always, he'd sported the perfect outfit for visiting a felon—a white linen suit and jaunty straw boater.

"Well, Ollie, this is quite a muddle you've got yourself into."

"I didn't do it all by myself, Jake. I had help."

"Are you, per chance, referring to the charming Mrs. Letty Thomas?"

"Letty Lying Thomas! She claimed I tried to seduce her. False! I never sent her love notes. Nor did I shoot her husband. What is wrong with the woman?"

"There's nothing wrong with Letty. She just has a long memory."

"What do you mean?"

Jakes' lips curled in a faint smile. "You have no idea who she is, do you? Really, Ollie, you should keep better track of your enemies. I know for a fact there are quite a few. Remember a woman named Helena Caryer?"

"Caryer?" Oliver's brows knit. "You mean the female spy who acted as courier for Rose Greenhow?"

LOUISE TITCHENER

"Yes, one of the more unlucky ones. She was caught with a Union battle plan tucked under her snood and jailed for conspiracy. Unfortunately, Helena had delicate health. Spending winter in the Old Capital Prison in Washington didn't suit her. She took sick and died of lung fever."

"What's that got to do with Letty Thomas?"

"Letty is Helena's daughter. Like I said, she has a long memory."

Oliver scratched his head. His cell was jumping with fleas. His own clothing had been taken from him and replaced with canvas overalls and a scratchy shirt. "I had nothing to do with Helena's incarceration. I barely knew the woman."

"But you did know her. Letty remembers you, Ollie. She remembers seeing you with her mother. She suspects you may have betrayed the woman."

Oliver's fists tightened on the iron bars separating him from Jake. He felt lost in a funhouse lined with distorted mirrors. Nothing was what it appeared.

He focused on Jake. "How do you know all this? What's between you and Letty?"

"We go back a ways."

"Knowing you, I'll bet there's more to it. She's invited you into her house. Has she invited you into her bed as well?"

Jake took out a handkerchief and held it to his nose. "A gentleman never discusses such matters."

"Maybe not, but if a husband found a gentleman like you in bed with his wife and objected too vigorously, he might well wind up with a bullet in his shoulder. Is that how Larry Thomas got shot?"

"You're the detective. Work it out for yourself. I didn't bribe the guard in this stinking cave to speak to you about the Thomas family. I came to warn you."

Oliver looked over his shoulder at the cell he shared with a couple of snoring drunks. He muttered, "Late for that, isn't it?"

"They're about to shove you into a convict work gang headed for a turpentine camp on the gulf coast."

Oliver was silent, trying to understand what this meant.

Still holding his handkerchief against his nose, Jake leaned closer. "Do you know what turpentine camps are like?"

"How should I? I'm a Yankee."

"You spent time in the south during the war."

"Not in a turpentine camp."

"Count your blessings. They're hell holes. Half the convicts consigned to them don't get out alive."

"You came here to cheer me up?"

"We go way back, Ollie."

"Not as friends."

"No, we've been adversaries. You've tried to put me behind bars. Once you succeeded. But a man can esteem his enemies. I respect you, Ollie. Sometimes I even like you. Despite our differences, I'd hate to see you expire in a convict camp."

Oliver gazed back at his visitor. Was Jake to be believed? "Are you offering to help me?"

"I'll try. But not right away. I'm here to find something. That job comes first. Once I succeed, I'll endeavor to lend a hand."

"Will you telegraph my housekeeper to let her know what's happened?"

"I'll try, when I can find the opportunity."

"I see. What exactly are you telling me?"

"You're a survivor, Ollie. I'm telling you not to give up. If I can be of assistance to you, I will. Eventually."

"Eventually?"

"Best I can do, Ollie old man. Best I can do."

CHAPTER THIRTEEN

CLOSE to nightfall the convict wagon pulled into a clearing. Oliver got a look at his new home. He saw a dozen hastily constructed shanties with thatch roofs and several smaller sheds. Later he learned these consisted of a cooperage, glue shed, pump house, spirit shed, stable, blacksmith shop, and commissary.

A man on horseback watched as the deputies who had driven the wagon jumped from their seats. He wore a sweat streaked white cotton shirt, canvas pants, leather boots, a wide-brimmed felt hat, and a sour expression. Oliver had overheard the other convicts talk about the "woods rider." This must be he. Oliver felt his hackles rise.

The man was of an age to have soldiered for the Rebs. He might have served in the cavalry. From the imperious way he sat his saddle and surveyed the scene, he was in charge. The deference offered him by the deputies, who had shown little regard for anyone until now, underlined his authority.

They stationed themselves with their shotguns at the ready. The shackled men climbed awkwardly down to the dusty earth. Some, crippled by their long hours in the jolting wagon, fell to their knees. Oliver managed to stay upright, but it was a trial.

"Look sharp, there. Don't dawdle!" the taller deputy instructed. He frowned up at the man on horseback. "What you thinking, Cap'n Arnold?"

Captain Arnold fingered the whip coiled across the pommel of his saddle. "I'm thinking' this is a mighty poor lot. Not a one looks good for more than a month or two."

"We do the best we can," the deputy replied. "That big buck over there knows how to box a pine. Worked in a turp camp before." He pointed at a tall, muscular Negro with wide shoulders and a sullen expression. He stood out from the other men, who were considerably less impressive physical specimens. All of them wore overalls badly in need of a wash and cotton shirts in the same condition.

Captain Arnold studied the big black man. "What's your name, boy?"

A shiver coursed across the man's throat. "Name's Nepp Percy, suh."

"What's your crime, Nepp?"

"Fightin' at a juke joint."

"Over a woman?"

"Yes suh."

"Well you ain't goin' to find any women around these woods. Even if there was, I guarantee you'd be too tuckered to mess with them. You'll get breakfast at 4:30 tomorrow morning'. After that it's out to the pines for boxing, chipping, dipping, and scraping 'til sundown. I expect you can teach some of these other poor excuses for men what that means."

As Captain Arnold's surveyed the collection of convicts, his gaze fell on Oliver. He lifted a thin eyebrow. "What have we here?"

The deputy stepped forward. "Name's Redcastle. He's a Yankee."

"A Yankee! A Yankee in these parts? Must be a hell of a fool. What's he in for?"

The deputy snickered. "Vagrancy. I hear he sent love letters to a married woman and tried to kill her husband."

Captain Arnold stared at Oliver. "Do tell. So he's a romantic fella'. A week or two out here and he'll get the romance drug out of him. That I can guarantee." He looked from Oliver to Nepp Percy and back. "Redcastle, I'm going to assign you to Percy, here. He is to be your instructor, and you are to be his school boy. Is that all right with you, Percy?"

"Yes suh."

"And you, Redcastle. Are you agreeable?"

"Yes."

"Yes, sir."

Oliver swallowed. His instinctive dislike of Arnold was making it hard for him to answer in a neutral voice. From the moment of laying eyes on the man, he had felt himself in even more serious trouble than he'd feared. In an isolated wilderness like this Arnold would rule the workers utterly. As this camp's woods rider, Arnold would have the power of life and death. Indeed, the man's own safety would depend on his maintaining an iron rule. To refuse his orders, or give him back talk, would be suicide. Oliver lowered his eyes. "Yes sir."

"That's better. I like a man to know his place. You fight in the war, Redcastle?

"Yes sir."

"At least you got the gumption to admit it. For all I know you might have tried to shoot me, years back. You think that's possible?"

"Anything's possible in war."

"Maybe you did shoot some of my friends. What do you think about that?

"Like I said, anything's possible in war."

"Don't I know. Well, you got yourself into a different kind of war now. Happens I'm the big general in this war. Just for the fun of it, say yes sir to me again."

"Yes sir."

Captain Arnold smiled, showing tobacco-stained teeth. "Has a right nice ring to it. As time goes on, I 'spect to hear it a lot out of all you riff raff. In fact, I'd like to hear it now. Say it now, all of you!"

That night Oliver slept on a straw pad which lay on the dirt floor of a tumbledown shack. It had been named "Skeeter Heaven."

"This place ain't worth spit," one of the other six convicts who shared the shack opined. He was a boy of around nineteen, a skinny lad with a badly healed scar across one cheek. The other prisoners addressed him as Collie because he liked collard greens. "Look at the bugs in this dirty ol' straw," he went on. "I ain't going to git a wink of sleep!"

"Oh shut your mouth on that, an older convict named Jupe exclaimed. They don't call this place Skeeter Heaven for nothing. The bugs in the straw ain't as bad as the skeeters flying in the window. They thicker than bees around a honeycomb."

This was true. Leaky shutters didn't stop the blood sucking insects. The smoke pouring from the stick and clay fireplace the convicts had used to heat their pork stew had kept the mosquitoes at bay. Now the fire had died, and nothing would halt them.

Oliver's stomach roiled. He'd been unable to eat the greasy pork concoction he'd been served. He'd offered his tin bowl to Nepp Percy. The big black man had taken the food without a word. Several minutes later he'd handed Oliver back his emptied bowl and muttered, "You be a chump not to eat. Man who don't eat don't survive."

Oliver knew it was true, but eating tonight was out of the question. One of the men who'd sickened on the journey lay curled up in a corner, moaning. The others paid no attention.

Oliver nursed the nausea rising up in him as he listened to disjointed snatches of their conversation. To his dismay he learned that pork, cornbread, and molasses would likely be their steady diet. "Supply wagon don't make it out here but once a month, and it don't bring nothing else," one of the more knowledgeable convicts vouchsafed.

If they wanted fruit or vegetables, they would have to forage in the woods for herbs and berries. Palmetto buds were said to taste like cabbage. Banban twigs resembled snap beans. But if you went berry picking in the woods, you had to be cautious. A man could find something that looked appetizing and get bellysick, or even dead, for his enterprise.

Instead of entering into the discontented parley, Nepp Percy composed himself on his mat. Soon he was snoring. Oliver tried to follow his example. But as he lay on his straw struggling to ignore the mosquitoes whining around his head, he considered the men sharing his misfortune. He had never before spent the night with a room full of Negroes. He knew that in other southern states white and black prisoners would be separated. Florida observed no such restrictions.

How would he and his fellow convicts deal with each other? At first he had feared they might make his life even more of a misery. Instead, at least so far, they ignored him. Nobody spoke to him or even looked his way. It was as if he weren't there at all. The only man who had addressed him directly was Nepp Percy, and then only after he'd consumed all the food from his and Oliver's bowl.

He turned his head toward the shuttered window. A thread of moonlight found its way through a broken slat. The same moon shone down on Baltimore. His housekeeper and his daughter would be expecting him home in a couple of days. What would happen to them if he never came back, and they never understood why?

He had left Mrs. Milawney with money for expenses, but that wouldn't last more than a month. Jake Jaggard had agreed to try and get a message to Baltimore about his predicament. Could he trust Jake to keep his word? Jake was a con man, an elegant liar. Deception was his stock in trade. It might be that he'd promised to help Oliver to keep him from telling anyone that he was a crook. Only a fool would trust Jake Jaggard.

Oliver closed his eyes and pictured Hannah Kinchman as she'd been the night she'd tried to shoot her husband. Her eyes had sparkled with rage, and her hair had been wild around her face. He hadn't seen her since. So far as Oliver knew, she hadn't been accused of anything. Was she still in Tampa? Any chance she might feel some remorse over the trouble she'd made and find a way to help?

No. He'd be an idiot to count on anything like that. If it hadn't been for Hannah, he'd on be his way back home. He imagined strangling her. Then he swallowed back his rage and acknowledged that he had only himself to blame. He should never have involved himself in her doings. Why had he been such a fool? He moved restlessly. Somehow he had to figure a way to get himself out of this hellish situation. But how?

CHAPTER FOURTEEN

A T 4:30 the next morning the clang of a bell roused the men of "Skeeter Heaven." They stumbled out for a lump of stale corn bread washed down with a tin cup of water. They were allowed a few minutes to use the privies. Then they were marched into the Florida scrub. Only the sick man was left behind. That night he would be gone, never to be seen again.

As a wagon rumbled behind them carrying supplies for the day, they slogged through a desolate checkerboard of swampy ground. Occasionally turbid streams intersected it, followed by sandy, monotonous pine forest. Other than the occasional scrub jay, and numerous flying and crawling insects, there was little sign of life.

It had turned cool during the night. A chilly breeze whispered through the vegetation. Many prisoners shivered as they walked. When they arrived at their work site, the sky had lightened enough to obscure the stars. Gray threads of dawn curled through the tree tops to float like ghosts in the resinous air below. The men shuffled restlessly and muttered under their breath. Oliver understood why they were perturbed. Dead pine needles whispered underfoot, almost like incoherent protests. Otherwise the forest was eerily quiet, the tall trees stretching away on every side, a silent watchful army.

"This place give me the creeps," Collie whispered. "Them trees is like spooks! They don't like us being here."

In the gloom Oliver could see the whites of Collie's eyes. His hair stood out from his head in spiky cornrows, making Oliver think of a frightened porcupine. He was saying what everyone in the group felt, Oliver included.

"Shut you mouth," a convict named Scoop hissed. "Don't make more trouble for us than we already got!"

The men in charge prodded the group into forming around a tree. It was now light enough for Oliver to get a clear look at the two guards. They seemed familiar. Where had he seen them before?

The shorter one named Lem said, "You men going to learn your first lesson. Mr. Nepp, here, is going to teach you good-for-nothings how to box a pine. Ain't that right, Percy?"

Nepp Percy gazed back with no expression. "Can't box no pine without a ax."

"You gonna' get your ax. "The guard leveled his rifle while his taller colleague unshackled Nepp . He took an ax with an elongated head out of the supply wagon. As soon as Nepp had it in his hand, the second guard stepped back and leveled his gun as well. Nepp Percy holding an ax was a formidable sight.

He shifted it back and forth in his large hands. When he'd found a satisfactory grip, he slammed the cutting edge into the base of the pine. After he finished up, the other convicts were told to examine the hole he'd made. Oliver was third in line. He saw that the hole, or "box," was cut at a downward angle about ten inches wide and four inches deep.

Later he would learn that the boxes were cut to hold turpentine. Over time the size of the box would increase as the top of the box was cut away to freshen the wound and maintain the flow of gum. The pines were being injured until they bled to death. He looked around at the doomed trees. Was the sense of dread that seemed to hang in the air his imagination? Or was it real? He shook his head, dismissing the idea as nonsense. Yet, he couldn't get rid of it entirely. There was something uncanny about this hushed kingdom of condemned forest giants.

They spent the rest of the day trying to master the art of cutting a box. Nepp had made it look easy. Oliver and the other men soon discovered that it was not. It took strength and accuracy to swing that ax so that the cut would bite at the right angle, width, and depth to hold a quart or possibly two of raw turpentine. A slight miscalculation and you were as likely to slash yourself as the tree. What's more, knowing where and when to box was complicated. Larger trees could support more than one box. However, if the gashes were too deep, the tree's life was cut short. If the cut was too broad, the face would rise out of reach, and the tree could no longer be harvested.

Growing up in Kansas, Oliver's chores had included splitting firewood. Now, after a few false starts, he managed to hack out a reasonable box. Others had more trouble.

"You'll do," the taller guard named Hoot remarked after he examined Oliver's work. Oliver stared at him, suddenly realizing why he looked familiar. Lem and Hoot had been the men who'd stopped the train headed for Tampa and hauled another man off it. Oliver wondered if they would recognize him. So far they hadn't seemed to.

Hoot was saying, "You and Nepp can work together. We'll start you out at fifty boxes a day. These others. . ." He shot a scornful glance at the trees some had damaged without success. "We'll just have to see what jobs they're good for."

Collie was the last to audition with an ax. He assumed an arrogant stance when he stepped up to the pine. Oliver knew his swagger was an act. During the war he'd met so many boys pretending to be fearless while inside they were terrified. He had been such a boy himself.

At sixteen he'd lied about his age to join the Union army. His superiors had recognized his skill with a rifle and "promoted" him to sharpshooter. At first he'd been cocky, wearing a red feather in his hat, preening like a silly young clown.

Later, after his first kill, that had changed. Oliver still had nightmares about those days—setting up to wait for the right moment, drawing a bead on the unsuspecting target, holding his breath until the wind dropped so the bullet could fly true.

Collie swung at the tree, but his aim went awry. He cut a gash in his leg. Screaming, he fell to the ground and grabbed his injured limb. Blood stained his pants and dripped down around his ankle, pooling on the carpet of pine needles at his feet. One of the guards laughed and called him clumsy. The other cursed him for a mug.

Scoop, the squat, muscular Negro with one blind eye who had warned Collie earlier, dropped beside him. He removed a checkered kerchief from around his neck and used it for a makeshift tourniquet.

"Here, what you doin'?"

Scoop shot a glance at the guard. "Stoppin' the blood. He's just a boy. You don't want a dead chile on your hands."

"Don't matter to me. One less to worry about."

"Listen here. You ain't as coldhearted as all that. He can't walk. Let him ride the wagon."

They argued, but eventually the guards gave in and let Scoop carry Collie to the wagon. He spent the rest of the day, propped between tools and boxed supplies, moaning.

An hour later the sun blistered through the tree tops. Faint with hunger, Oliver plodded through the dry, whispering forest. He vowed never again to give his dinner away, no matter what turned up in the bowl. Beads of sweat burned his eyes, dampened his belly, and pooled in his armpits. Pine resin stuck to his skin and clothing. The odor seared his nostrils. His pants were starched with it. Later he and his cabin-mates would find humor in setting their resin soaked pants up in a corner. The stiffened pants would stand at attention like the bottom half of a topless soldier.

As the endless hours crawled on, the other men were just as disheartened as Oliver. Earlier in the morning there'd been some talk among them. Now they were mostly silent, gazing stonily as Lem and Hoot sneered at their botched efforts to cut a proper "box."

"If you fools can't cut a decent box, maybe you can learn to chip," Hoot declared. A pine would bleed only so long as its wound was fresh. In seven or eight days the gum would crystallize like blood forming a scab. "Chipping" freshened the wound. It was done with a hack, a circular piece of iron with a sharp lower edge, and involved cutting the bark away just above the box. It, too, required a degree of skill that only two more of the men were able to achieve.

"Guess the rest of you can scrape and dip," Lem opined. "Those are jobs even women can do. We'll keep tryin' to get you all taught to be more useful, but right now it don't look promising."

"As if I care a damn," one of the prisoners muttered under his breath. At this point in the late afternoon nobody cared. They were all too exhausted, and dispirited to think anything mattered. They plodded from tree to tree, muscles throbbing, sweat pooling in every fold and crevice. Only the squawk of a Jay and Collie's whimpers broke the strange, burdensome silence.

Later, just at dusk, they heard sounds made by another work crew. It was so surprising to hear human voices that all the prisoners straightened. They turned their heads toward the noise. Oliver knew the camp housed other men, though he hadn't actually seen them yet. When they'd been roused for breakfast, it had been too dark to see much of anything.

"You men rest easy," Hoot warned. "I'm going to see if there's trouble."

When he returned he addressed his colleague who had remained to stand guard. ""Fella' fainted and they're trying to figure what to do with him."

"Which one was it? Spooner?"

"Yeah, wouldn't you know." The guard looked at Redcastle. "We got another white man in camp. He's nothing but trouble. Even tried to escape once. We caught him. He won't be trying that again. Maybe you two should get acquainted. Name's Spooner. Reuben Spooner."

CHAPTER FIFTEEN

THAT night the discovery that Reuben Spooner was in the turpentine camp kept Oliver wide awake. He had to speak to the man. How? The guards herded Skeeter Heaven's inmates to the turpentine trees before dawn. Darkness had fallen when they returned. By that time they could barely put one foot in front of the other. In camp the guards, Lem and Hoot, were still keeping a close watch on them.

As the next few days dragged past, Oliver, Nepp Percy, and Scoop were assigned the job of boxing. The other convicts in the group either worked as scrapers or odd jobs men.

"Scrape" was gum that had hardened on the tree. The prisoners used a blade attached to a long handle to dislodge and gather it into a special wood box. The receptacle had an open top and was designed to sit at the base of the tree.

Workers dragged these vessels, each holding between one hundred or more pounds of scrape, through the forest. The laborers who weren't scraping or cutting boxes cleared tree limbs from the bases of trees and burned the debris. Others collected wood needed to make barrels. It seemed there was no end of jobs that needed doing, most of them involving hard labor.

Back at the camp, skilled workers distilled the gum and scrape. Oliver never saw this operation because he was out all day "boxing." Nepp described it to him.

"Think boxing is bad? Working the distillery is worse. Gets so damn hot in there! The fumes near choke you! I see a boy burned to death when the turp boil over!"

The distillery was a two story wood structure near a stream. It had a wood furnace with a copper still above it on the second level. The distilling operation required skill, as workers needed to heat the gum evenly and at the right temperature. Raw turpentine doesn't boil until it reaches three hundred sixty degrees Fahrenheit. Since stills had no gauges, there was always the danger of flames.

Oliver wondered what would happen if the distillery caught fire, and the flames spread? He'd observed that with every passing day restrictions on the prisoners grew more lax. Men couldn't do their jobs in shackles. After they freed the prisoners of restraints, the guards watched to see if they made trouble. When they appeared passive, Lem and Hoot spent more time smoking and telling jokes.

That changed, of course, when Captain Arnold, the woods rider, appeared atop his bay stallion. His life depended on keeping the prisoners in strict routines, and he knew it. At the sound of hooves pounding the forest bed, the guards assumed a militant stance. Arnold could only cover so much territory in a day. When he wasn't around to demand proper order, Lem and Hoot grew careless. The chaos of a fire might offer the opportunity to escape. Oliver wanted nothing more. But he knew he couldn't do it alone.

He set about establishing a better relationship with his fellow boxers. At first they ignored his attempts at conversation. That was natural. He was white, a member of the race oppressing them. But working long hours day after day in the forest of victimized pines created a reluctant camaraderie. Eventually, they responded to some of his questions.

Nepp Percy used the fewest words, but gave the best answers. "You ask me where we be. How come you so ignorant?

Don't you see where the sun lie? We on the west coast." He turned back to the tree he was abusing and struck it a ringing blow.

Oliver set the head of his ax into the pine needles and leaned on the shank. "I'm not from Florida. I see we're southwest of Tampa. Where? In the middle of the state?"

Nepp spit to one side, then glanced back over his shoulder. "Didn't you hear me? We on the coast."

Next to him Scoop giggled as if he'd had a very amusing thought. "White man wants to go swimming? We close to the Myakka, but I wouldn't go swimming in no rivers. I wouldn't take no bath in the creek near the distillery shack, either. Alligator eat you for lunch."

Ignoring the significant looks they shot each other as they both laughed, Oliver said, "By the coast you mean we're close to the Gulf of Mexico? Does the creek here run into the Myakka? Does that run into the Gulf? How close is the Myakka?"

Nepp shrugged. "Maybe five, six mile. All these creeks probably run into the Myakka. But that be miles of black bear, snakes, gators, wild cats, wild pigs, and wild people. They lot of unfriendly folks in these woods, and most of 'em live near water. Wouldn't be no stroll in the park to hit the beach. 'Sides, you try and run for salty water, they'll shoot you, or string you up. Or worse." He indicated Lem and Hoot smoking a few yards off.

Scoop rolled his eyes. "Bad things happen to a man who runs. Cap Arnold keeps dogs. They git you in no time."

"I didn't say I was planning to run."

"No, but you thinking on it. I can see the wheels turning."

"You can't tell me nobody ever escaped from this place."

Nepp shrugged. "There's ways of foolin' a dog. These woods full of runaways—runaway slaves, runaway soldiers, runaway servants, runaway thieves and killers. These woods more dangerous than the camp."

"And that's saying something," Scoop added.

"What you three wagging your tongues about?" Lem had come up behind them. "I hope you jokers ain't planning no trouble. It's not mealtime yet. We ain't out here for a picnic."

"We ain't planning trouble, boss." Nepp turned back to the tree where he'd been working. Oliver and Scoop gave the guard the same assurance and resumed their tasks.

Oliver's ax sliced into a fresh pine. He had to escape. Even if his life didn't depend on it, his daughter's did. What would become of Chloe if he didn't turn up in Baltimore soon? Acid welled at the back of his throat. He coughed, knocking his ax blow askew. He stared down at the bad cut. The wounded tree seemed to reproach him. He had to get out of this place. He had to find or create an opportunity and make the most of it.

First, he had to get a true picture of his location and how best to make his way to safety. He couldn't go east to Tampa. That would be suicide. He had to head west, toward the closer left coast of the state.

Never having visited the area, he didn't know what he would find. The Homestead Act had lured settlers there, but how many? Was it still a wilderness inhabited mostly by wild animals?

An image of one of Mrs. Milawney's bountiful breakfasts presented itself so forcefully it made his eyes water. He could smell the coffee, feel the steam rising off one of her honey muffins, and taste the sweetness of fresh squeezed orange juice.

Those oranges had come from the west coast of Florida. So there would be shipping. Where there were ports there would be a telegraph. If he could get access he could wire for help. But to get to the coast alive he'd need a weapon, if not to defend himself then at least to feed himself. How was that to be done?

It had to be accomplished. But first he had to speak to Reuben Spooner. He'd come here to find the man. His own reception in Baltimore would be better if he could bring Spooner back. Or, failing that, bring back news of him.

The guard, Hoot, broke into his thoughts. "Here Redcastle, you ain't cut but two boxes in the last half hour. This last one is a mess." He poked a finger at the splintered wood and frowned. "That's nowhere near good enough. What you day dreaming about?"

A horse snorted, and Hoot stiffened. He and Oliver both turned in time to see Captain Arnold ride into the clearing and draw up a few feet away.

"What's going on here?" The woods rider scowled down at them. Despite the heat, he wore a shirt with long sleeves. Frayed suspenders held up his stained canvas pants. A well-worn leather cartridge belt circled his fleshless waist. A shotgun and a coiled whip lay over the pommel of his saddle. The glint of gold engraving at the top of the stock of another rifle holstered on the far side of the horse and visible near the woods rider's knee caught Oliver's attention.

Hoot drew himself up. "Nothing much, Cap. Just getting Redcastle here to step up the work."

Captain Arnold contemplated Oliver. "Redcastle. That name sounds familiar. Something special about you, Redcastle?"

Oliver shook his head.

The woods rider turned back to Hoot. "He giving you trouble?"

"He ain't made his fifty boxes a day yet. Yesterday he only made forty-three."

Arnold's lip curled. "Another useless slug! That's no surprise. When it comes to getting work done, give me a black over an uppity northern white ass any day. That Spooner fool is worse. He near set fire to Snake Haven last night. The boys in that cabin hate the son of a bitch! Wouldn't surprise me if he turned up strangled in a day or two."

"Guess you wouldn't shed no tears, Cap."

"I wouldn't." Captain Arnold focused on Oliver, his eyes pale blue pebbles in the winged shadow of his hat. "Hear that,

Redcastle? Maybe you think because you're white, you'll get special treatment. Think again. You don't work I'll lay my whip on you just like the others. Now pick up that ax!"

Oliver hurried to the next nearest tree and began cutting. So Spooner was in a shack they called Snake Haven. Judging from what Arnold had said, he needed to find that place and soon.

Captain Arnold and the guard continued talking. As Oliver deepened his first cut, he heard Arnold say, "Guess what? We got the darky preacher come to camp again. This time, he got his ma and his granny with him, if you can believe. Says the old woman's a healer. They're fixin' to give the men a sermon tonight. Won't that be a hoot?"

CHAPTER SIXTEEN

THAT night the men straggled into camp at sunset. After they'd swallowed their usual meager portion of pork stew, the guards herded them to an open area next to the river. Even Collie, hot with fever from an infection that had set into his ax wound, was propped up against a tree. In the torchlight his skin looked gray. His eyes rolled up, showing only the whites.

The gathering spot was behind the distillery, so Oliver finally got a good look at that building. It appeared no different from the other ramshackle structures around it. But it had two stories. The window openings had no shutters.

It stank of turpentine and smoke, as if the lifeblood drained from the pines saturated its wood. While Oliver scrutinized the building, speculating about the effect a torch might have on it, men from the other shanties were steered into the space. The crowd swelled. He listened to the mutterings of the others shuffling around him. If this meeting were being held early in the day, they might have been receptive to a change in routine. Now, after back breaking hours in the piney woods, they only wanted the oblivion of sleep.

The moon slipped from behind a thread of clouds as a final group of convicts led by guards filed into the dell. Oliver spotted another white man in the collection. He limped along several paces to the rear of his dark-skinned fellows. Though a guard prodded him forward, he hung back, as if he didn't want to join his group. Oliver could see why. The others didn't fancy him. They either refused to look at him, or shouldered him out of the way when he got close.

Oliver squinted through the gloom. Was this Reuben Spooner? He saw a scrawny, wild-eyed man dressed in rags. He didn't look like the well-groomed image in his tintype. Yet, his matted hair was the right color, and so was his body type—making allowances for several weeks of near-starvation. Oliver suspected he didn't look much like his tintype, either. And he'd only been in the place for a week.

Oliver edged toward Spooner. He was within a few yards when Hoot, the guard, poked him in the back with the barrel of his gun. "Hey, Redcastle, you're s'posed to stay put."

"You told me to make friends with the other white man here. This is probably the only chance I'll get."

Hoot looked from Spooner to Oliver and back. He shrugged. "Guess it can't do no harm. But make it quick. Meeting's going to start, and that man ain't going to be around much longer." He sniggered. "Turp camp don't seem to agree with him."

"I can't imagine why," Oliver muttered under his breath. He threaded his way through a knot of prisoners, being careful not to step on any toes. Every man in this place was either defeated unto death or ready to explode. The slightest misstep was dangerous. Finally, he tapped Spooner on the back.

He jerked around as if bitten by a snake. His eyes were red-rimmed, his mottled features streaked with sweat and grime. "What? Don't touch me!" His voice rose hysterically.

After apologizing and making sure of Spooner's identity, Oliver introduced himself *sotto voce*. In as few words as possible, he explained that William Walters had sent him to Florida on behalf of Spooner's family.

Spooner's expression shifted. Leaning forward, he whispered, "I thought they'd forgotten me. But why are you here? Are you undercover?"

"Long story." He glanced back at Hoot who was frowning. "I can't talk now. Tell me where I can find your bunkhouse."

"Third to the left of the distillery."

That ended the conversation, as Hoot had rapped him on the shoulder. "That's enough gabbing, Redcastle. Get back with your group. Meeting's about to start."

Oliver returned to the Skeeter Heaven cluster and faced the river. Three individuals had stationed themselves there with an air of silent purpose. While they stood gazing at open bibles cradled between their palms, the milling crowd began to quiet.

"Let 'em speak their piece. Sooner we git this over, sooner we can git some sleep," Nepp muttered.

With his gun snugged in the crook of his arm, Hoot had come around to the front of the crowd. "All right, you men, settle down. We got Preacher Alvarez here. These two women are his wife and Granny. They come to try and save your miserable souls. Shut your mouths and listen up."

The garbled murmurs around him were only background noise for Oliver. He examined the three figures preparing to address the crowd. Without a doubt, the tall, good looking man in the center was Rigo Alvarez, the cart driver who'd first introduced Oliver to Tampa. The woman to his left looked like Maizie, the enterprising Negress from whom he'd purchased fried chicken for lunch with Hannah Kinchman. And the wizened little black woman on his right? Was he dreaming? Could that be Hannah in disguise?

The question remained unanswered until an hour later. In a gentle voice that gradually toughened, Rigo exhorted the crowd to change their ways and follow the heavenly guide. He was by turns friendly and conciliatory, angry and scornful, eloquent and exalted.

Oliver was impressed. He found himself comparing Rigo's performance with that of his own preacher father. He, too, had been a riveting speaker. But his morality was as uncompromising with his family, and every soul he touched, as it was with himself. His listeners had respected his inflexible right-eousness, but they hadn't been softened by him.

When it came to his sons, Oliver's father had not believed in sparing the rod. He had beat Oliver once too often. After a particularly brutal session with the strap, he had run away from home to join the Union Army. That was how he had become a sharpshooter, a killer of men he didn't know.

It was impossible to believe that Rigo would use leather on a boy who'd committed a minor infraction. As he spoke, he radi-ated goodness and understanding. He had connected with this audience. All but the most hardened of the convicts stopped shuffling and listened. Only Collie remained oblivious, whim-pering from time to time but otherwise appearing to be asleep.

There were no doctors for the men in the camp. Nepp and Scoop had tended the boy, washing his wound and feeding him by hand when he would accept food. But over the last week his leg swelled and turned an angry red. None of the camp's overseers helped. At first, they'd wanted him to work despite his injury. When they realized that was impossible, they ignored him. Oliver, who'd seen the effects of gangrene during the war, doubted he would survive.

Finally, Rigo reached the climax of his exhortation. His voice reached a crescendo. He raised his arms and lifted his face to the starry skies. For the first time, Oliver noticed the beauty of the Florida night sky, like a black velvet jeweler's case pricked with diamonds. The warm southern breeze blew softly on the faces of the captivated men. The scent of distilled pine resin, before so noxious, seemed cleansing—even purifying.

"My brothers, come to Jesus and be baptized, Come be washed in the blood of the lamb. Have the courage to step forward and be healed."

All this time the two women had been silent statues, heads bowed, eyes closed. Now they began to sway from side to side, gently at first, then more vigorously. They hummed, then be-gan to sing. "What a friend we have in Jesus."

"Step forward," Rigo implored. "Step forward and accept His blessing!"

Three men did step forward. After a moment, several more followed. The woman Oliver suspected of being Hannah Kinchman in disguise, opened her eyes and stared at him. Oliver stepped forward, too.

The two women formed a receiving line for Rigo. As each of the men who wished to be baptized stumbled toward the beckoning preacher, the women squeezed their hands. They patted them on the back and whispered encouragement into their ears before guiding them into his care. When Oliver's turn came, the woman he now knew was Hannah whispered, "Gun buried behind the privy. White rock on top. Boat hidden in broom weed, next to cleft Myrtle Oak and big live oak with split trunk, half mile south of camp. Good luck."

CHAPTER SEVENTEEN

THE next morning Collie woke up raving, lost to the wretchedness of his condition. His leg had turned an ominous color. Poisonous looking threads spread toward his knee. When the guards came, Scoop begged them to do something for the boy. "Can't you see he's in a bad way? Child needs a doctor!" They refused. Collie was left to his misery, the others herded out to the turpentine fields.

Normally more talkative than the others, Scoop was silent. When Oliver expressed sympathy for the suffering Collie, Scoop shrugged. There was an ugly set to his mouth. "Boy will likely be dead soon."

Each man was assigned a patch of trees. Oliver's was in an isolated area. While he worked, he racked his brain. The rise and fall of his ax punctuated the violence of his thoughts. Collie's suffering only added to his determination to get out of this place. How was he to recover the buried gun behind the privy without being discovered? How was he to escape the camp and find the boat hidden in broom weed? And what the hell was a cleft Myrtle Oak?

The night before Rigo had baptized the men in line, offered up a prayer for all the inhabitants of the camp, and departed. The women drove a wagon, and Rigo rode a mule. Oliver presumed they would set up camp somewhere between here and Tampa. Whatever their plans, they would likely make it safely back to town.

His own situation was considerably more doubtful. He had to break out of this brutal prison. He had to negotiate unknown territory filled with alligators, snakes, and every manner of biting insect. Then there was the problem of Reuben Spooner. How was he to get both himself and Spooner out of camp?

Distracted by questions whirling through his head, Oliver didn't hear Captain Arnold enter the clearing behind him until his horse was breathing down his back. Oliver's ax faltered. His cut went awry, wounding the tree he was working on in the wrong direction.

"Say, Redcastle, that's the second time I've seen you butcher a pine. Are you purely stupid, or are you trying to make trouble?"

Oliver straightened and turned to face the night rider. Arnold slouched atop his stallion looking down from what seemed a great height. Except for the ironic slash of his thin-lipped mouth, the shadow of his hat made his expression unreadable. His deeply browned hand rested on the loose coil of the leather whip embracing the pommel of his saddle. The guards stood on either side of him, cradling their weapons and taking in the scene with an air of anticipation.

Hoot said, "He don't look like no sharpshooter."

"Looks can deceive. That's what my old momma used to say. Lookee here, Redcastle, you got a real unusual name. Sarge who runs the distillery says he heard it before. He used to ride with me, so I trust his recollections. Sarge thinks you might be the Yankee sniper they called the Red Feather boy? Could that be true?"

Oliver resisted the impulse to deny. Arnold wouldn't ask if he weren't already convinced. "That was a long time ago. The war is over."

"Some things are never past. Not if you lose everything. Not if a bunch of no account Yankees burn down your home, rape your women, shoot your friends. Not if they tear up the world you was raised with. That stays with you, rides your shoulder and whispers in your ear."

Lem and Hoot nodded. "That's right, Cap!"

He flicked them a scornful glance. "Did I ask you two to chime in with your half-assed opinions? Me and Mr. Redcastle are having a man to man conversation. I asked him if he was the Red Feather boy, and he didn't tell me no." Arnold's gaze shot back to Oliver. "Did you now?"

Oliver became aware that none of the other convicts in his section were in sight. He couldn't hear the noise of their axes. He, the woods rider, and the guards were alone in this part of the woods. "I was sixteen when they called me that."

"We was all young kids in those days. Me, I was fourteen when I joined up. My mam wanted me to stay home, but I knew my duty. I did my share of killin', but the men I sent to their grave had the ability to do the same for me. So it was fair. Snipers, they're a different kettle of fish, ain't they? Nothing fair about shooting a man in the head from half a mile off, is there?"

Oliver agreed, but didn't imagine the woods rider wanted a philosophical discussion, or an apology. "I didn't choose the job. My superiors chose it for me."

"They chose you because you're a cowardly son of a bitch with a good eye and a cold heart. Do you deny it?"

Oliver met the woods rider's narrowed gaze squarely. "Like I said, I was sixteen."

"You're not sixteen now, Redcastle. Can you still shoot? Or have you forgotten how?"

"Could be I have. I don't keep in practice. Certainly not in this place."

"That's too bad because the boys and me have a little wager. Red Feather boy used to be our worst nightmare. Kept us awake at night worrying he might be aiming to kill us while we was asleep. When you get on in years, you got to put your bad dreams to rest. Know what I mean?"

Oliver tensed. Where was this headed? "Don't think I do."

"We think you've probably lost your touch. You've lost your touch, and we haven't lost ours. We think any one of us could outshoot you now."

"You could be right."

"We could be wrong. Let's give it a test. Let's us have a shooting match. You against the boys, and if they can't take you on, I will."

Oliver looked from the woods rider to Lem and Hoot. He saw the barely suppressed excitement in their expressions. His spine went cold. This was not going to be a shooting match. They planned to kill him. He said, "I don't have a gun."

"Lem here says you can use his Spencer. That rifle good enough for you?"

"Yes."

"Well, I should think so. Spencer's a damned fine weapon. I tell you what. Since you're a special kind of shooter. I'm going to give you a special kind of gun." Smiling to himself, the woods rider pulled a rifle out of the holster attached to his saddle and tossed it to Oliver. "What do you think?"

Oliver examined the firearm he'd managed to snatch out of the air. He'd noticed the beautifully carved and engraved stock before. Now that he saw the whole weapon and felt its perfect balance between his hands, he could appreciate its quality. It was a gentleman's long range rifle, hand made by a master craftsman.

"You like it?"

"It's beautiful."

"English. Used to belong to a sharpshooter on our side. He didn't make it out alive, so now I got his weapon. I keep it clean. So it's in pretty good shape."

Oliver nodded. He'd heard about these guns. The Confederacy had imported them for its best marksmen. This was the first one he'd seen. "These rifles are rare and valuable. I'm surprised you're letting me touch it."

"Seems right, you and the previous owner being in the same line of business only on opposite sides. No bullet in it now. When Lem puts one in, Hoot will have you covered. You try any funny business he'll drop you in your tracks. Understand?"

Oliver nodded his understanding and watched while Lem paced off fifty yards and nailed a paper target to a tree. The woods rider said, "We'll start slow, just to see where we're at." The woods rider took the whip off his pommel. "Oh, and Redcastle, don't think you can miss your target, and we'll forget who you are. If I think you're not doing your very best, I'll have you nailed to a board and whipped raw back at camp.""

Fifty yards was not a challenge for any of them. Lem, Hoot and Oliver all hit the target close to the center. At one hundred yards the quality of the shooting began to vary.

"Guess that lets you out, Hoot," the woods rider declared. "You wasn't even close to the center. I'm disappointed in you, boy. Thought you was better than that."

Hoot scowled. "Wind kicked up just when I pulled the trigger."

"I didn't feel wind. You're out. Now it's between Lem and Red Feather boy here. You pace off another fifty yards."

Grumbling, Hoot stalked into the woods. Oliver watched him find a tree at a greater distance. He glanced down at the weapon balanced between his hands. Why had woods rider given him this magnificent gun? It gave him a clear advantage over the guards. Normally it took a bit of time to become comfortable with an unfamiliar firearm. This rifle was so beautifully made that with it he felt confident of hitting his goal. Arnold must know this. What did he have in mind?"

At one hundred and fifty yards Lem's shot was slightly off center. When Oliver took his turn and brought back the target the woods rider studied it with raised eyebrows. "Why, that's plumb where it ought to be. I'm impressed." He turned to Lem. "But not with you. I'll take over from here. You go pace off another fifty yards."

"He's got a better gun than I do."

"Did I ask you for an excuse? No, I did not. I asked you to pace off another fifty yards."

"That'll put me in the next county."

"Shouldn't matter to a real sharpshooter. I'm anxious to see how Red Feather boy does at a serious distance—that is, now that he ain't a boy no more. Or maybe I should say, now that he's my boy. That's right isn't it Redcastle? Now you're my boy."

Oliver stared at Captain Arnold, at the faint sardonic smile on his weathered features. He understood what was about to happen. He'd been a fool not to figure it out sooner. He turned and watched as Lem set up the mark. He had plenty of time to study it as it took the guard several minutes to make it back to the shooting stand. It was imperative that Oliver make the shot, or at least convince the men watching him that he'd made it.

CHAPTER EIGHTEEN

Even with the best of long distance guns, a shot at two hundred yards requires special preparation. The gun must be fixed and stationary. If there is any wind at all, the shooter must either compensate for it, or wait for it to drop. To compensate, the shooter must know the gun very well. This weapon was new to Oliver.

He picked up a fallen log and went down on his belly to position the log as a brace. How familiar this felt. He'd done it so many times during the cursed war. Waiting for his mark to appear. Waiting for the conditions to be right. Now, he squinted through the gun site. The target looked infinitesimally small. At his back his captors made sarcastic comments.

"How's your eyesight these days?" the woods rider inquired. "I know mine ain't so good as it used to be."

Oliver watched the slight movement in the uppermost pine needles. Not much breeze, but enough to disturb a long distance shot. He had to wait for the drop. This would be nerve-wracking if the men observing kept up the mockery. He couldn't be distracted. He had to close his ears.

Luckily, the drop came a few seconds later. He fired.

"Whoeee! I do believe I saw that paper wiggle!" Hoot exclaimed.

"Wiggle is one thing, bullseye is another," Captain Arnold said. "Why don't you go get that target and bring it back, Redcastle. Keep in mind I'll be watchin' you real close to see you don't put no holes in it that aren't already there. Oh, and take the gun with you. I like to see the way you carry it. Looks real professional."

This request confirmed what Oliver already suspected. He got to his feet, picked up the gun and started walking. As he made his way through the trees his shoulder blades itched. They could easily shoot him in the back, but he doubted that was the scheme. He thought they planned to shoot him as he was returning. That way the killing shot would have been aimed at a man carrying a stolen gun recently fired. They could claim he'd been shooting at them.

Was he mad to imagine this scenario? Why would they go to so much trouble to make a murder look like self-defense? In this remote place the woods rider could do what he wanted. Or could he? Oliver was helpless in the south, but both he and Spooner had powerful connections in the north. Perhaps William Walters or Pinkerton was already making inquiries. Captain Arnold might have been alerted about them. Perhaps that accounted for his caution.

Or maybe I'm cracked, and this is what it seems, a shooting match. Oliver stopped at the tree where Lem had nailed the target. A small stab of satisfaction mixed with the prickles of menace between his shoulder blades. The bullet hole was close to center. So he could still shoot. That would not help now as the gun he carried was empty. So what to do—walk back and hope for the best, or make a break?

His feet decided. They raced toward a screen of greenery, dodging between the trees, weaving a zigzag course through a thick stand of scrubby sand pine. Behind him shouts of rage ricocheted through the pines. A volley of rifle fire shot a flock of scolding crows into the sky. They scattered between puffs of cloud.

Neither Lem nor Hoot possessed long range guns, so their bullets left Oliver unscathed. Fifteen minutes later he stumbled on the broken-off stump of a fallen tree overgrown by a stand of red cedar and wild morning-glory. It made as good a hiding place as any. He slipped between the cedars and waited, panting. Gradually his breathing grew regular. Trickles of sweat pooled in his armpits and ran down his back and belly.

An inquisitive hornet buzzed around his head, then settled on his sleeve. He could hear Lem and Hoot calling to each other. It sounded as if they had separated and were searching in opposite directions. He listened for the woods rider's horse, but no thudding hooves interrupted the buzzing of insects in the late morning heat. Meaning what? Arnold was letting the guards search while he took his ease? Or had he gone for reinforcements? Dogs? Oliver inhaled and let out his breath slowly. He'd heard that Arnold kept bloodhounds penned in back of his cottage.

"See anything?" Lem's voice—much closer, no more than a few yards off. Oliver forced himself to breathe more quietly. After a few seconds, Hoot answered, "Nothing yet."

"Son of a bitch must be around here," Lem muttered.

He was even closer. His booted feet crunching over dried pine needles punched into the stillness. Hoot's voice came from a greater distance. He had to be at least a hundred yards off in the opposite direction. Lem, though, was entirely too close. Through the screen of wild morning glory Oliver marked his progress. He picked up a fallen pine cone and rolled its nubby shape between his sweating palms.

Lem spotted the stand of cedar and headed toward it. A few feet from Oliver's hiding place he poked at the roots of the evergreens with his foot. Oliver listened to his labored breathing, saw the sweat staining his hatband and armpits. Oliver pitched the pine cone at a scrubby growth of firebush at Lem's heels. The guard whirled and leaned down to investigate the noise. Oliver hurtled out of the cedars and swung the butt of his useless rifle at the back of Lem's head. The blow connected with a loud thump, and the guard crumpled to the ground like a fallen scarecrow. Oliver seized his Spencer.

Now he had a weapon he could use to defend himself. Had he killed a man to get it? He checked Lem's pulse. Still going strong. He had no liking for the man, but hoped to hell he'd wake up in an hour or so. There was no time to wait and see. Oliver removed a pair of cartridge magazines from Lem's belt. He glanced at the sky to get his bearings and started to jog in the direction where he judged he'd find the river.

Panting, mind racing, Oliver pushed through what seemed like an endless tract of pine barren. He heard voices, and the thwack of men swinging axes. It was distant, like murmurs from another planet. The trees around him had already been boxed. The resin leaking from them stained the air. The sharp odor stung Oliver's nose. His eyes watered.

He had been wondering how he would evade the bloodhounds the woods rider might set on him. He passed a boxed pine overflowing with resin. It was almost as if he heard a voice offering a solution. He set the Spencer on a stump and dipped his hands into the gummy substance.

As he smeared it onto his skin and clothing, he looked up at the tree in gratitude. It was a strange sensation, staring up at the quivering tufts of green needles with the sun slanting through. His watery eyes saw halos of greenish-gold light.

A wave of dizziness overwhelmed him, and he fell to his knees. For several minutes he stayed inert, balancing on his hands and knees breathing in the sharp scent. Then he pushed himself to his feet and picked up the Spencer. After a last glance at the tree from which he had accepted an offering of resin, he pushed on.

He arrived at the river mid-afternoon. He spent the next two hours looking for the cleft Myrtle Oak next to the patch of broom weed where Hannah claimed to have hidden a boat. The river was a narrow, overgrown, muddy stretch of water. As he explored, he saw nothing to match Hannah's description. Though, she hadn't given him much of a description.

What's more, he wasn't sure how far south of camp he'd come. Hannah had said he'd find the boat and the Myrtle Oak a half mile south of camp. Should he follow the flow of the river and turn left? Or should he turn right? It went against instinct to head back toward the camp. The boat was his only chance. He had to find it.

An hour later he stumbled on the Myrtle Oak. It was not like an oak at all, but rather a scrubby evergreen growing in a dense thicket on the river bank. He found it only because he recognized the stand of broom weed adjacent to the split trunk live oak that Hannah had described. Exhausted, he dropped down on the muddy bank and looked around. At first he saw nothing. After a few minutes he noticed something red poking out of the tangle of leathery green leaves next to the broom weed.

The more he stared, the more boat-like the red shape looked. He forced himself to his feet and peered into the greenery. He'd found Hannah's gift. It was a bright red two-person racing shell complete with oars.

CHAPTER NINETEEN

THE boat contained an oilskin bag. Oliver fished a bottle of water and a small sack of biscuits from it. He gulped some of the water, saving half for future needs. He'd been considering drinking from the muddy, weed-choked river—despite the small alligator he saw sunning itself on the opposite bank. "Thank you, Hannah," he muttered as he wolfed one of the biscuits.

The cry of dogs interrupted his investigation of the boat. After ramming the craft well back into the leaves, he headed for the live oak. The increasing volume of the yelping dogs gave him strength to ascend the tree. Did they have his scent despite the precautions he'd taken with the pine gum?

He'd smeared so much of it on himself that his stiffened clothing made climbing more difficult. At last he achieved a perch on a branch high enough off the ground to offer cover from a casual passerby. Men with dogs who'd scented prey were unlikely to be casual.

Oliver spent the next hour in suspense. He was lucky. The dogs never found him. The gum had fooled them. Once again, he offered thanks to the trees. Then he closed his eyes, leaned back against the oak's broad trunk and dozed. He opened his eyes when late afternoon shadows cast dark fingers on the olive green surface of the river. All was quiet now. The sound of the hunters had faded. He was alone, and free to head west toward the Gulf of Mexico and possible escape.

That was what he wanted. He knew he couldn't. Despite the risk, he had to go back to camp and rescue Reuben Spooner. At dusk Oliver descended from his perch and extracted Hannah's boat from its hiding place. Its light weight surprised him. Was it even made of wood, he wondered. He ran an exploratory hand over its slick surface. It felt like wood, but it didn't weigh like wood. He turned his attention to the oars. They were very long and mounted in a fashion he'd never seen before. It took him several minutes to secure them.

As he slid the craft into the water he mused that, of course, it wasn't Hannah's boat. The name "Rapture" had been painted on its side. Rapture must belong to Larry Thomas. He was the only person in Tampa likely to own such a craft. How had Hannah managed to confiscate it? Hannah Kinchman was a resourceful woman.

Once Oliver had adjusted to the long oars and the sliding movement of the boat's seat, Rapture slid through the water like an arrow. Even rowing upstream while dodging fallen logs and overhanging branches, he made good time. Close to camp he steered under the cover of greenery to sip what was left of his water and munch a biscuit. He was grateful to find a second water bottle and a bag of jerky that would help renew his strength.

As he chewed on the dried meat, he made a plan. It was rough and full of peril. At least it clarified how much he was willing to risk to save Spooner. He concluded that he would cut and run if the case looked hopeless. But he had to try.

After dark, he guided Rapture close to the section of camp where the outhouse that serviced "Skeeter Heaven" was located. He secured the craft to a tree, then listened. If the dogs were anywhere near, his task was hopeless. They'd hear him prowling and give warning. His only recourse would be to abandon Spooner and make a run for it.

He didn't hear dogs. Still out searching for him? More likely, their handlers had camped and would continue their hunt in the morning. He scrambled out of the water and stood dripping on the bank, listening for several more minutes. Either the dogs were asleep or they weren't in camp.

His first stop was the outhouse to find Hannah's buried gun. Moonlight filtering through a scud of cloud picked out the white rock she'd described. The dirt beneath the rock had been disturbed recently. His probing fingers touched oilcloth wrapping a six-shot Colt 45 and a pouch filled with bullets. Thank you Hannah! He tucked the Colt into his waistband. Next he had to get Spooner out of his bunkhouse.

Again, he strained his ears for the dogs. Hearing only the murmur of voices and the faint call of an owl, he began to dodge through the shadows. The buildings he passed were dark, snoring from exhausted convicts the only sound.

As he approached the ramshackle hut where Spooner was quartered, the voices he'd been hearing grew louder. Lit by faint moon glow, half a dozen men circled another man. They were taunting him, shoving him back and forth, aiming not-so-playful kicks at his ankles and the backs of his knees. The victim was Spooner.

"Trouble man! You ain't nothin' but a trouble man!" one of the attackers chanted.

Oliver's first impulse was to rush in and help Spooner. But that would bring disaster on both of them. A moment later Spooner collapsed to the ground and curled into a ball, his arms wrapped over his head.

One man gave a whoop. Several others laughed.

"He look like a hedgehog."

"He got no more sense than a varmint!"

"Listen to that! The man cryin' like a baby!"

Oliver heard the whimpers, too. He peered through the shadows at Spooner's crumpled figure and felt himself torn between pity and scorn.

His abusers seemed to be affected similarly. "Man is use-less," one of them grumbled. Another spat on the ground and turned away. "I got to get me some sleep."

"What we goin' to do about the fool? Can't leave him out here."

"Why not? Good a place as any."

"Oh, leave him be. He wants to come in, let him. I don't care no more. Fool can rot out here for all I care."

Muttering similar slights, Spooner's tormentors straggled back into their sleeping quarters. Anybody who went to Spooner's aid would be visible from the bunkhouse. Oliver stayed hidden, waiting to see what happened next. More idle remarks floated from the hut. After what seemed like a long time, the noise subsided. A little later Oliver heard snoring.

Spooner remained curled on the ground. Oliver considered whether he should risk being seen when Spooner moved his arms and peered through his fingers. He propped himself up and looked around. Perceiving that he was alone, he began to crawl toward the shadows where Oliver hid.

He darted out when Spooner was close. Clapping a hand over the other man's mouth, he dragged him behind a tree. Spooner bucked like a mule with a wasp under its saddle. Oliver shoved him face down onto the ground and planted a knee in his back. "Quiet! I'm here to help you!"

When his hissed words finally sank in, Spooner stopped thrashing. "My hand is coming off your mouth. Don't yell!"

Spooner started wriggling. "For God's sake, man, settle down. It's Redcastle. I want to help you escape."

Finally, the injured man quieted. Half expecting he would start screaming, Oliver removed his hand. Instead, he shuddered and muttered in hopeless tones, "We can't escape. There's no escape from this hell."

"We can try. It's now or never."

"How?"

"I have a boat hidden. Come with me."

"Can't. Can't walk." He tried to sit up but collapsed back onto his belly.

"I'll help you." Oliver pulled him to his feet. "Put an arm around my shoulder."

It had been almost too easy to extract Reuben Spooner from the turpentine camp. As Oliver dragged the feeble man back to the river, he kept looking over his shoulder, expecting an alarm to be raised. The camp brooded like a somnolent dragon.

Spooner was a dead weight. Hoisting him into the fragile and tippy racing shell was a struggle. To stabilize the lightweight boat, Oliver had to push it onto the mud bank.

Ignoring Spooner's groans and whining protests, Oliver finally managed to arrange him in the stern. The space was tight. Two active rowers would have been pressed for legroom. "Rapture" wasn't designed for an occupant who sprawled like a rag doll with wet stuffings.

Finally, Oliver was able to get into "Rapture" himself and push off into the water. At that moment a flare of hot light blazed into the night sky. An inferno scorched the darkness.

CHAPTER TWENTY

SHEETS of flame vented into the blackness, some exploding in dazzling orange balls. Outlined against the burning distillery, Oliver saw two familiar figures. One threw up his hands to caper amidst the flames like an exultant imp. Scoop. The other seized Scoop by the shoulders and, after a brief struggle, dragged him out of the firelight. Nepp Percy.

Shouts and screams spewed from the darkness. Figures emerged, popping in and out of the firelight like shadow puppets . Another explosion shook the ground. In a moment the river would be lit like a Roman candle. Oliver turned away and began rowing with all his might.

He never looked back. Aided by the current, a breeze at his shoulder, and the adrenalin coursing through his veins, he pulled at the oars with all his might. The bloodshot light of the fire helped him avoid snags and other hazards. It seemed to take a long time, but once he was free of the conflagration, he had to rely on moonlight to steer. There was enough of that to allow progress despite the many obstructions in the waterway.

At his back Spooner, having lost consciousness, gabbled in his sleep. Otherwise, he was dead weight. The hours crawled past to the rhythm of the oars. Dawn was just beginning to thread the sky with gray when Oliver's exhaustion overtook him. The oars, so light at first, seemed made of lead. Somehow he managed to steer the boat into a clump of water locust and tie up.

A glance over his shoulder showed that Spooner was still asleep, his mouth open, his face bruised, a bloody cut creasing his forehead. Oliver had no room to stretch out, so he closed his eyes, slumped over the oars, folded his spent arms under his cheek and went unconscious. Three hours later a thump on the head jolted him awake.

"I'm hungry."

It was several seconds before Oliver was able to gather his thoughts. Reuben Spooner's bruised and irritable face, chock-a-block with his own, packed his field of vision. Hydrated, well fed and cleaned up, Spooner was probably a good looking man. There was nothing good looking about him now.

"I'm hungry. Thirsty as hell, too. Anything to drink in this damn boat?"

"There's a bag of food up front."

"Jesus, God, thank you!" Spooner lunged past Oliver, upsetting Rapture's delicate equilibrium. The rolling boat plunged Oliver head first into the water, interrupting his furious protest. When he came up for air and cleared his eyes, he saw Spooner thrashing nearby. It took longer than it should have to drag him onshore, as he was doing everything he could to make it difficult. Finally, Oliver righted the boat and rescued the oars and food. The oilskin bag had floated to the surface and become snagged in a patch of weed. Most of the food was still edible, though the biscuits were soggy.

Spooner gulped the drinking water until Oliver wrested it from him. "We need to preserve this. It's the only clean water we've got."

Reluctantly, Spooner nodded agreement. "I swallowed half this creek just now. It'll make me even sicker than I already feel."

"Whose fault is that? Where's you sense? You can't jump around in a boat like that!"

"Not much of a boat, if you ask me. More fit for a pair of china dolls than a couple of grown men."

"Rapture's the only ship we've got and our only hope of getting out of this place alive."

"Rapture? It's called Rapture! Whoever named it must have been loony!"

"Maybe, but it's fast. With both of us rowing it'll be even faster."

"I feel too sick to row."

Oliver stared at the man he had just risked his life to liberate, the man who had initiated his present predicament. He was beginning to understand why Spooner's bunk-mates had disliked him so much. He said, "Sick or not, we're both going to paddle our way out of this hell hole. It's that or die. What's more, you're going to sit in front of me, so I can see you're pulling your weight. Otherwise, I'll feed you to the alligators."

"How are you going to do that?"

"Shooting you and pushing you overboard." Oliver patted the Colt 45 tucked into his waistband. Fortunately, he hadn't lost it when the boat tipped.

"William Walters is paying you to rescue me."

"William Walters isn't here."

"Your bullets are probably waterlogged."

"Care to test them?"

Spooner grimaced and turned away. They packed up what remained of their supplies. Oliver forced Spooner into the front seat of Rapture and settled himself in the stern with the rifle, and oilskin supply bag .

"Start rowing."

"How? These oars aren't normal. Neither is the seat."

"You'll get the hang of it. I did."

They pulled out into the stream. The air was at rest, only the twitter of birds disturbing the hush of the emerging day. Dawn streaked the tender flow of water with silver and lavender-tinged gold. The overhanging trees filtered cool light. Oliver thought of cathedrals. Pools of darkness created sanctuaries of shadow.

Despite Spooner's protests, he seemed to know how to handle the oars. When Oliver commented on his proficiency, he shrugged. "I've rowed boats like this before."

"Then why pretend you hadn't?"

"I told you. I'm too sick to man the oars."

"You're doing fine now."

"You're sitting behind me with a damn gun. I've got no choice."

"Don't you forget it." They sculled on for half a mile before Oliver spoke again. "You might show a little gratitude. I risked my life to save you."

"Then, you're a fool. We've no chance of getting out of this place alive. Certainly not in this boat!"

"What do you mean?"

"It's made of paper."

"What?"

"It's a racing shell. They make them out of paper stuck together with glue and varnish. Fine for college boys on calm rivers. Not for a rough place like this."

As he spoke they narrowly avoided a dead tree blocking half the waterway. When they were beyond it Oliver said, "If we're sailing a paper boat we're going to have to be very careful."

"You mean you are. You're the one steering."

"Exactly. And you're the one causing trouble. Walters sent you down here to take a look at his investment. Not to disappear into a turpentine camp. How'd you manage that?"

Spooner was silent. When Oliver finally poked him in the back with the barrel of the gun, he shuddered. "Answer me."

"It's a long story."

"We've got a long day ahead of us. First tell me how got hooked up with William Walters."

"None of your damned affair!"

"It's entirely my affair. It's the reason we're both in this mess!"

"He and my family have done business together."

"Doing what?"

"You wouldn't understand."

"Try me."

"My folks have an import-export business. They deal in fancy goods: wines, specialty foods, expensive trinkets for the ladies, laces, silks—that sort of thing."

"And your family supplies Walters with…?"

"Wine. When he serves Port and Sherry, it came from us."

"Why would he send a wine merchant to Tampa?"

"My family has done business in the south. I was their agent and familiar with the territory. I was going anyway. I had other business to attend to."

"What other business?"

"That's confidential."

Oliver stared at Spooner's back with narrowed eyes. They paddled in silence while he mulled over what he'd just learned. Finally he asked, "When did you begin acting as your family's agent in the south?"

"Not recently."

"When?"

"It doesn't matter."

"I think it does. During the war the blockade meant southern cities accustomed to the good life—cities like Charleston and Jacksonville— were starved for fancy goods. They were willing to pay anything for their luxuries. Traitor merchants from the north made a fortune supplying them. That's what you were up to, isn't it?"

"I don't need to answer. The war is over."

"The war is not over down here. Not by a long shot. It won't be for another hundred years."

The pop of a gun burst the river's tranquility. They heard the distant barking of excited dogs.

Chapter Twenty-One

OLIVER hurried the boat into a screen of willow. He muttered, "I thought they'd be too busy with last night's fire to bother looking for us."

"What fire?"

"Good God, man, didn't you see it? Nepp Percy and a fellow named Scoop, set fire to the distillery. It went up like a bomb."

Spooner grimaced. "I knew something like that was afoot, but I was too sick to care."

"You knew about a plan to fire the distillery?"

"They talked of it in my cabin. They said a kid died for lack of medical treatment, and his friends wanted revenge."

"A kid named Collie?"

"Don't know." Spooner sounded disinterested. "That sounds right."

The dogs started howling again, this time closer. The cries had a chilling quality to them. Oliver knew that sound. The dogs weren't hunting blind. They'd found their quarry.

"Maybe they're not after us," he whispered. "A lot of prisoners probably took off during the confusion last night. Certainly Nepp and Scoop would have."

"Doesn't matter. If the hunters follow the water, which they're bound to do, they'll find us."

"Not if we are ahead of them."

"Are you crazy? Out on the river we'll be sitting ducks. They'll shoot us. Or worse, take us back to camp and make examples of us."

"We have to outrun them."

"In a paper boat that's about to fall apart?"

"Let's hope that Rapture lives up to its name." Oliver pushed out of the willows and steered the shell into the current. "Time to stop whining and show what you can do."

Spooner never quit complaining. But he did put his back into the oars. They both knew their lives depended on putting miles between themselves and the scent hounds. Even with the current in their favor, making headway wasn't easy. In places the waterway was little more than a weed-choked stream. In other spots fallen trees with dense branches seemed to reach out to snag Rapture and rip her apart. Several times Oliver felt certain the fragile boat had been fatally punctured. Miraculously, it stayed afloat.

For what seemed like hours they heard the cry of the dogs behind them. The sun was high when the sound finally died away.

Spooner stopped rowing and hung his head over the drifting oars. "I can't go on."

"We're ahead of them now, but they may still be hunting us."

"I don't care. I need to rest. I need food."

Oliver felt the same. Strength seemed to drain out of him like whiskey through an un-stoppered bung hole. "All right," he agreed, and steered Rapture toward the river's edge. "We'll have something to eat and drink."

"And take a rest. I need to take a rest."

They got out of the boat. The water felt good on Oliver's feet until he looked down and saw a copperhead wriggling nearby. For a moment he wondered if he was having delusions.

Spooner pointed at it. "Jesus Christ! Those things will kill you!"

Hurriedly they dragged the boat up onto the mud bank. While Spooner collapsed onto the ground, Oliver fumbled with the wet tie on the oilskin bag. His fingers felt thick and awkward. His hopes were crushed when he finally got it open and saw that the remaining biscuits were nothing but mush. The jerky was wet but still edible. He divided it between himself and Spooner. They finished it off in silence.

"There's a little more water left, but this is the last of our food. We'll have to find more."

Spooner rolled his eyes. "How? Fight off the alligators for fish?"

"I have guns. I'll have to shoot something. But I can't fire a gun now. I don't want to make noise until I'm certain it won't attract the wrong kind of attention."

"Nothing but the wrong kind of attention in this place."

"Exactly. We should push on."

"The hell with that! I need to rest. You want me back in that damned boat you'll have to carry me." Spooner set his face into a stubborn mask.

Oliver felt every bit as tired as Spooner claimed to be. More since he'd rowed all night and had little rest the day before. He hadn't the strength to force the man. Finally he said, "All right. We'll relax for a bit. But not for long."

Spooner grunted, closed his eyes, and leaned against a tree trunk.

Oliver did the same. Afraid of falling asleep, he made himself speak. "We were in the middle of a conversation when we heard the dogs."

"So?"

"So, let's keep ourselves awake by finishing it. You did business in these parts during the war. How'd you get into trouble after Walters sent you back?"

"I don't care about staying awake. I want to sleep."

"We can't afford to fall asleep. Not with a pack of dogs after us."

"My troubles are complicated. Too complicated to explain."

"Let me guess. During the war you cheated someone down here, sold them bad wine or bad food. They recognized you when you came back. That's how you wound up in the camp."

After cursing Oliver, Spooner declared, "I never sold bad anything. The goods my family offers are always top notch."

"Something you did pissed somebody off."

"Like I said, it's complicated." Spooner sighed. "All right, it's personal."

"Personal?"

"Having to do with my family."

"What family? Your folks in Baltimore?"

"No. Family down here." He closed his eyes again. "My daughter."

"What daughter is this?"

"Her name is Rosella."

Oliver stared. "Rosella Beauchamp? Callie Beauchamp's daughter?"

Spooner's eyes popped open. "How do you know that?"

"I've been introduced to both ladies. Callie Beauchamp is a Negress. How does she happen to be the mother of your daughter?"

"How do you think? When she was young she was beautiful."

"When she was young somebody owned her."

"Yes and he gave her to me."

"You'll have to explain that."

"I don't have to explain anything to you, you nosy bastard! It's none of your damned business!"

"You want to get out of here alive, you'll tell me everything."

Spooner turned his face away. He sighed. "During the war I visited a plantation near Charleston. The owner wanted to restock his wine cellar. We didn't conclude our business until late, so I spent the night. My host sent Callie to me."

Oliver lifted his eyebrows. "I'm guessing this obliging host didn't send her just to fluff up your pillow."

"It wasn't like it sounds. Callie didn't come willingly. She had no choice. But afterward, we fell in love. I visited often. When I left for the last time, she was pregnant."

"You didn't try to take her with you?"

Spooner looked irritated. "I offered to buy her, but her owner wouldn't sell. When the war ended we'd lost touch. Callie took our daughter to Florida. She'd heard they were hiring freed slaves to work the salt flats. She eventually got easier work with the Pedrosos."

"I'm surprised she didn't go north and try to find you."

"She knew better. You know what it's like. There's no way I could marry her or acknowledge our child. Besides, by that time I was already married."

"In other words, she knew you were a bastard. That's what you just called me."

"Maybe that describes us both."

Oliver was silent, considering the truth of this statement. He couldn't avoid comparing his own story with Spooner's. He hadn't known that his daughter's actress mother was pregnant with his child. But he wasn't certain he would have married Marietta Dumont had he known. After all, she'd left him for another man. He couldn't be certain that Chloe was really his.

Perhaps he might have forgiven Marietta's unfaithfulness if she hadn't abandoned Chloe, then had her maid foist the child on him. The maid had lied to him. She had claimed that Marietta was dead. As he soon discovered, she wasn't dead—only down and out. How could he ever trust her after that? No, he wasn't a saint, but he wasn't as bad as Spooner, either. Aloud, he asked, "Did Callie let you know you had a daughter?"

"She sent me a note."

"You never saw your daughter until you came to Tampa?"

"That's correct. Stop grilling me. Why should you care about any of this?"

"How did you meet?"

Spooner took his time answering. Finally, he said, "She was a maid at the hotel where I stayed."

Oliver examined Spooner's face. His eyes remained tightly closed, but he had exchanged his hostile expression for one that suggested unease. A red flush crept up his neck and suffused his features. Oliver remembered something he'd heard from Callie and blurted, "Oh, I see. Rosella's a good looking girl. You didn't realize she was your child and tried to get her into bed."

Spooner recoiled as if he'd stepped barefoot on a wasp. "I'm sick of talking to you, you son of a bitch! I'm not going to say another word."

"You don't need to. I can guess the rest. Not only did you try to get Rosella into bed, you probably succeeded. Maybe you even raped her."

"Go to hell!"

"Her mother found out and complained to Arnold Pepperwhite. He's a powerful man in Tampa. Considering he has a yen for Rosella himself, he probably arranged to make sure you never bothered her again."

"I said go to hell! I wish I'd never laid eyes on you or this whole cursed state."

"Callie Beauchamp is thinking along similar lines. She couldn't have been happy about you committing incest with her daughter. "

"Shut your damned dirty mouth!" Spooner clenched his fists and turned his face away.

A rustling in the greenery nearby distracted Oliver. After a few seconds of listening intently, he said, "We should probably go."

"I'm not going anywhere with you! You can't make me. I hate the sight of you! I'd rather float down the river with one of those water moccasins."

"We can't stay here."

"I can. Shoot me if you want. I'm not getting into that boat!"

Oliver considered his options. He had been a fool to raise Spooner's hackles. Stirring him up would only make more difficulties. He wasn't even sure why he'd done it. Guilt about his own illegitimate daughter perhaps? He told himself he'd never felt guilty about his relationship with Marietta. Yes, he'd been in love with her. He could admit it to himself now. In love with her beauty, her charm, her daring spirit. Yes, he'd been smitten.

It was she who'd left him, never telling him she was pregnant. If she truly was at that time—for how could he be certain? Regardless of who Chloe's birth father might be, she was his daughter now. He was doing his best to raise her up right, even considering relocating his business for the sake of her health. Why should he feel guilty?

But maybe he did. He closed his eyes and allowed himself to think about his relationship with Marietta and their daughter. Where was Chloe now? Did she and his housekeeper, Mrs. Milawney, think he was dead? It was painful to picture Chloe with no proper guardian to protect her. Marietta claimed to want her back, but she was as reliable as dandelion fluff in a hurricane. He had to get out of here. He couldn't fall asleep. He couldn't.

He forced his eyes open. The sun was low in the sky. He'd been dead to the world for hours. His head jerked toward the spot where he'd left Rapture. It was gone, and so was Spooner along with his rifle and what remained of their supplies. What's more, he could hear the dogs in the distance.

CHAPTER TWENTY-TWO

SPOONER had stolen away with the boat. Oliver blinked up into a thick canopy of tangled greenery. Maybe this was just a nightmare. No, it was real. He was alone in the wilds of Florida with no boat, no food, a wet pistol full of wet bullets, and scent hounds hot on his trail.

He staggered to his feet. Think, he told himself. He clutched the pistol still in his waistband. It might be useless, but at least he had it. Spooner had probably left it to him only because he feared to interrupt his deep sleep by prying it loose. Oh Lord, how could he have been so senseless?

Late afternoon sun slanted through the lattice of trees rimming the water. Pale columns of light arrowed into the river's bed. He knelt at the edge of the embankment and splashed droplets into his eyes. He could see his face distorted like a fun house reflection. The river had its own special odor—decay and mushrooming life fermenting into a dank perfume. Near his elbow a colony of ants swarmed on a rotting log.

He scooped up handfuls of mud and smeared it on his clothing, feet and ankles. Its odor might confuse the dogs.

How far had he and Spooner come in Rapture? Was he anywhere near the coast? He knew he had to start moving. It was either that or let them find him. Not with Chloe depending on him. Best to follow the water, he thought. It would take him to the coast.

At the cry of a hunting dog in the distance, he willed his limbs into action. He waded in shallow water when he could, skirting clumps of bushes and trees, jumping over bramble carpeted logs when he had to. Stray branches lashed his arms and face into a crisscross of welts. Mosquitoes hummed in his ears. He staggered to his knees several times, but always managed to get back to his feet.

The sun sank lower, and the sky lost its blue glint. He had stopped hearing dogs. So most likely they had been tracking other escapees. Once those were rounded up, Captain Arnold would focus on him and Spooner. Arnold was not the sort who would give up easily. Where was Spooner now, Oliver wondered as he stumbled around a clump of bulrush. Would they meet again?

It was almost dark when he finally crashed to the ground. This time he was unable to rise to his feet. All he could do was close his eyes and sink into oblivion.

"Wake up, mister. You look dead, but you got yourself a heartbeat."

Oliver tried to ignore the voice, but it was persistent. He dragged his eyelids up. A young girl's face swam into focus. Beneath the rim of her straw hat she had round brown eyes and a pug nose. Freckles sprinkled her tanned cheeks. She sat back on her heels and turned her head.

"Lookee. He opened his eyes, Daddy."

"I see that." The voice was a deep, rich Mississippi drawl.

"Pears sick, don't he? What you wanna' do?"

"We could put him outa' his misery. Roll him into the crick and forget about him. That would be easiest."

"No Daddy! Man needs help."

"Pansy, why is it you take in every ailing, good for nothin' critter you find? I thought you wanted to go frog huntin'. This ain't no frog."

Oliver finally managed to turn his head and look at the person the girl called "Daddy." He saw a hulking figure in baggy pants held up by what looked like Confederate army suspenders. A wide brimmed hat made his block of a face inscrutable. Under the suspenders he wore a stained union suit and a red neckerchief. The vision blurred and fell apart as if dissolving in oil. "Please," Oliver managed to say before he slid back into unconsciousness.

An hour later Oliver became aware that something was moving underneath him. Somebody had draped him over a mule. His face rested in the animal's prickly barb of mane. He groaned and struggled to sit up. Too weak to do more than hump his back, he collapsed. A hand seized his neck and heaved him into a sitting position.

"Time you had something to drink, Mister. Pansy, get the canteen while I hold his head."

Oliver mumbled a protest but was powerless to evade the iron grip on his neck and shoulders. His face was yanked up to the sky. Water streamed over his lips and chin. He choked but managed to swallow some of it before he was released back onto the mule's neck.

"Think he got some. 'Pears dead to the world agin. Let's push on home before skeeters eat us alive."

Oliver woke up the next morning. A ribbon of sun coiled through a window slit. Shielding his eyes, he blinked up at it. Silver threads glimmered in the light. A spider busied himself with a fly trapped in the web.

Where was he? For several long seconds he had no idea. Some of what had happened yesterday came back—his confrontation with Spooner, waking up to find the man had disappeared with the boat, forcing himself to stumble along the river's edge. But what had happened after that? Had he been captured? Was he in a prison?

He battled to his feet and stood swaying on watery legs. When he'd managed to steady himself he looked around. He was in a shed with a thatched roof. The hides of skunks, squirrels, possums and what might have been a bobcat upholstered the wall above a collection of feed barrels. That's what accounted for the musky odor of the place.

He peered through the window slit. The structures outside were not the ramshackle bunkhouses of the turpentine camp. Instead he saw what appeared to be two good sized, unpainted but solidly built houses. Both had porches appointed with rocking chairs.

Between them was a barn with a fenced-in area containing three mules, two cows, and a sway-backed horse. Nearby were several small huts thatched with palmetto. Chickens roamed around them. He spotted a large vegetable garden and what appeared to be a pen for hogs. Palms and Florida scrub encircled the complex, giving it an exotic look, as if a Midwestern farm had been set down in a tropical forest.

The door behind him banged open. He jerked around and saw the same imposing figure who'd rescued him yesterday. "My woman's fixin' to get breakfast on the table, Mister, if you'd care to eat."

Oliver croaked, "Please. I'm hungry!"

"Bet you are. Thirsty too, I'll warrant."

"Very thirsty. And dirty. I haven't had any way to get clean in days."

"First things first. You'd best fill your belly. Name's Handy, Micah Handy." He did not extend his hand but kept his arms dangling at his side.

"Oliver Redcastle."

"Can't say yet whether I'm pleased to meet you, Oliver. But I like your name."

"Well, I'm delighted you meet you. You saved my life."

"We'll see about that. And I do see you need soap and water. Clean clothes, too. The rags coverin' your hide are fixin to fall right off. Ain't fit for anything but the fire."

Micah pointed out the privy. It turned out to be capacious, four-holed, and well-used judging from the odor and the army of flies buzzing in every corner. When Oliver emerged, he followed his host to the larger of the two houses. Inside it was plain but clean. The pine floors were swept, and the walls had been whitewashed. The furniture was spare and roughly made, but the fragrance emanating from the outside kitchen was divine. Moments later he was tucking into a tin plate of what his hostess called "white bacon." It was really salt pork fried to a crisp brown, its hot grease poured over grits, sweet potatoes and corn bread. The food was delicious, but he found he could only eat a small amount.

"Best not to fork up more'n you can handle," the female Micah described as "My woman," advised. "You'll be gettin' the same thing for lunch and dinner. When I cook up a batch in the morning cool, it feeds us the whole day. Sometimes more." She was almost as tall as Micah and even wider. Her ruddy face might have been pretty once but was now weathered into a rugged majesty that an artist might appreciate. She had pale blue eyes deeply creased in the corners.

After Oliver apologized for the state of his appearance, she chuckled and told him her name was Arnette. It was plain to see that Arnette had not led an easy life. Even so, she seemed comfortable in her loose-fitting, home-spun dress. When she finished serving coffee, she left the room promising to fix him a bath. The young girl named Pansy was nowhere to be seen.

Micah drew up a chair across from Oliver. "Well now, I judge it's time to talk."

Oliver started to repeat his thanks. Micah held up a silencing hand. "Thank my girl, Pansy. Weren't for her, I'd left you where you lie. Never know what a man's about in this place. Scalawags light here like flies to a carcass. We heard of trouble in the turp camp down river and 'spect you're part of that. Am I right?"

Something in Micah's fixed gaze told Oliver it would not be a good idea to lie. He nodded and gave an edited version of who he was and how he'd escaped the camp.

Micah leaned back and sipped his coffee. He set the tin cup down and folded his brawny arms across his broad chest. "So you're a law man from up north. Mighty nervy of you to mosy down thisaway. Most in these parts soldiered for the Confederacy and hate the north."

"The war is over."

"You think that, you're a fool. War will never be over 'round here. Believe me, I know."

"You fought for the Confederacy?"

"I did. Seventh Battalion of Mississippi Infantry. After the defeat at Corinth, I deserted."

Oliver sat up. "You're a deserter?"

"I am," Micah declared, "and not shamed of it neither. Between the starvation rations, idiot captains, and having to wade through rivers of blood, any man with sense would have done the same. I was raised in Mississippi, but not by the people wantin' war. The Rebs broke us poor farmers. They made themselves a tax by which they stole whatever they fancied. When I got home I found they'd took my horses, hogs, corn. They even cleaned out my smokehouse. My family was all but starved. Fact, I lost a child from starvation. They did me and other poor folk more hurt than the whole Union army."

Micah's heavy black brows knit and he clenched his fists. "I 'spose you know about the Twenty Negra Law?"

"Probably, but can't remember exactly. . ."

"Every twenty slaves owned on a plantation exempted a white slave owner. So that made it a rich man's war and a poor man's fight. I never owned a slave in my life. Married one but never owned one."

"You married a slave?"

Micah chuckled and then winked. Suddenly his eyes held a twinkle. "Well, kinda'. I got me two families. Step outside and I'll show you."

CHAPTER TWENTY-THREE

MICAH led Oliver to the porch and pointed. "See these two houses? Built the one we're in out of good pine and then did the same for the other. Built them both with my own hands."

"Well, sir, they look like fine houses." Situated on either side of the barn, they appeared almost identical. One had a coral honeysuckle vine clinging to the porch rail. A collection of tin cans planted with flowers adorned the other. "You're a good carpenter."

"I got a family lives in each. Maybe you wonder about that, seeing as it ain't legal to have more'n one wife at the same time?"

"That is true in most states, though I don't know laws in Florida," Oliver answered. Where was this going?

Micah sneered. "Laws don't mean squat in these parts 'cept when some varmint wants to use 'em agin' you. But I ain't actually breaking the law. Arnette and me, we're legal married as can be. We was married when we was both kids."

"She seems like a fine lady. Excellent cook, too."

"She bore me six little babies, and only three died. She keeps the hogs outa' the garden and manages the chickens. Man couldn't ask for a better wife. We married up real young, but Arnette was older than me. She was right pert then. Our age difference didn't figure. But when she went through the change she left my bed." Micah shrugged. "This ain't no easy life. Man gets lonesome. Needs comfort." He squinted. "You been through tribulation, but you still look like a strong, healthy fella. You can take my meaning."

Oliver nodded. He could understand. The wandering life he'd led hadn't allowed time or place for a wife or a real home. There had been women before and after Marietta, but never opportunity to build anything lasting. He'd hoped to make a home for himself and his daughter in Baltimore. Now he feared losing that, too.

Micah took a wad of chewing tobacco out of his pocket and stuck it in the corner of his mouth. He stood in silence for a minute or two, working at it. Finally, he cleared his throat. "You got a wife waitin' for you?"

Oliver shook his head.

"Alone in the world then?"

"Pretty much."

Micah gave him a considering look. Oliver could feel the man assessing him, drawing conclusions. It was unnerving. Oliver was reticent by nature. In his profession he'd had to be. Knowledge about a man was power over him.

Micah spit out the tobacco. "Well, back in the time I was speaking of, Arnette and I had a talk, and she showed the sense the good lord gave her. She agreed to find me a woman for my needs. That's when I took up with Moya." He pointed at a small, neat looking figure sitting on the porch of the second house. Oliver couldn't see her face, but he could tell she wasn't white. "She looks busy. What's she doing?"

"Stuffing mattresses."

Oliver squinted, watching as she shredded palmetto with a fork, cut off the hard parts, then pushed the fronds into a ticking."

Micah said, "Moya's been a good woman. She's a good mother, and she keeps a clean house. Her pap was Seminole.

Her mother was half black and half white. So, she and the three little ones she's given me are a mix. My kids by her could pass, though. If they had to. Pansy's Moya's oldest."

"Pansy's Moya's daughter, and you're her father?"

"That's right. You look surprised. What did you think of Pansy? "

"I'm grateful to her. The two of you saved my life."

"Yes, but what did you think? I bet you never figured her ma was part Negra."

Oliver thought back to the young girl who'd found him. He remembered little but her brown eyes and kindness. He was sure he owed her his life. "No, I didn't. How many children do you have?"

"Six in all. Three boys by Arnette and two boys and a girl by Moya." He scratched his ear. "The older boys are a fret."

"How so?"

"Since they been growed they been tomcattin' around with anything they can find. They need proper wives to settle them down. I've been on the lookout, but so far no luck. Moya's kids are young yet, ceptin' for Pansy. She's almost sixteen."

"That's young."

"Not around these parts. Pansy's the right age for a husband if we could find her a good one."

"You say your legal wife found Moya for you?"

"Sure did. She run from her master after the war and headed south to look for her father's people. Found us instead."

Arnette came around the corner of the house and signaled. Micah shaded his eyes to see her against the sun, then said, "Women got you a tub of hot water ready if you'd care to clean yourself."

Oliver agreed and followed Micah to the shed where he'd awakened earlier. A tin tub had been set up, half-filled with warm water. A rickety wood chair next to it held a bar of strong smelling homemade soap. At Micah's urging, Oliver stripped off his filthy garments and stepped into the bath.

Micah scooped up the discarded clothing. "I'll take and burn all this. Bring you in some clean duds."

"Thanks."

Fifteen minutes later Oliver sat with his head tipped back and his eyes closed, enjoying the bath, when the door clicked open.

CHAPTER TWENTY-FOUR

EXPECTING to see Micah, Oliver turned his head. Pansy walked in and smiled at him. She was holding a ragged towel and looked very different from the waif in men's clothes he dimly remembered. A pink ribbon confined her dark curls. A dress of the same color showed off her pert bosom and tidy waist. Waddling along beside her was a fat skunk. It regarded him with shoe-button eyes. They sparkled like shards of mica in the gloom of the shed.

Catching Oliver's startled expression, Pansy said, "Don't be skeered of my skunk. Bluebell don't have her stink sack on her no more, and she don't bite. Plus she's right friendly. I come to scrub your back and give your hair a wash."

Oliver looked in vain for something to cover himself. He'd been so eager for a bath that he hadn't noticed the lack of a cloth to dry himself, or worried that Micah had not replaced his discarded attire. The cooling water in the tub barely covered his thighs.

"Pansy, I'm naked."

She chuckled. "Well, I know that. Hardly nobody takes a bath with clothes on them."

Oliver tried to sink deeper into the small tub. "I mean that you shouldn't be here, alone with a naked man more than twice your age. It's not proper."

She snorted. "Proper don't mean much in these parts. I got brothers. Naked don't mean much to me, neither. I see Jeb and Earl walking around without their pants. I even see Pa that way sometimes."

She crossed to the tub and cocked her head. "You already washed your hair." Her gaze traveled over his body with open curiosity. "You need to put on some flesh. You're mighty thin but still a fine looking fella'. You got good wide shoulders and muscles up your arms. Know what? I like your looks better'n I do my brothers, and they're handsome according to what I'm told." Her grin widened and she patted the top of his head. "Now I'll wash your back."

"Pansy, I appreciate your kindness, but I insist you leave."

"You don't like gettin' your back scrubbed?"

"I do, but. . .I'm sure your pa wouldn't want you alone with a man who's got no clothes."

"Oh, that's all right. He told me to come tend to you." Blue-bell left Pansy's side and wandered about the tub, stopping now and then to stare at the wall covered with hides. Oliver wondered if some of the furry remains nailed to the boards might have belonged to her brothers and sisters.

Pansy busied herself preparing the soap and towel. She said, "Pa told my ma to put a ribbon in my hair and let me wear my best dress. You like it?" She danced away to the middle of the room, spread her arms and performed a slow whirl so that her skirt belled out around her bare feet.

Despite himself, Oliver was charmed. Pansy looked so blissful. Her innocent delight at having a clean dress, and a ribbon in her hair, enchanted him. A smile twitched his lips. He suppressed it. "Child, I'd like to speak to your pa. Would you ask him to come in, please?"

"Oh, I can't do that until you're washed. He told me to make sure you got a good scrub before I left." She grimaced. "What Pa wants Pa gets. He wants you clean, so I got to get you that way." She circled around back of the tub, applied soap to his neck and shoulders, and began kneading gently.

Oliver pressed his knees together and took another tack. "Your pa thinks you might be lonely out here in the woods."

Pansy slowed her circular scrubbing motions. "Lonely? Why, no. I got lots of friends."

"Your brothers?"

She laughed at that. "My brothers ain't my friends. They're my chores. I got to take care of them when my mam gets the megrims. Samson and Zeke can be trouble, let me tell. Tendin' them scallywags night and day makes a person feel like she's been kicked into a corner and sat on."

"Your mother isn't well?"

"Sometimes she gets the headache. Specially when she's spent the night with Pa." Her hand slid down his wet arm. He noticed what appeared to be a brilliantly colored lacquer bracelet. On closer inspection he saw that it had scales.

"Is that a coral snake on your wrist?"

"Used to be. When I was a little baby Pa found me playin' with it. He killed and stuffed it, and I been wearin' it ever since."

"Corals are very poisonous. You're lucky to be alive."

"That's what they say. My mam thinks it a miracle I never got bit. Reckon I was one lucky little baby."

Oliver nodded his agreement. He recalled a Greek myth about an infant playing with snakes. Was it Hercules? A peculiar light-headedness swept over him. Somehow he'd stumbled over the edge of creation and dropped into a world distinct from all he'd known.

He inhaled, tasting an atmosphere steeped with the ripe odors of greenery. It harbored creatures unseen but resident in every particle. Was it winter? The season of snow began to seem like a faraway hallucination. In this realm of paradox and hidden energy, old rubrics did not apply. Even time seemed to circle like a lazy river that disappeared into secret wells, then resurfaced when least expected. Light struck a spider web festooning the corner above him and fractured into golden splinters. He shivered as Pansy's hands slipped down his back and began to knead his knotted muscles.

"You feel real tight. I'll loosen you up."

That was what he feared. He pressed his knees together and asked, "I can understand why your younger brothers might not be your favorite companions. What about your older brothers?"

"My older brothers? You mean Pa's other family? Jeb, Hi and Earl?"

"Yes."

She snorted. "Oh, they ain't my friends. All they think about is killin' plume birds for their feathers." Her voice thickened with anger. "It's so mean the way they shoot the mama and daddy birds and leave the babies to be et up by varmints. I hate it."

Oliver pictured the egret feathers so popular for decorating female hats. How many fashionable ladies would enjoy those hats if they knew how birds had died to provide them?"

"And," Pansy went on, "when they're not killin' the poor pretty birds they're botherin' the Murkels."

"The Murkels?"

"Sixteen Murkels live over by Duck Hammock in a little old one-room shack with a dirt floor. Pa says they're no account trash. But Hi and Jeb like the oldest girls, Emmy, Thelda and Lula. They sneak out at night to visit them."

"I see. What about you? Are you friends with any Murkels?"

"Fanny's all right. She's the youngest. Sometimes we go frog hunting. She knows all the best spots. Promise you won't tell Pa! He wouldn't like it."

"I won't tell."

She thought for a moment, her clever hands pausing against his slick shoulders. Bluebell had found a pile of spilled chicken feed and was sniffing it, her plumed tail twitching with interest.

"Oh, git away from that!" Pansy darted at the skunk, swatted her furry backside and scooped up the feed. After she'd dumped it back into a barrel, she turned to Oliver. "Bluebell knows she only s'posed to eat what I give her. She starts gettin' into the feed, and Pa will skin her."

"Pansy, you were going to tell me something else. What?"

She stilled, thought for a moment longer, then shrugged. "Why, just that Fanny isn't my only friend. I got another one. Antonio."

"Antonio? That's a Spanish name."

"Antonio is Cuban."

"Cubans live here?"

"They got a fish camp down where the river empties into the big water. Pa don't like them. He thinks they're spies."

"Spying for Cuba?"

"Well, Cubans were here before us, I guess."

"Are they spies?"

"Don't know." Pansy wrung out the washcloth and replaced it on the stand next to the tub. "You got a beard growing. I could give you a shave."

"No thanks. I'll do that for myself."

"What about a haircut? I could give you a haircut. I cut my brothers' all the time."

"Do you have scissors?"

"Sure do. I got 'em right here in my pocket." She extracted a rusty implement that looked more appropriate for shearing a sheep than giving a man a haircut.

Oliver said, "All right." He waited until she had been clipping at his hair for a minute or two and then asked, "You mentioned that Antonio is your friend. How good a friend?"

Pansy didn't answer. Oliver waited to see if she would when the door to the shed smashed open, and Micah stormed in. "What's going on here?"

CHAPTER TWENTY-FIVE

MICAH planted himself in front of Oliver's tub. He cradled a shotgun in his arms, his expression forbidding. "Young man, why are you stark-naked and alone in this shed with my innocent daughter?"

Oliver's bath water had cooled. He felt goosebumps rising along his arms and bare shoulders. The small tub forced his bare knees against his chest accordion-style. He wanted to hoist himself up, but couldn't without being even more exposed. Pansy stood next to the tub staring at her father in amazement. "Why, Daddy, you tole me to. . ."

Micah shot her a furious glance. "Shut your mouth and don't interfere. You hear me?"

Pansy's jaw dropped. She took a step backwards. Micah's attention reverted to Oliver. "Yankee, you have a funny way of returnin' a favor, seducing my innocent young daughter."

Oliver started to protest, but Micah raised his shotgun in a most menacing manner. He demanded, "Did I not, as a good Christian, save your life when you was like to die out in the swamp? Did you not eat at my table and take shelter on my property? Answer me, yes or no?"

Oliver said, "Sir, I think you know I'm naked in this tub at your request, and your daughter…"

Micah aimed his shotgun square at Oliver's bare chest. "Shut your damned mouth, and don't open it until you're ready to give me a decent Christian man's answer. Are you ready to do right by my little girl? Are you ready to make her your lawful wife?"

At this, Pansy gasped and blurted, "Daddy, I don't want to marry nobody!"

Micah shot her another hard look. "I ain't asked what you want or don't want. Now git yourself outa' here, and tell your ma to take that sinful dress offen you, and git those ribbons outa' your hair! You hear me?"

When Pansy bobbed her head, he added, "And take that godawful skunk with you, and don't let me see her again lest I blow her head off!"

Pansy snatched up Bluebell and rushed from the shed. When she'd slammed the door behind her, the two men faced each other in angry silence. Micah leveled his shotgun. "You can stand yourself up now."

"You took my clothes away."

"That's right. Now do as I say and stand yourself up like a man."

The confining tub had cut off the circulation in Oliver's legs. They would have collapsed beneath him if he hadn't braced himself with his arms. At last he managed to rise to his full height and stand in the cold water with pins and needles shooting through the bottoms of his feet.

Micah looked him up and down. At last he drawled, "Well now, I reckon, once we feed you up, you're going to make my little girl a right fine husband."

"Pansy is hardly more than a child. I'm too old for her. I fought in the war. We both know how long ago that was."

"You ain't got no choice in the matter. So make up your mind to it. And make up your mind that if you ever do her wrong, I'll blow your head off. If I ain't around to keep my promise, one of my boys will do it for me. You hear?"

"Pansy doesn't want to marry me."

"She's my child. She'll do what I say."

"You can't force me."

"Of course I can. I've sent the boys to fetch the preacher. He'll be here in two days. When he come, we'll have ourselves a wedding. I've already told the women to start their cooking."

Once again Oliver was confined to the shed, this time under guard. Micah had drafted his three sons into a twenty-four-hour watch. Oliver had already met Jeb and Hi. They were strapping, bearded young men with their father's taciturn manner and their mother's fresh complexion and pale blue eyes. Like their father, they all wore loose pants held up by suspenders, or tight leather belts made out of gator hide. When Earl turned up to guard Oliver he seemed different from his older brothers. He was smaller, red-headed, more freckled, more excitable, and quite a lot less formidable. He arrived to take his turn from Hi just after sundown.

"About time," Hi grumbled. "You ain't no more reliable than a rabid coon."

"Ma just finished dinner. I'm on time as I could get. I ain't looking forward to spending the night with the damn skeeters."

"I hope they eat you alive. Serve you right for going behind my back with Thelda."

"Can I help it if she takes a shine to me? You know how that girl is."

"I know you're a mealy mouth, lyin' skunk. What you mean 'how that girl is'?"

"Hotter than a frying pan in a forest fire." Earl's snicker was abbreviated by what sounded like a punch in the mouth.

"Oof. Stop that! I'll tell Pa."

"Go ahead. You know Pa don't like you. Thinks you look too much like that Yankee soldier stayed at our place while Pa was gone."

"I ain't no Yankee! You got no call."

"You're not to say my girl's like a frying pan. Open your dirty mouth again, and I'll squash you like a bug! You hear?"

"Ah, c'mon Hi. It was just havin' fun."

"Thelda is mine. Try havin' fun with her again, and I'll fix you so you'll never have no more fun. Understand me?"

Oliver pressed his ear to the window slit closest to the brothers and listened to them wrangle. A few minutes later Hi stomped off. Oliver heard the rustle of footsteps. The boy appeared at the window wiping away a dribble of blood at the corner of his mouth. Despite his injury, he looked jaunty—his ragged straw hat pushed back at a rakish angle.

"How you doin' in there Yankee?"

"Well enough."

"Guess you and me is going to spend the night here."

"I look forward to the company."

"Do tell?" Laughing, Earl performed a spirited jig. When he finished hopping from foot to foot, he pressed his sharp-chinned, freckled face close to the open slit. Oliver could see the flecks of yellow in his small green eyes. "Lookin' forward to your wedding day, too?"

"What do you think?"

Once again Earl exploded into a hyena laugh that set his whole skinny body to quivering. "Whoee! I think I'm going to have me a Yankee brother-in-law. Not that I ever wanted one. But Pa has his own notions. Oh yes, he sure do! Nighty night, Yankee."

Stuffing his hands into his pockets and whistling, Earl struck a cavalier attitude and strolled around the other side of the shed. Oliver heard a thump as he settled onto a stool. A few minutes later he heard a faint scraping sound. Whittling?

Oliver closed his eyes and considered his situation. Tonight would be the time to try a getaway. How? The dogs were bound to set off an alarm. He didn't wish to injure a member of Micah's family. He only wanted out of this outlandish situation. But it was hard to see how he could escape without a fight. Certainly, he'd have to disable Earl. Hurting the boy did not sit well, but if he had to, he would.

Three hours later the moon glinted through the trees, and Micah's compound was quiet. Only the buzz of Earl's snores broke the murky silence. Oliver had tested every corner of his prison. The hut was more solidly built than it appeared. The door had been barred with a stout piece of oak. He couldn't break it without an uproar. He had found a piece of board abutting the dirt floor that he might pry loose. Could he do that without making a commotion? He doubted it. So he had located a feed scoop and set about digging himself an escape route. If he worked all night, he might make a crawl space he could wriggle through.

"Mister?" The whisper floated in through the window slit.

Oliver straightened.

"Mister? Are you there?"

"I'm here." Oliver peered into the narrow slot of darkness. The moon came out from behind a cloud. He saw Pansy's shape in the shadows.

She leaned close to the narrow aperture and whispered. "I got to talk fast. Earl's asleep but he might wake. I'm going to help you get out. Can't do it tonight. Tomorrow when the preacher comes they'll be fixin' his dinner. That's when we'll make a run for it."

"We?"

"I'm going with you."

"But Pansy. . ." Oliver didn't finish his warning. The crunch of a footfall sent the girl scampering into darkness. He heard a different female whisper, throaty and playful.

"Earl, hey Early, wake yourself up. I got something nice for you."

CHAPTER TWENTY-SIX

Earl's soft snores rumbled to a stop. After a long pause, he muttered, "Hello there, Thelda. Fancy seein' you here. Does your pa know you're out after dark?"

"Pa don't know and Pa don't care."

"What about Hi? He bust me in the mouth over you!"

"What Hi don't know won't hurt none. "

"But. . ."

"I got somethin' mighty nice for you, Earl. Somethin' I know you like."

"Now what would that be?"

"That'd be me. Me like this. See?"

As Oliver listened to Thelda's steamy whispers, his imagination churned. He pictured a sultry tropical temptress, a barefoot Venus dressed in flour sack rags, but all the more alluring for her rusticity. Was she young and beautiful? Hi and Earl seemed to think so. Or was she just, as Earl said, 'hotter than a frying pan in a forest fire.' Whatever the truth, she was having her effect—not just on Earl but on Oliver, too.

Earl muttered, "I can't see nothin' in the dark. What you doin' with your top?"

"I'll come closer. Now can you see?"

"Sure can. Ah, Thelda, that's sweet, but Hi will skin me if I mess with you."

"We won't tell. Now be nice, and let me kiss away the hurt on your poor ol' mouth. Why, I do b'lieve your lip is split."

"It is."

"Let me fix it."

Oliver heard a smacking and then a soft chuckle. "Well, well, what do you know? Looks like guard duty ain't goin' to be so bad after all."

Thelda giggled. Then Oliver heard a whole lot of whispering, moaning, and rustling.

The next morning, Micah peered through the window slit of Oliver's prison, "How you doin in there, boy?"

"What do you think?" Oliver had spent half the night trying to ignore the activity outside and dig his way to freedom. He had not succeeded in making a hole big enough to wriggle through. Now he was filthy, exhausted, frustrated, and cross.

Micah squinted, trying to see into the gloomy interior of the shed. "Look here, son, "Preacher be here soon. Come next mornin' you'll be a married man. So I come to tell you to clean yourself up. I know you did it once, but didn't last. After sleepin' with the skunk hides in there you stink."

Oliver was too infuriated to speak.

Micah shook his head. "I know you're fit to be tied, but ain't that the way with all us men? Women rope us in, and we drag our feet. Like it or not, it's nature's way."

"Pansy did not rope me in. She's just a child. You roped me in."

"Son, it amounts to the same thing—seeing as I'm her pa and have her best interests. Now let's get you cleaned up." Micah unbarred the door and poked his head into the dark interior. "Come on along with me. Arnette's set up a tub back of the house. I got you some fresh clothes. We'll get you fixed up fine!"

Oliver staggered outside and stood blinking in the bright sunlight. Micah poked him in the back. "Come on now, thisaway. When I said you stink I was not deceitful. You smell like a ripe polecat."

Prodded by Micah, Oliver stumbled around the side of the house. Chatting about the wedding preparations as if Oliver were looking forward to them, Micah steered him toward a tin tub filled with water. "Now, son, strip off them dirty pants and git in there. When you come out squeaky clean and smellin' sweet, we'll feed you up good. You need to put on some flesh. Don't want Pansy to think she got into bed with a washboard." He guffawed at his joke.

Excited male voices broke into the old man's hilarity. Micah turned his head. His sons, accompanied by dogs, hurried out from the trees. All carried shotguns. Earl, who looked none the worse for his hectic night, supported an axe on his shoulder.

He jogged past his brothers and approached Micah, sparing only a brief glance for Oliver. "Pap, we got company."

"What company? You mean the preacher's here already?"

"Not the preacher. Damn pusillanimous preacher must have tipped off Cap Arnold . He's got his dogs and a posse headin' thisaway. Hear that?"

The howl of a hound floated in on the wind. The dogs at the boys' heels pricked their ears. They began to whine and mill about. After giving them a stern reprimand, Earl stared at Oliver, "What you think he's after? Think he's wantin' this fella'?"

"That could be." Micah focused on Oliver and knit his heavy brows in thought. "Take him back to the shed and lock him in."

"But they'll want to search."

"I'm fixin' to see it don't come to that. Arnold ain't nothin' but a damned Regulator pretendin' to be law. He and his gang give us nothin' but grief. I hate the ground he walks on. Now, do as I say. I gotta' get my shotgun."

Micah hurried off with his other sons and their dogs. Earl grabbed Oliver's arm. "You heard, Yankee. I got to lock you up."

When Oliver resisted, Earl threatened him with his ax. "You fixin' to get your head split?"

"You wouldn't do that to your future brother-in-law."

"Don't try me. I don't fancy no Yankee brothers. Ask me, Pansy could do a whole lot better, even if she is a half-breed."

Oliver considered taking the ax away from Earl. He thought he could do it, but he didn't want to hurt the boy. Still, if there was no other way—

A female voice interrupted their dispute. "I ain't no half-breed, Earl. Happens I've got the same pa as you!"

Earl turned his head. "Pansy, what you doin' out here? You're not sposed to see the bridegroom on your weddin' day."

Pansy circled around and confronted her brother. She was no longer dressed for seduction, but wore trousers, a felt hat and boots. Planting her feet so as to block his path, she glared at him. "Let him go!"

"Let who go?"

She jabbed a finger in Oliver's direction. "You don't want him to be my bridegroom and neither do I. Let him go."

Earl looked thunderstruck. "Pansy, you know I can't. Pa would skin me."

"What do you think Hi's going to do when I tell him you spent the night with Thelda?"

CHAPTER TWENTY-SEVEN

E ARL'S eyes popped. He took a step backward. "I ain't!"
Pansy fixed her hands to her hips. "Don't lie. I heard
her sneak in, and I heard the ruckus the two of you made."

"So did I," Oliver offered.

Earl's horrified gaze swiveled from his sister to Oliver and
back. "You wouldn't tell Hi. You know how daft Hi gets. He
might shoot me dead."

"He might," Pansy agreed. "So you'd best let Mr. Oliver go."

Pansy and Earl argued the matter for several more minutes.
To Oliver's surprise and delight, Earl gave in. He demanded
only that Pansy tie him up in the shed. He wanted it to look as
if he'd been forced to release his prisoner against his will. Once
that task had been completed, Pansy steered Oliver away from
the house and onto a path through the trees.

She broke into a run . "We got to hurry!"

"I'm hurrying ," Oliver said, trotting after her.

"I mean we got to really hurry! We got to get to the boat
and out into the big river before Pa and the boys know we're
gone."

Pansy had hidden a weather-beaten pirogue in bushes at the
edge of a creek a half mile or so from her father's homestead.
A pile of flour sacks stowed by the mid-ship seat weighed the
craft down. "What's in those?" Oliver asked as they struggled
to push the overladen vessel out into moving water.

"Supplies," Pansy muttered. "Food and water."

After they climbed aboard, Oliver asked, "Where did you get the boat?"

"Stole it from Murkels."

"Stole it? I thought the Murkels were your friends."

"Only Fanny. We used this boat to hunt frogs, so I knew where she kept it."

"She won't like you stealing her boat. She won't be your friend after this."

Pansy shrugged. She stood with her back to him, staring straight ahead as they poled the flat bottom vessel through the shallow muck of the weed-choked creek. "I ain't comin' back, Mr. Oliver. No more than you are. I'm leaving this place for good."

Oliver was silent, thoughtful as they worked the boat out into moving water. When it finally lifted off the sticky bottom and slid into the flow, he said, "Pansy, I don't know what you're planning, but you can't go with me. I can't stay here in Florida. I have a daughter at home in Baltimore. I've got to do everything I can to get back to her."

She shot him a hard look. "I'm not aiming to go with you. "You're going with me, Mr. Oliver."

"What do you mean?"

"You'll see. But first we got to get so far the dogs can't find us."

"How far is that."

"Depends."

"On what?"

"On how much trouble Cap Arnold give Pa and the boys." A popping sound could be heard in the distance. Pansy turned her head to listen. She aimed a knowing look at Oliver. "Somebody giving somebody else some trouble. We got to get us as gone!"

For several hours they paddled a sinuous stretch of water, perpetually steering around obstacles and going with the current in a southwesterly direction. Pansy plied her oar steadily, never slacking off or showing any sign that her arms were tired. Oliver knew they must be, judging from his own sore back. After they rounded a bend where the screen of trees overhead thinned, he broke the long silence between them. "Your father called Arnold 'a damned Regulator.' What did he mean?"

A swirl of water slung them past a twisted branch that snagged a splintered edge on the side of the pirogue. When they'd freed themselves, she said, "Regulators are mean varmints who gang together to make life a misery for folks they don't like."

"They don't like your family?"

"Not hardly." Pansy sounded bitter. "Pa has more than one wife. My mother isn't a color that suits ol' Cap Arnold, so he's been looking to run us off our land." She pointed at a tangle of greenery. "I think it's time we stopped to eat. We can tie up to one of them trees. It'll give us a screen if we need to hide."

Oliver agreed. It had been a long night and an even longer morning without breakfast. The flour sacks amidships held biscuits, two water jugs, and strips of dried meat. After Oliver polished off one of the biscuits, he asked, "Arnold didn't come to your place looking for me?"

"I don't know. Maybe he did. But it's not about you, not really. It's about me and my ma. Always has been." Pansy took a long drink of water from the jug, then passed it to Oliver who took several swallows.

He handed back the jug. "Arnold and his men want to run you off because part of your family is mixed race?"

"They don't put it so polite, but yes. Weren't that the boys are mighty handy with their rifles, and Pa is a stubborn ol' badger, we'd be gone by now, or swinging from a tree. The boys do what Pa says, but they don't like it. They don't like me, or my mother, or my little brothers. Guess that's natural. Arnette, she don't dare complain. Pa would knock her silly if she did. But she hates us."

"That's not what your father said to me."

Pansy rolled her eyes. "Pa lives in his own world and sees only what he wants to see."

They finished their lunch, washed up and climbed back into the boat. A few minutes later Oliver ducked a low hanging branch and brushed a veil of Spanish moss away from his face. "What about your mother? Does she know—?"

"'Course she knows! She knows everything, and she knows what I'm doing," Pansy exclaimed. "She's the one packed our grub. She's the one tole me I had to git away if I wanted a life. Why ask so many questions? You should be happy you ain't married to me by now!"

Oliver bit back his next question and said, "Pansy, I'm sorry. I am grateful you helped me escape. I know it wasn't easy for you. I know it was dangerous."

"Not was, is. Is dangerous! We got to paddle hard. We can't stop agin' until we're clear away!"

Again, silence descended interrupted only occasionally by the call of a bird or the splash of a fish. Once Oliver heard what Pansy told him was a panther screech.

As shadows lengthened the humidity increased. Oliver began to feel that the air they slid through was almost as liquid as the green water flowing beneath them. The creek had gradually broadened, a hopeful sign that they were heading toward a larger waterway. Eventually the pirogue floated out into a much wider river.

"I don't think Pa and the boys are coming after us," Pansy said. Her voice was expressionless, neither sad nor happy.

"Pansy, I'm sorry to ask more questions, but what about your mother?

What will happen to her when your father finds you gone? Will he know she helped?"

The girl turned to look at him. Tears filled her dark brown eyes. Her expression was somber. "She say she can take care of herself."

"Can she?"

"I don't know. Hope so. But there's nothin' I can do to help. Not now. Maybe not never."

"I'm sorry."

"Me too. But like she always say, you come into this world , you got a long, hard road ahead. We got to stop before it gets dark and find us a tree where we can spend the night. It ain't safe to sleep on the ground."

"Pansy, tell me where we're going."

"You'll see come sunup."

"You mean we'll arrive at our destination in the morning?"

"You'll see."

CHAPTER TWENTY-EIGHT

OLIVER spent a miserable night balanced in the crotch of a live oak. The screech of panthers, and the rustle of creatures lurking in the palmetto thickets around his leafy perch had kept him wide awake. Snakes? Lizards? Bobcats? Wild pigs? Several times he heard what sounded like hogs snuffling around the base of his roost.

The next morning Pansy, who'd reposed in an adjacent tree, appeared untroubled by their irksome night. She'd looked somber at breakfast and hadn't said much. But she carried herself with alert authority. Oliver admired her resilience. She steered their pirogue into an inlet screened by a clump of cabbage palms. The inlet opened into a bay cut off from a broad expanse of blue water by a long sandy spit.

His eyes widened. He inhaled the scent of fish and salt air, heard the cry of gulls wheeling overhead and the gentle slap of waves on the golden shore. He'd left the Florida jungle behind. He'd arrived in a new and very different world.

"Is that the Gulf of Mexico before us?"

"No, but we close. Big water is on the other side of that island out there."

Oliver squinted. Yes, he could make out a stretch of land in the distance. So the turquoise water he saw had to be a bay protected by a barrier island. As their pirogue nudged up against the shore, he focused on the cluster of huts roofed and walled in palmetto thatch. They had been erected in the sand. A makeshift dock stretched into the bay. Nearby, a schooner floated at anchor.

An old man wearing stained cotton pants and a loosely woven shirt spurted from one of the huts. Smiling broadly, he hurried toward them shouting a lengthy greeting in Spanish.

To Oliver's surprise, the girl answered in the same language. As Pansy jumped from the boat, the two carried on a lively exchange, pointing several times at him. Then the old man hugged Pansy, kissed her on the cheek, and hurried away.

Oliver pushed himself out of the pirogue and waded up to the dry sand. A border of broken shell grazed his bare feet. Hopping past it, he asked, "Where are we? Who was that? Where did you learn to speak Spanish?"

For the first time that day, Pansy smiled at him. "You look awful tired Mr. Oliver. Would you like to rest a while?"

"Yes."

"Me too. Fernando, that's the old man I was talkin' to, he's fixing us up sleeping places. I figure we might as well rest us until the men come back."

"What men? Come back from where?"

"From fishing. "They'll be back by suppertime."

Oliver looked about him, trying to understand where they were and what was going on. The odor of fish filled his nose. He saw strings of mullet hanging up to dry. "This is a fishing camp," he said aloud.

"Sure is. The Cubans sail here because their water back home is pretty much fished out. Fish in the bay jump into their nets. Here comes Fernando. He say he's fixed you up a place to rest yourself."

Oliver spent the next several hours dead to the world. He sprawled face down on a thatch mattress . It might have been the most luxurious bed possible. Neither the ants crawling across his face, nor the sand fleas exploring his bare toes mattered.

When he finally opened his eyes, spiky shadows filled the corners of his enclosure. He rolled over and gazed up at the thatch roof. Voices drifted in on the warm salt breeze. Groaning, he got to his feet.

Outside, the sun shot crimson threads into a scrim of lavender clouds parallel to the water. With an appreciative eye on the beauty of the setting sun, Oliver headed toward the sound of voices. Weaving his way past several lean-to's piled high with salted fish, he spied a half dozen men gathered around a campfire.

They spoke in Spanish, laughing, nudging each other as if sharing a joke. One picked out a languorous melody on a guitar. Another tended a frying pan full of sizzling fish. Pansy was a member of the group, coiled close to a dark-haired young man, her own dark hair brushing his shoulder. When Oliver stood looking down at her, she turned her face up to him and smiled.

"Why, Mister Oliver, did you get a good sleep?"

"I did."

"You look a whole lot better." She grinned and Oliver was struck by the sparkle of firelight reflected in her eyes.

"I feel a lot better."

"That's good, cause we got more travelin' to do."

"Traveling?"

"I'll explain. First off, I want to meet you up with Antonio. He's my fiancé. We're going back to Cuba to get married. What do you think of that?"

Oliver extended his hand to the handsome young Cuban. "I think Antonio is a lucky man. Congratulations to the both of you." He couldn't stop himself from asking, "How did the two of you meet?"

"Met when Antonio and his Uncle Fernando came our way to do some plume hunting and meet up with a friend." Pansy beamed at her fiancé. "We took to each other right away."

Oliver looked from one bright young face to the other. They did seem suited—each young person vibrant and impatient for life. "How long ago was that?"

"Oh, more'n a year. We been meeting ever since."

Oliver wondered how they had managed without alerting Micah's family. He asked, "You kept meeting because Antonio and his uncle kept coming your way to plume hunt?"

"Oh no." Pansy shook her head. "They both give that up when I told them how bad it was for the poor little birds. Antonio came to see me, and Fernando came to meet up with his friend. Antonio taught me to speak his lingo."

"Well, I can hear that you do it very well. That will come in handy when you're living in Cuba. Will you let your parents know?"

Her expression sobered, and her gaze dropped. "I'll write to Ma when we get to Cuba."

Antonio tapped Pansy's shoulder and whispered into her ear. She listened and then turned back to Oliver. "Antonio said I should introduce you to the other Yankee in camp."

"The other Yankee?"

"Fella' turned up here a few days ago, real sick. Oh, here he is now."

Oliver saw a familiar figure approaching from the other side of the camp. He stared in surprise and mounting outrage. It was Reuben Spooner.

CHAPTER TWENTY-NINE

TWENTY four hours later Oliver sat cross-legged on the bow deck of the *Estrelita*, the schooner he'd spied at anchor near the fish camp. Schooners had a reputation for speed. But the *Estrelita* plodded through the tranquil water of the Gulf. Overloaded with salted fish, as well as half a dozen fishermen, and three unexpected passengers, it was headed for Key West, or "*Cayo Hueso*," as the Cubans called it. There it would drop part of its cargo before sailing on to Cuba.

Oliver guessed that unless the wind freshened enough to blow away some of the fish smell giving him a headache, the *Estrelita* wouldn't be docking in Key West for several more days. Still, they were on their way, and that lifted his spirits. The Cubans, most of them members of Fernando's family, had been Oliver's saviors. They'd fed him well. They'd brewed excellent coffee for his breakfast and provided him with a change of clothing. They'd even given him an instructive tour of their salting operation. What's more, they'd done it all with smiles.

After sailing with them through their fishing grounds, he could appreciate their attraction to this stretch of west Florida coast. Legions of fish swarmed its blue water. Abundant sea fowl thronged the beach, and sharks swam around in schools. It truly was a fisherman's paradise.

"God, this damned boat stinks to high heaven!" Nearby to Oliver, Reuben Spooner sprawled in the shade of an ancient canvas sail that drooped in the stagnant wind. He appeared even thinner and more unwholesome than he had back at the turpentine camp. Purplish scars blotched his wrists and ankles. His hair hung in lank strings around his feverish eyes. Beneath his shirt his ribs protruded like tines on a broken fork.

"Bad enough I have to listen to their foreign gabble day and night!" He poked an accusing finger at the Cubans clustered at the stern of the sailboat. None of them looked troubled by the sun frying the deck and the boat's lack of progress. One kept a nonchalant hand on the wheel while the others played a spirited game of dice.

Oliver rolled his eyes. "You're one ungrateful bastard, Spooner! If it weren't for Fernando and his family you'd be alligator meat by now."

"I can take care of myself."

"I hear you stumbled onto their camp almost naked—no boat, no food and covered head to foot with bloody scratches, bruises, and bug bites. They fed you, clothed you, nursed you, and now they're hauling your sorry carcass to safety."

"No different from you. You look as if you're ready for the bone yard."

"At least I made it here in a boat."

"So would I have if you hadn't stuck me with a toy made out of paper. Damned thing dissolved right under me."

Oliver glared at Spooner. "I stuck you with a paper boat? You mean you pinched it from me. Slunk off leaving me to perish in the damned Florida jungle!"

"If you'd showed me some respect instead of treating me like your prisoner.

"Oh shut the hell up!" Oliver turned away and stared at the limp jib. The breeze had slackened even more. In fact, they were becalmed. The blazing sun hammered the top of his head. He moved to get some protection from the staysail. The shapeless rotted canvas looked ready to fall apart at the slightest stress. Maybe it was just as well the wind was faint.

Sighing, he leaned against a coil of rope and considered his situation. Better than before, he thought. Now he could plan to get home. Though he'd never been to Key West, he knew it was a trading center. The Union army had used it as a base to battle Confederate blockade runners. Perhaps he could find a way of getting word to his family.

That would take money, and his pockets were empty. He couldn't ask the Cubans for money. They'd already been kind enough. He'd have to pick up work in Key West. Then there was the matter of Spooner. Now that he'd reconnected with the man, he supposed he was responsible for him. One way or another he had to get both Spooner and himself home.

Sighing again, Oliver closed his eyes. His mind drifted back to yesterday evening when Pansy had introduced him to Antonio. He seemed like a nice young man. It was astonishing that he'd won Pansy's young heart on a plume hunting trip. Even more surprising that she'd been able to pick up his lingo so quickly. They'd only met a few times. Maybe she wasn't telling him the whole story. If there was more to it, and there probably was, Oliver decided he didn't care.

He hoped the young man would do right by the girl, marry her as he promised so that the two of them could make a life in Cuba. It seemed likely since Fernando, the patriarch of the family, approved of Pansy. Of course, Cuba right now was in political turmoil, what with people like Marti stirring up rebellion against the Spanish.

Oliver's eyebrows knitted. Why would Antonio and his uncle leave the safety of the coast? Why abandon their flourishing fishing business to meet with a friend in the wilds of Florida's interior? Pansy said it was to hunt plumes. They could hunt plume birds as well, if not better, on the coast. Something was odd about that. Something was odd about everything lately.

It was as if time had become a snake eating its own tail. It looped in and out. People and places he had put behind him kept bobbing up like persistent corks. He could not have been more surprised to see Reuben Spooner. Had the fates elected perpetual torment with the vexatious man?

The gentle rocking of the boat and the hot stillness of the air put Oliver to sleep. An hour later shouts dragged him out of a troubled dream. When he opened his eyes he saw that his fishermen benefactors had gathered on the port side of the *Estrelita*. They were exclaiming in Spanish and pointing. One of them brandished a telescope which two others were trying to claim. Spooner had joined them and was endeavoring to peer between their heads. Clustered as they all were, Oliver couldn't see past them to identify the object galvanizing their attention.

He looked to *Estrelita's* stern where Fernando stood alone, manning the wheel with one hand and holding a second telescope to his eye with the other. Oliver made his way to the back of the boat. Once past the crowd at the bow he saw what had captured their interest.

A small passenger steamship, like ones he'd seen in Tampa, drove through the calm blue water. Oliver's eyes narrowed as he studied its twin rakish smokestacks and distinctive profile. He'd seen this boat docked in Tampa's harbor. It was a refurbished blockade runner named *Gypsy Dancer*. *Dancer* had almost caught up with the *Estrelita* and would soon leave her in its wake. Chortling, Fernando offered the telescope to Oliver and said in Spanish, "Two women and a beautiful *Senorita*."

Oliver put the instrument to his eye and saw what Fernando meant. Three women stood at the steamship's rail, smiling and pointing as their boat chugged past. As the overloaded schooner floundered in its wake, Oliver recognized all three of them. The lovely Rosella Beauchamp and her mother were standing on either side of Hannah Kinchman.

CHAPTER THIRTY

THAT night a storm whipped the Gulf into a frenzy. Winds thundering out of the north smashed the wallowing *Estrelita* to her side, pushing her masts almost parallel to the churning sea. To Oliver's surprise, Fernando ordered his small crew to replace the tattered jib. When the new sail filled the *Estrelita* fought her way north and began to right herself. Instead of lowering her rotten sails, as Oliver would have thought prudent, the Cubans trimmed sails for the new course.

Oliver had been suspicious of the aging schooner's sea-worthiness and doubtful of his host's seafaring skills. Clinging to the rail, drenched by stinging plumes of spray, he began to understand Fernando's bellowed orders. The old man steadied the wheel. Ignoring the saltwater streaming from his hair, he roared commands. His crew staggered about the beleaguered schooner, barely avoiding being washed overboard as they hauled in the huge mainsail.

The *Estrelita* righted herself, partnered with the screaming north wind, and plunged through the roiled water. Oliver breathed a sigh of relief. The beamy *Estrelita* was no match for the speedy, pencil-thin Baltimore clippers, but her extra width made her much more stable. No longer doubting Fernando, or *Estrelita*, he blinked needles of water out of his eyes and looked around for Spooner. He found him below deck, wedged between two barrels of salted fish. He had curled himself into a fetal position and lay there moaning and muttering. Oliver could do nothing for him. He found a spot for himself and trusted the Cubans to continue dealing with the threatening weather.

Hour after hour *Estrelita* plowed due south through the storm tossed waters of the Gulf. Oliver woke regularly to the pounding of the waves, and Spooner's relentless groans and whimpers.

During this time Oliver's thoughts focused on Baltimore and what seemed like the dream of a former life. He wondered about his daughter. Where was Chloe now? Mrs. Milawney would have run out of housekeeping money. How was she managing? He trusted she wouldn't abandon Chloe. Who would take care of the child if she couldn't? He clenched his fists. He had to get a message to them as soon as possible.

What about his client, William Walters? What lies might the people in Tampa have told him? Had Walters sent someone else to investigate the trouble in Tampa? What a mess!

Oliver's thoughts drifted to *Gypsy Dancer*, the steamer that had passed *Estrelita* earlier in the day. A picture of Hannah, Rosella and her mother standing at the rail rose before his mind's eye. They had to be bound for Key West. Why? What had happened in Tampa after Hannah had smuggled a gun to him in the turpentine camp?

Had she succeeded in shooting her runaway husband? Had Rosella thought better of her alliance with Arnold Pepperwhite? Had her mother given up working for the Pedrosos? Where were they now? Had *Gypsy Dancer* been affected by the storm? He sank into a troubled sleep. Blurred images of Baltimore, of his young daughter, and of the three women aboard *Gypsy Dancer* snaked through his dreams. Then a beautiful, auburn-haired woman with glimmering green eyes replaced them. Marietta, the mother of his child. The woman he couldn't banish from his dreams.

The next morning, Oliver awoke to sunshine streaming from *Estrelita's* open hatch. Every joint in his body ached. Seawater sloshed about beneath the wooden racks bearing the containers of fish. He was wet from head to toe. He extricated himself from his bed on the rim of a wooden palette. Opposite, Spooner lay unconscious, snoring noisily. After contemplating the man's lank wisps of dirty hair and the dribble of spit on his unshaven chin, Oliver made his way topside.

The chameleon Gulf had transformed itself into a paradise of sunny skies and blue waters. A brisk breeze continued to blow *Estrelita* south. The fishermen, so vigorous during the storm, lay scattered about the deck. They were all unconscious, several curled up like sleeping infants. One was even sucking his thumb.

Dead to the world, Fernando sat with his head resting against a roll of canvas. His eyes were closed and his hair, stiffened with saltwater, wreathed his head like a crown of seaweed.

At *Estrelita's* stern, Antonio manned the wheel. Pansy sat next to him, her head resting against his knee as she tore hunks off a round of bread.

"Good Morning Pansy and Antonio, we seem to have survived the storm," Oliver said making his way toward the twosome.

The girl smiled and offered him a piece of bread which he accepted.

"Mornin' Mister Oliver. Lordy, I was scared outa' my wits all night. Thought we was going to die."

"Me too."

Pansy chuckled and rolled her big brown eyes. "It's fine now, isn't it." She pointed up at the cloudless sky. "Tony says the storm was good. It blew us close to Key West. He thinks we'll make port by the end of the day."

Antonio nodded and grinned. "*Si,*" he said and gave Pansy's shoulder an affectionate squeeze.

Oliver wondered how much English the young man understood. Maybe more than he was letting on. After eating his bread, he said, "I see the rest of the crew is sleeping. Can Antonio handle the boat all by himself? I'm not a sailor, but I can try to help if he needs me."

Pansy shook her head. "Oh Tony's all right for now. The wind is blowing us straight where we want to go, and he's been sailing *Estrelita* since he was a tyke. Haven't you now?" She smiled up at her fiancé.

He smiled back. "*Si muchacha.*"

The wind stayed fresh, driving them southward. Oliver went below several times to check on Spooner. He remained insensible. Just as well. Awake, he did nothing but grumble.

By noon Antonio sighted a strip of land in the distance and gave a shout. Fernando stood up and rolled his thick shoulders. After kicking a couple of his men into wakefulness, he picked up his telescope. For a full minute he stood with his feet planted wide on the vibrating deck, staring intently.

"*Banditos!*" he exclaimed and hurried back to seize the helm from Antonio and hand him the telescope. The younger man took several seconds to study whatever was happening in the distance. He turned to his uncle with a scowl. The two began a tense conversation in Spanish.

Oliver tapped Pansy's shoulder. "What are they talking about?"

"Antonio says there's a steamship stuck near the coast, blown into shallow water in last night's storm. It's about to be attacked by wreckers."

"Wreckers!" Oliver had heard about the wreckers who plundered ships gone aground. They made their living preying on unfortunate mariners. Some had even grown rich despoiling vessels who'd come to grief on the treacherous shoals and reefs rimming the keys. Rumor had it that wreckers sometimes planted false navigation lights on those reefs to lure boats to ruin.

Fernando relinquished the wheel to his nephew. He began bawling orders. Antonio swung the wheel so that the boat came about toward land.

"We're going in," Pansy cried.

"To do what? Fight off the wreckers?"

"Maybe. I don't know." She shot him a worried look. "We'll have to see."

They made good speed. The thin blue line of distant land grew more distinct. Once again Fernando took the wheel. He steered *Estrelita* forward in a zigzag course while Antonio hung over the foredeck calling out warnings in Spanish.

"Why aren't we going in straight?" Oliver asked Pansy.

"Antonio says it's treacherous when we get close to an island. Very shallow with coral reefs. The steamboat is hung up on one." She pointed, and Oliver squinted into the distance.

"There's more than one boat there."

"The wreckers came in a couple of old schooners. 'Course, they know where to steer them old sailboats so they won't get caught. That poor steamer. It's stuck good. The wreckers are lowering rowboats to board her."

Several shots rang out . Oliver saw puffs of smoke over the water. "Gunfire! Who's shooting? The wreckers?"

"Looks like the other way round. Looks like that steamer is putting up a fight." Pansy had commandeered one of the other telescopes on the *Estrelita*. She put it to her eye and began to describe what she saw.

"Lordy, there's women on that steamer. One is shooting her gun off."

CHAPTER THIRTY-ONE

"LET me see!"

Pansy relinquished her spyglass, and Oliver squinted through it. He recognized the distressed vessel. It was the *Gypsy Dancer*. He saw a man, possibly the steamboat's captain, brandishing a club to ward off boarders at the foredeck. He was accompanied by two other sailors, one carrying what appeared to be a coal shovel while the other had a shotgun.

Two rowboats lowered from two anchored schooners were coming at *Gypsy Dancer* like wolves at a wounded buffalo. Oliver scanned *Gypsy's* deck looking for the women he'd seen earlier. There was no sign of Rosella and her mother, suggesting they were hiding below deck like sensible females. But a figure he recognized stood amidships staring down a sturdy wrecker trying to climb over the steamer's rail. The fool woman was menacing him with her pistol. Hannah!

"Good God," Oliver groaned. He turned to Pansy. "Are there guns aboard this ship? We'll need them if we're going to take on a gang of determined wreckers."

"Not that I know," Pansy shouted. She was staring to the south and pointing. "But look, maybe we won't need them! Maybe we won't have to fight the wreckers!"

Oliver followed her gaze. He saw a sidewheel paddle steamer race out of the pass at the southern edge of the key where *Gypsy Dancer* was aground. Billows of smoke came off her. She headed toward the melee firing a big gun.

"She's got a cannon!" Pansy exclaimed. "She's firing at the wreckers. She's going to save that old steamboat!"

As the battle at sea unfolded, the Cubans danced about the deck, pointing and shouting. Firing regularly, the paddle steamer closed in on the grounded steamboat. Finally, the wreckers leapt back into their boats and rowed to the safety of their schooners. The Cubans gave a cheer.

Oliver watched this turn of events transfixed. He raised the telescope to get a better look at the daring commander of the rescue vessel. He recognized the small, sturdy figure immediately. It was the man who'd introduced himself to Oliver as Wendell C. Hartley, the man who'd shot Jose Marti. It was the man Hannah had described as a former blockade runner named Chester Glass, a Key West wrecker himself.

After chasing off the wreckers, Glass threw a line to *Gypsy Dancer* and hauled her off the reef where she was snared.

"What if she sinks?" Pansy exclaimed. The girl leaned over *Estrelita*'s rail with the spyglass glued to her eye. With her tidy figure and air of excitement, she was a fetching sight. The loose canvas trousers she wore only seemed to enhance her budding femininity. The wind swirled her dark curls around her well-shaped head. Her brown skin glowed in the sun. Glancing over his shoulder Oliver smiled as he caught the admiring glances Antonio was shooting his fiancé. He hoped the young man truly appreciated Pansy. This spunky girl was leaving everything she knew to start a new life with him.

Aloud, Oliver replied to her question, "Depends on how well armored her hull is." He didn't mention that he knew *Dancer* had been a blockade runner and a very successful one. Chances were she had been reinforced well enough during her war time service so that she would stay afloat despite her encounter with a reef.

So it proved. Once *Dancer* had slid free, she fired up her engines, steamed off behind her rescuer, and disappeared through a pass between the chain of islands. The Cubans cheered, then weighed anchor and turned back to deep water. *Estrelita* headed toward Key West.

That evening Fernando guided *Estrelita* through a broad channel into Key West's famed harbor known as Key West Bight. Oliver took in the jam-packed port. Unlike the miles of desolate coastline *Estrelita* had just navigated, Key West's harbor bristled with masts. The wind had dropped. It was still steady enough to allow Fernando to ease *Estrelita* through the thicket of Caribbean trading vessels and small fishing "smackees" returning from the coral reefs.

They passed shrimpers and men standing in rowing boats with long forked poles. He pointed at one, and Pansy, who stood next to him humming with excitement as she took in the colorful scene, explained, "Them's for catching sponges. See, that fella's got a bunch on strings. I hear they got a sponge auction right here in the harbor. Folks up north prize them sponges, so they fetch a good price."

"*Hola, Roberto!*" Antonio called out as they glided past an ancient Caravel bobbing at anchor. A dark haired sailor aboard the caravel returned his greeting. As the two shouted friendly remarks at each other, Oliver wondered how many Cuban vessels were in the harbor. Nearby, he spied a cutter flying a British flag. A French flag fluttered atop another mast. This isolated little place appeared to be a meeting ground for the world.

Remarkably, *Estrelita* found a spot to tie up on a finger dock. Even more surprising, her landing place was next to *Gypsy Dancer*. It was almost as if *Dancer* had been saving a berth for her. Though, of course, Oliver told himself, it had to be coincidence. There was no reason to think the two vessels had any connection.

Despite her misadventure, the steamship looked no worse for wear. There was no sign of Hannah, Rosella or her mother.

The ship appeared deserted. Only a single sleepy looking deck-hand lounged against the wheel to keep guard.

A few minutes later, after Oliver had rounded up Spooner and thanked his Cuban benefactors, he stepped onto the dock. Spooner followed, exclaiming as he hoisted himself onto the weathered boards, "At last, dry land! Look at those damned turtles. My god, they're huge!"

Oliver frowned at the enormous animals crawling a few steps away. To get near enough to *Gypsy Dancer* to ask after Hannah, he had to walk around them. He threaded a wary path. When he got close enough to call out to *Dancer's* sole deckhand, the man replied, "Ladies went off to a hotel in town."

Pansy clung to a piling. She laughed as he made his way back through the turtles. "Them's Green Turtles. I never seen Greens before, but I heard about them. Watch! Don't step on that whopper! He won't like that. Turtles is big business here."

After skirting the largest of the animals, Oliver asked, "Why are they on the dock like this?"

"Cause they just been catched." She jumped onto the pier and knelt to get a better view of one of their wrinkled, sleepy looking faces. "They're kinda' cute."

"What will happen to them?" Oliver asked.

"Oh, they'll go into cans, mostly. Or they'll be made into soup. First they'll go into kraals, so they'll stay fresh. That's what Tony said."

"Kraals?"

She pointed at a large wood container built next to a shed. "It's filled with water. See, those fishermen coming out of the shed? They're getting ready to put them turtles away in the kraals."

For one so concerned about plume birds, she appeared non-chalant about the fate of these gentle giants. When he pointed this out, she said, "Oh, but they taste good. It's not like they stick 'em in a fancy lady's hat! That's mean!"

A moment later Antonio joined her and the two young people made plans to go into town. Before they left, Pansy gave Oliver a hug and wished him well. Antonio shook his hand. Then the couple strolled off with their arms around each other's waist.

"That'll never work," Spooner commented when they were out of earshot.

"What do you mean?"

He rolled his eyes. "Look at those two. She's just a kid and not all that pretty. Once the spick gets her to Cuba, he'll tire of her."

"They're engaged to be married."

"That'll be the day. He'll never marry a girl like that."

"Like what?"

"No money, no relatives worth spit, doesn't dress like a female. She's a half-breed. What's she got to offer?"

"Your daughter is a half-breed."

"What's that got to do with anything?"

"It's got to do with your hypocrisy. When you dismiss Pansy like that you're talking about the way you judge women, not the way Antonio judges them. Pansy's smart, strong and young. I think she's very pretty."

Spooner sneered. "Then why aren't you on bended knee?"

"I have a home and a daughter of my own to get back to in Baltimore. Which reminds me, we need to find work."

"Work!" Spooner looked horrified.

"I haven't got a penny to my name, and neither do you. I need to pay for my dinner and a place to lay my head tonight."

"That's your problem, not mine. " Spooner looked around. Grinning slyly, he took a gold piece out of his belt. "I think this'll buy me a mighty fine dinner."

Oliver snatched the coin and held it up to the fading light. "It's Spanish. Where did you get this?"

"Where do you think?" Spooner tried to retrieve the gold piece, but Oliver held on tight. They struggled. Finally

Spooner gave up, stamped his foot and sputtered a string of curses. "Damn you! Interfering bastard! You've no right! It's mine! Give it back!"

Oliver glared. "It's not yours! You stole it from Fernando and his crew, didn't you? After all they did for you! They saved your life! You are one ungrateful wretch!"

"What have I got to be grateful for? I've had nothing but trouble since I got to this hell hole. And you're a big part of my trouble!"

"You're just about all of mine! I'm taking this back where it belongs."

Spooner turned bright red with fury. Ignoring him, Oliver climbed back onto *Estrelita*, hailed Fernando and returned the coin to him. After the old man thanked him heartily and wished him well, Oliver returned to the dock. Shadows were lengthening, and Spooner was gone.

CHAPTER THIRTY-TWO

OLIVER hiked the length of Key West's busy harbor. Spooner was nowhere to be found. He was sorry to have lost him, but not very sorry. It was a relief not to have to deal with the troublesome man. Meanwhile, other problems needed solving. How was he to get word to his family and fill his empty belly?

Luck was with him for a change. Tied up at a wharf next to a South American boat unloading bunches of green bananas, he saw a Baltimore clipper named *Mermaid*. He recognized her bare breasted figurehead. He had visited the ship several times in its Fells Point home berth. In fact, he had met the ship's captain in Baltimore and spent an afternoon with him in a tavern.

Oliver stood staring at the familiar vessel, struggling to remember the captain's name. Suddenly the solidly built, ginger-bearded man strode down the gangplank and walked directly toward Oliver. He was about to pass by when Oliver stepped in front of him. "Captain MacDonald, Captain Dirk MacDonald!"

MacDonald stared at him in obvious irritation, no spark of recognition in his sharp blue eyes. He was dressed in much the same costume he'd worn in Baltimore— a slouch cap, light blue chambray shirt and dark blue trousers. In concession to Key West's tropical weather, he'd foregone his customary navy blue pea coat with shiny brass buttons.

Oliver realized how he must look in comparison. Dressed in the rag tag clothing the Cubans had given him, unshaven and unwashed for several days, he wouldn't resemble the detective MacDonald had met in Baltimore more than a year earlier.

"It's Oliver Redcastle," he said a little desperately. "We met last March while I was investigating an insurance fraud case involving your sister ship, *The Blue Muse.*"

MacDonald scratched the back of his head. "Redcastle?"

"Yes. I don't expect you recognize me. As you can see, I'm in some distress here."

MacDonald took a step closer and stared into Oliver's face. "Good God, man, what's happened to you?"

"It's a long story."

"Not a good one from the looks of you." MacDonald paused a moment, gathering his thoughts. "See here, I'm headed into town for my supper. Come along and join me. You can tell me this long story of yours over a mug of ale."

Oliver felt like hugging the man. He accepted the invitation, fell into step next to him and asked him where he was bound.

"Back to Baltimore. We'll spend all night loading those bananas coming in from Costa Rica. *Mermaid's* hold is half full of rum and coffee now. Once the bananas are aboard, we'll sail with the morning tide, making stops in Charleston and Norfolk. If the wind stays fair, we'll be back to Fells Point in a week."

MacDonald couldn't have said sweeter words. An hour later the two men sat at a scarred wooden table in a noisy open air cafe near the waterfront. They had selected a dark corner for privacy. The remains of the conch soup and hogfish sandwiches the captain had ordered for them were pushed aside. A large pitcher half full of ale sat between them. They each sipped from mugs filled with the brew. MacDonald leaned over the table in order to catch every word of Oliver's story.

"You've had a hell of a time! I don't wonder you look like a half starved wild man. What will you do about the legalities?"

Their conversation was interrupted by a loud quarrel that had broken out in a corner opposite. Two rough looking sailors, one of them a muscular West Indian, the other a wiry Asian, wrestled each other to the sawdust floor. Around them other men, equally diverse in origin, shouted insults. It looked as if a melee might break out. A moment later the two brawlers got to their feet, slapped each other on the shoulder and, to the sound of jeers and thunderous laughter, resumed their seats at the bar.

"I can't get over this place," Oliver commented. "We're on a tiny spot of land in the middle of an empty sea. Yet it's vibrating with life, filled with people from every corner of the earth. This could almost be a bar in Fells Point."

"Except for the conch soup." MacDonald smiled. "All seaports are the same. When rough men have been too long at sea they act alike no matter what part of the world they come from. Key West is just Fells Point with palm trees and warm winters. But you haven't answered my question about your legal situation."

"Perhaps because I've been asking that same question of myself. If I can get to Baltimore, I think I can have all that put to rights. William Walters will use his influence to overturn this wrongful conviction. I'm sure of it. I'm here on an assignment from him, and he has influence with the people who railroaded me."

"I'm sure you're right. Everyone knows that what passes for law in Florida makes the Wild West look like a church social. But first you have to get back home. I can help you with that. Be on the *Mermaid* when she sails at dawn. How does that sound?"

"It sounds wonderful. Thanks."

"Don't be late. We have to go with the tide to get around the reefs and shoals. If you're not aboard, I can't wait for you."

"I'll definitely be there."

The two men shook on their agreement. Captain MacDonald left the café to get back to his ship. Oliver remained at their table, savoring the offer of passage home he'd just received.

He refilled his mug and looked around, bemused by the colorful scene. He took in the mixture of people, the clinking of glass, the raucous outbursts of laughter, the differences in dress, the amazing variety of headgear. He observed the occasional woman sitting with a sailor, blending her shrill merriment with his, her hair tumbled and her clothing in disarray. Chickens wandered in and out, pecking crumbs of food on the sawdust floor. Birds landed on the tables to snatch away a crust. Dogs strolled in and out.

Once again he had fallen into a different world, a world apart from everything he'd experienced. Even the air, warm with its tang of salt and seafood, its stew of odors from the harbor and Caribbean spice from the kitchen, smelled different.

He couldn't believe his luck in meeting Captain MacDonald. Soon he'd be back in Baltimore. Florida would only be a memory. Was Chloe still well? Jake Jaggard had said he would get word to his housekeeper. Had he? What about Hannah? What was she doing here? Would he ever see her again?

A familiar laugh came to his ears from across the room. Turning toward the sound, he saw Jake Jaggard, Sir Harvey Lexton and Reuben Spooner. They stood at the bar. Their heads were together as they shared an earnest conversation and a pint of ale.

CHAPTER THIRTY-THREE

OLIVER pushed his chair into the shadows. He sat back to observe Spooner and his companions. The threesome stayed at the bar for another hour, bursting into laughter from time to time. Something seemed to amuse them greatly. Oliver wondered if he was the subject of their hilarity. Spooner had certainly made a fool of him.

While the minutes crawled past, he had plenty of time to scrutinize them. Jake Jaggard had foregone his usual top hat and tailcoat. All the same, in well-cut twill pants, a spotless bleached muslin shirt, and a wide brimmed felt hat cocked at a jaunty angle, he was the best dressed man in the room. Lexton wore a similar outfit, though with less panache. Spooner, by comparison, looked even more disreputable than he had earlier in the evening. Oliver glanced down at his own rag tag garments. Sartorially speaking, he and Reuben Spooner were a sadly matched pair.

To justify his lengthy stay in the café, Oliver purchased another mug of ale with the coins Captain MacDonald had lent him. He sipped it judiciously. It was more than half full when the men he watched finally got up from their stools and exited the café. Once they were out of sight, he followed. They were just rounding a corner when he emerged into the darkness outside.

The sun had set. A cooling breeze, zesty with the odors of seaweed, fish and spicy cookery whispered past Oliver's brow.

The darkness seemed to make the harbor even more animated. Groups of people strolled about talking and laughing. Women in Spanish dress frilled with scarlet and gold, some with children, clustered around a vendor selling sweets. Lanterns twinkled on the masts of ships. Knots of eager sailors looked for entertainment.

Despite the deepening night, other sailors, less fortunate, lugged cargo from one ship to another. When Oliver passed Captain MacDonald's *Mermaid,* the crew was hoisting bananas with only the light of the moon and a few flickering lanterns to guide them up the narrow gangplank.

Oliver would have stopped there, would have dozed all night on the dock to be sure of being on the ship set to depart in the morning. But dawn was many hours away. Having spotted Spooner in cahoots with Jaggard and Lexton, he wanted to find out what they were up to.

Several times, between the people blocking his path and the accumulating gloom, he lost sight of his quarry. He had just spotted the three men rounding a sponge warehouse when something else caught his eye. *Estrelita* bobbed gently where she was tied, but her crew was not at rest. Nor were they unloading salted fish, supposedly Fernando's reason for stopping at KeyWest before heading home.

In fact, they were not unloading *Estrelita.* They were stocking her. They were supplying her with crates from Gypsy Dancer, the steamer that Chester Glass had pulled off a reef. So there was a reason why *Estrelita* had been able to tie up next to the former blockade runner. It had not been coincidence.

Oliver ducked behind a shanty nearby and watched. The Cuban Schooner's crew dragged container after container out of *Dancer's* hold. The wooden boxes looked heavy, judging from the effort they cost their sweating bearers. Barking orders from time to time, Fernando surveyed the operation closely. He opened several boxes and inspected their contents, then nailed them shut. The men groaned as they heaved their burdens onto *Estrelita's* deck, then maneuvered them into her hold.

The contents of those cases didn't require delicate handling. They weren't full of breakables, bottles of rum or the like. They hid something much sturdier—and Oliver guessed what it might be. He now understood the reason why Antonio and his uncle had left their fishing camp to wander north. Antonio had chanced to meet and fall in love with Pansy. But he hadn't been to hunting plume birds. He and his uncle had been hunting quite a different prize.

Oliver straightened. He started to step out from behind his shelter. Someone jammed the barrel of a gun into his side. He stiffened and made to turn his head.

"Be still," a female voice ordered.

"Hannah?"

"Yes, it's me. Now be sensible and don't make trouble."

Olilver gritted his teeth. "I'm not the troublemaker here. Those boxes are full of guns. What the hell is going on?"

"What do you think?"

"I think Fernando and his family aren't just fishermen. They're followers of Jose Marti."

"Perhaps."

"Perhaps, my eye! They're transporting guns to the Cuban rebels. Chester Glass is part of the ring supplying them."

"Excellent, Oliver. You've made a fine deduction."

"You mean I'm right? But Glass was paid by the Cuban government to get rid of Marti! I saw him try to shoot the man. Why would he be helping him acquire arms?"

"'Tried' is the operative word. Glass is a slippery fellow and likes to play a double game. Gun-running is lucrative, perhaps even more lucrative than assassination. I suspect Glass wasn't really trying when he shot Marti. Or perhaps he changed his mind when he got the opportunity to help supply guns. Now, let's get out of here before they see us. There's a café nearby where we can talk."

Oliver turned in time to see Hannah tuck her revolver back into her handbag. She looked up at him with a Mona Lisa smile. A strand of hair fluttering at her forehead caught his eye. He said, "So that's why you were aboard the Gypsy Dancer. You were keeping an eye on all this for Pinkerton."

"That's why they sent me here."

"Do you intend any action?"

"Regarding the guns? My instructions are not to interfere. Washington has no love for the Spanish oppressors in Cuba. They want to know what's going on so they won't be caught short if there's trouble on our shores. Right now the trouble is about to be shipped away.

"All right, but why were the Beauchamps on *Dancer* with you, and where are they now?"

Hannah chuckled. "My goodness, aren't you the curious cat. The Beauchamps are stowed on *Estrelita* and about to sail to Cuba aboard her. It wasn't easy persuading Rosella to give up her red-faced, crooked benefactor, Mr. Arnold Pepperwhite. She was certain he would make her into another Sarah Bernhardt. In the end her mama persuaded her that her acting ability wasn't his chief interest. A man like Pepperwhite will make promises to a girl like Rosella, then discard her without a second thought. Now, don't be stubborn, Oliver. Come with me. We both have a lot of catching up to do. Don't you agree?"

Oliver nodded. "Indeed, I do."

CHAPTER THIRTY-FOUR

A few minutes later they sat across from each other at *The Naked Blonde*, a dingy café tucked away in an alley. Oliver thought it must have been named after the bare-breasted ship's figurehead looming over the bar.

Fishing nets, cork floats and other seafaring trappings hung from the weathered board ceiling and festooned the unpainted walls. A starved looking tabby cat slunk along the periphery of the dirt floor, eyeing a crow pecking crumbs from a table-top. Nearby a group of sailors ogled Hannah. She seemed oblivious.

"You have admirers," Oliver pointed out.

Hannah rolled her eyes. "Admirers who've been at sea for months without a woman. Hardly a compliment."

"The swarthy fellow with a green parrot on his shoulder appears particularly smitten."

"Does he?" Hannah kept her gaze glued to Oliver's face. "He surely thinks I'm a prostitute he can tempt with pennies. Even if I were available for pennies, he's not my type."

Oliver smiled. "What is your type?"

"At the very least, a man who's encountered a bar of soap recently."

"That would leave me out."

She continued to scrutinize him closely. "I should say so. But then I don't think you ever wanted to be left in. Not really."

"What do you mean?"

"I'm referring to your beautiful Marietta."

Oliver was taken aback. "She's not mine."

"She's the mother of your child."

"What has Chloe's mother got to do with anything?"

"Oh, I think Marietta Dumont has a great deal to do with a great many things where you're concerned. I believe you've never recovered from your love affair with her. Not really. Admit it, Ollie, she's always been the one for you."

"You're wrong." That came out a little too fast and a little too strong.

Hannah laughed. "Am I? I ran into her recently. She was in a traveling carnival, dressed in pink tights, working for a knife thrower."

"A knife-thrower?" An image of Marietta, her luscious figure exposed, her hair pinned to a target for the benefit of a gawking circus audience made Oliver slightly sick. "Why would she do that? She's a stage actress!"

"She's no longer young, Oliver. She probably had no choice."

"I saw her six months ago. She was as handsome as ever."

"I'm sure. She has the kind of face that will be fine-looking at ninety. But parts get scarce for an actress past her prime. I should know. That's one of the reasons I took up with Pinkertons. A lady detective doesn't have to be young and beautiful. In fact, it's better if she isn't. It's better if she can blend in and be taken for granted, like most women are and always have been."

Oliver looked up at the ceiling, barely hearing what Hannah said. How could a woman as gorgeous as Marietta ever be past her prime, he wondered. An enormous cockroach perched on one of the beams. He focused on it. It seemed to stare back with equal interest. Finally, he said, "Let's not talk about Marietta. Not here, not now."

"All right. I see she's a sore subject with you. So, what shall we discuss?"

"You, Hannah." Oliver detached his gaze from the cockroach, leaned back in his chair and studied her in the light of the oil lamp. "You're looking well."

Her tanned cheeks had a healthy flush. Her hair, too, was streaked with golden lights from the sun and not so tightly confined as usual. The loose strands at her forehead made a kind of halo in the lantern's radiance. She wore her usual shirtwaist and dark skirt. But in the heat she'd rolled her sleeves up to her elbows and opened the neck of her collar. In fact, she looked amazingly cheerful, relaxed, even happy. He tried to remember when he had seen Hannah Kinchman looking so fine.

He said, "Florida appears to agree with you."

She folded her hands in front of her and rested her elbows on the scarred wooden table. "I wish I could say the same for you. You're skinny as a rake and badly in need of a bath, a shave and a haircut. I've never seen you so unkempt."

He ran a hand over the stubble sprouting from his cheek. "I haven't been vacationing at a luxury hotel."

"I know that. At least you've escaped from that horrible turpentine camp. At least you're alive. I'm glad, Oliver. I was worried about you."

He hooted. "You? Worried about me? You're the one who consigned me to that nightmare."

Hannah's brow wrinkled. "You put yourself there. I risked my own neck to give you a means of escape."

"A damned chancy one. Though, I admit I should thank you. It couldn't have been easy to get that boat into the wilderness."

"True. Oliver, let's not argue about what's past. I did what I had to do. You followed your own impulse. Unfortunately, your impulse turned out badly."

"You imply shooting up Haines' party turned out well for you."

She smiled slightly. "In fact, it did."

"May I ask in what way?"

"Later. Right now I think we should talk about your problems. I don't mean Marietta. I'm sorry I brought her up since she's such a sensitive topic. I mean the difficulties you're in at present."

"You mean the difficulties you created for me? That I'm an escaped criminal? That my reputation is forever blackened?"

"Well, yes. But it's not as bad as you fear. Truly. I believe I may have solved that trouble for you."

"Really? How?"

An exhausted looking old woman wearing a food-stained apron brought the mugs of ale and seafood gumbo Hannah had ordered for both of them. Oliver had already imbibed sufficient ale, but to cool his rising temper, he took a long drink. Hannah scooped up a spoonful of the gumbo, savored it, then closed her eyes and smiled. "Um, this is good. Spicy, but good. Aren't you going to have some?"

"I'm too on edge, waiting for your answer. Don't keep me in suspense. How do you think you've solved my troubles?"

She set down her spoon . "Very well. I've been in touch with the office—not an easy thing down here in the wilds. I've had a message delivered to William Pinkerton. I'm sure he'll take care of your legal problems. He has the contacts, and he owes you a favor."

"Who delivered the message?"

She lifted an eyebrow. "That's my affair. Just be glad that it's done."

"When I get back to Baltimore, I won't be clapped into chains and returned to Tampa?"

"I believe that when you get back to Baltimore your reputation will be white as snow, or rather, no worse than it was before you visited Tampa. Now try the stew. It's delicious, and you look as if you haven't had a square meal in weeks."

He picked up a spoon and sampled the concoction. It was good, though perhaps a bit fiery for his taste. He said, "I may be in Baltimore quite soon." Between bites he explained his arrangement with Captain MacDonald.

Hannah clapped her hands. "What a stroke of good fortune! Sounds as if your luck has changed for the better, Oliver. Honestly, I'm happy for you."

"Thanks, but I'm still furious with you. You'll not mollify me with a bowl of soup. What are you doing in these parts, anyway?"

"I've explained that to you."

"You've told me you're here to keep an eye on this pack of Cuban rebels. I wonder if there isn't more to it. In fact, I think you mentioned Marietta to distract me. It hasn't worked. I want to know the truth."

She shrugged. "Actually, something else has come up. But it needn't involve you."

"Would it, by any chance, involve Reuben Spooner, the man I was sent here to find?"

Her expression sharpened. "Why do you ask?"

"Because when I met you tonight I was following Spooner and two other gents —Jake Jaggard and Sir Harvey Lexton. I had dealings with Jaggard when you were my assistant in Baltimore. Perhaps you remember?"

She hesitated, then nodded. "I recall his reputation. He's a con man and a scoundrel."

"True, but the ladies find him charming."

"I have never been charmed by the man."

"Good, because it was obvious Spooner, Jaggard and Lexton were up to something shady. I can't help but think that you know what it might be."

"If I do?"

"Then tell me."

"Why should I?"

"After what I've been through on your account, you owe me."

"Oliver, if you want to get safely back to Baltimore, you're better off not knowing."

He leaned across the table, slammed his fist down and glared. "Don't play games with me, Hannah. Walters sent me here because of Spooner. When I get back to Baltimore I'll have to report on the man. Tell me what's going on!"

"Or what?"

A hand crashed down on Oliver's left shoulder. A gravelly voice commanded, "Simmer down, muchacho. This fella' givin' you trouble pretty lady?"

CHAPTER THIRTY-FIVE

O LIVER used his left hand to pull off his assailant's grip, springing to his feet as he twisted toward him. He found himself staring at the imposing red beak and beady eyes of a large green parrot. "Damn fool!" the parrot squawked. "Hit him with a stick! Poke his eye out!"

The discourteous bird clung to the shoulder of a disheveled personage wearing a torn shirt and canvas trousers so encrusted with spots and streaked with faded patches that the original color of his filthy clothing could only be conjectured. His greasy cap floated atop a head of stringy shoulder length black hair. A full beard, grizzled and uncombed, partitioned his mottled cheeks and large, sun-stewed nose. His eyes, dark irises swimming in twin yellowish pools sewn with red veins, glowered into Oliver's angry gray gaze. "Name's Gator Ned," he said as he reached out to restore his grip. "And you ain't a goin' to forgit it."

Oliver knocked his hand away. "I don't care for your touch, Ned. Keep it to yourself."

"Don't care for my touch, eh?" Gator Ned flashed a snaggled fence of beige teeth. His sour breath plumed over Oliver. "Don't want to have no finger laid on you?" Ned barked a sharp laugh. His parrot squawked out a colorful string of curses. Between shouts of encouragement, Ned's companions at the other side of the room hooted. "Atta boy, Piggles! Tell 'em what's what!"

LOUISE TITCHENER

They were a motley group—one peg-legged, another so battered by the sun his features were lost in a sea of flaky wrinkles and withered tattoos.

"Settle down there you damn fool bird," Ned instructed his pet. He turned back to Oliver. "Bet you plan on laying a finger or two on Missy here, ain't you boyo?"

Hannah rose to her feet and cleared her throat. Both men looked at her curiously. "Sir, I must insist that you leave our table and return to your own."

Ned leered. "Gawd in heaven," he exclaimed. "The lady's got a mighty pretty little voice. Ned come over here to help you out, Missy." Piggles clacked its enormous yellow beak as if to emphasize the point.

"I am not in need of assistance, sir."

"Oh, but I see that you are. This fella' here ain't showing you the proper respect. Now I'm a man knows how to treat a lady. Ain't that right, fellas?" He turned toward his companions who began rising to their feet.

"Sure does," the man with the tattoos assured Hannah with an enthusiastic thumbs up. I seen him treat a lot a ladies. They got some mighty interestin' treatment! Ha,ha!"

The situation that had seemed merely awkward, began to look threatening. It became more so when Ned reached out with the obvious intent of seizing Hannah's wrist and dragging her to his side. Oliver knocked the interloper's hand away. "The lady doesn't wish to be touched."

Ned scowled. "I say she does. I say she can't wait to be touched by a real man." While the parrot shrieked "Hit him with a stick! Poke out his eyes!" Ned shoved Oliver back and lunged again for Hannah. Oliver regained his balance, stepped forward on his left foot, and launched a right uppercut that sent Gator Ned reeling back. He crashed to the floor where he lay looking astonished. Piggles flapped to the ship's figurehead decorating the bar, perched on one of her enormous peeling breasts and chanted "Uh oh, uh oh!"

Roaring curses, Ned struggled to get up. His cohorts bellowed displeasure and rushed at Oliver.

A bullet cracked. Its sharp report froze everyone in place. "Lordy," Ned exclaimed as he finally managed to rise to his knees. "I do believe the lady just shot into that there fishing net on the ceiling. Now put that peashooter down, Missy," he coaxed. "You don't want to get your pretty self hurt."

Hannah aimed her pistol at Ned and reached for Oliver. "Let's get out of here."

Hand in hand, with Hannah pointing her weapon at the unruly sailors, they backed toward the exit. When they were within a few feet of their escape route, one of their tormentors shouted, "Rush 'em, boys!"

Hannah fired at his feet. As the bullet cracked, she and Oliver turned and sprinted into the darkness.

"Why did you waste a shot on him?" Oliver panted as they raced through an alley and back toward the harbor. "That little gun only has two bullets and that was your last."

Hannah had restored her gun to her handbag and picked up her skirts. "So we could escape, obviously!"

"Shooting only made them angrier. They'll catch up with us. We won't have anything but our fists to fight back."

"Not if we outrun them," Hannah panted. "They're a gang of misfits, Oliver!"

Misfits or not, the furious sailors were in hot pursuit. Their pounding feet and shouted threats reverberated in the narrow alley. When Hannah and Oliver finally emerged into the open, she pointed at a pile of lobster crates. Catching her meaning, Oliver steered her behind them. The crates could be used as weapons, he thought. Perhaps if he threw them hard enough at their pursuers, he could do some damage. Or maybe the ruckus would summon help.

Meanwhile, Hannah was fishing in her skirts. "I've got more bullets hidden in a pocket in my petticoat if I can just find them."

Gator Ned and his mob emerged from the alley. The moon had slid behind a cloud, draping their hiding place in blackness. The mob of ruffians rushed past and disappeared into the gloom.

"Well, that was entertaining," Hannah muttered, still searching for the hidden bullets. "Bother, I know I've got them here somewhere."

"Entertaining? The last thing I need is a midnight dust-up with a crew of amorous hooligans. You are one troublesome woman."

She looked up from her fruitless search. "I'll take that as a compliment."

"Take it any way you want. Drop your skirt. We haven't time for the bullets. Let's get out of here before they come back."

"Agreed." She straightened. "Follow me."

"Why this way?"

"Before the ruckus started you insisted I tell you about your three delightful friends, Jake Jaggard, Sir Harvey Lexton and Reuben Spooner. Isn't that so?"

"Yes, but they're not my friends. Nor are they delightful."

"Do you still want to know what they're up to?"

"I do."

"Very well, then come along."

Hannah led Oliver along the waterfront. The hour was late. The crowds giving the area a holiday flavor had thinned into the occasional drunken sailor leaning on a woman he'd most likely purchased, or a lone figure hurrying to an unknown destination.

The character of the harbor had changed as well. Its thicket of masts, which had thrust themselves at the clouds with brio earlier, now shifted uneasily in the murky water. Their shrouds clacked in the rising breeze. A crescent moon slipped behind a rag of cloud, and the night deepened.

"Where are we going?" he asked.

"You'll see."

"That's *Estrelita*." He paused to stare at it. "Appears buttoned up tight now."

"Yes, they've loaded their cargo. They'll be gone at dawn's light."

Hannah proceeded past the centrally located docks, the ones that were in relatively good repair. She led Oliver into an area of the waterfront less populated. Here the conditions were far less pleasing.

The snaggled pilings of the docks, if you could call them that, protruded from the water like broken fence posts. Oliver guessed they'd been beaten to bits by storms and then abandoned. The few water craft tied up at them were small fishing smacks of the poorer sort. Or they were boats that had been forsaken. All was quiet at these desolate moorings— except for a flurry of activity at the far end of the group.

"There are your friends," Hannah whispered, pointing. Very busy, as you can see."

CHAPTER THIRTY-SIX

OLIVER squinted into the darkness. Perhaps one hundred yards off, at the last of the derelict moorings, he saw three figures moving about. It was too dark to make them out. "Those men are Jaggard, Lexton and Spooner?"

"They are."

"What are they doing?"

"Guess." Hannah was obviously enjoying herself.

"I've no time for guessing games. Tell me."

"Here, there's a sail repair shack where we can get a good view." She pulled him behind a hut sheltering spools of rope and rolls of canvas. The moon reappeared. Oliver could make out some of the activity in the distance.

"That looks like Spooner and Jaggard standing on the dock."

"Yes. Appears they're having a serious discussion."

"More likely Spooner is carping about something. Peevishness, that's his specialty." Oliver squinted at a figure stowing boxes of supplies on the smallish sailboat tied to the dock. Lexton? Another figure he couldn't identify walked the boat's deck, apparently checking lines and canvas.

"I think they're getting ready to cast off," Oliver muttered. "Their boat is long, maybe thirty-five feet or so, but very narrow. Four men will crowd it. What sort is it?" He leaned forward, trying to get a better look. "It's got an unusual profile with those straight, flaring sides and hard chine. I know I've seen one like it."

"You've probably seen a similar craft on the Chesapeake where they're more common. It's a sharpie, used for oyster tonging."

Oliver raised an eyebrow. "A sharpie? Why would they take a shallow draft boat into these waters? A shallow draft would surely be unsafe in the open ocean."

Hannah leaned a hand on the shed's weathered wall and smiled to herself. "Well, it's got a centerboard and a very seaworthy name, *Stormbird*. But you're right, it's designed for shallow, tidal water, not for the deep water and heavy weather you could expect in the Atlantic. It's my belief they're not planning to sail into the open ocean. They're planning to keep *Stormbird* close to land and hug the Gulf shore while heading north."

"Back to mainland Florida?"

"Back to the southern tip, the Everglades where the land is like a wet sponge, and the creeks are shallow, treacherous and alive with snakes and alligators. A sharpie will take them further into that kind of terrain than a boat with a fixed keel."

Oliver frowned. "You think they're sailing into the Everglades? Why?"

"For a very good reason, my friend. Treasure."

"Treasure!" Oliver took advantage of the moonlight to glance back at Hannah. She looked happy, excited, very pleased with herself. His curiosity sharpened.

"What's going on? You told me Pinkerton sent you to Florida to keep an eye on the Cuban revolutionaries. How do Jake, Lexton and Spooner figure into that picture? What's the connection? How do you know they are headed to the Everglades looking for treasure? What treasure are you talking about?"

"Curiosity killed the cat." She did not turn her head to look at him, but kept staring at the busy scene on the sharpie's dock. "It's a long story, Oliver, and you have a boat to catch come dawn."

"You haven't led me out here to keep me in the dark."

She shrugged. "It's really none of your affair. You're better off not knowing."

"Too late for that now. I'm guessing the Cubans were only part of your mission. Spooner admitted to me that his family smuggled luxury goods to the Confederates during the war. That family is still in business and probably still dealing in illegal stuffs. Someone arranged the sale and transport of the arms I saw going aboard the *Estrelita*. Was it Spooner? Was that part of the reason he was directed here? Or was it Chester Glass? Or perhaps they're all in on it, including my employer, and I was sent on a fool's errand from the beginning."

Hannah sighed. "Oliver, you've guessed a lot of it. Why dig for more? I promise it doesn't affect you. If you're worried your client is somehow involved, I can assure you he's not. Walters sent Spooner here to investigate the railroad. He had no idea Spooner had an agenda of his own. He sent you purely out of a concern for his agent. You can go back to Baltimore, make your report and return to your family. You record will be clean. Walters will probably pay you well when you tell him what you've been through. Why isn't that good enough?"

Maybe it was, Oliver thought. Maybe Hannah was giving him good advice. He gazed down at her, struggling with himself. He wanted to shake the whole truth out of her. He wanted to know what Jake and the other two were up to. What good would it do him? He'd already been absent from home far too long. He had no idea how Chloe and Mrs. Milawney were faring. They might be in trouble. He had to take this opportunity to get back to them. He had to be aboard *Mermaid* when she sailed out of Key West on the morning tide.

Oliver sighed. "All right. Keep your secrets. I'll leave you here, if that's what you want. I'll head back to the *Mermaid* and stop interfering."

She held out her hand. "Good. You've made the right decision."

"I hope so, but I'm not so sure. I'll worry about you." He took her fingers in his, feeling the fine bones beneath the warmth of her soft skin. He could also feel strength in her small hand. A callus roughened her trigger finger—a reminder that she was more than the fragile woman she looked. He couldn't stop himself asking, "Will you be all right?"

He heard her low chuckle. "That's not a question I can answer."

A rough voice exploded out of the darkness behind them. "No, sweetie, it ain't."

Oliver jerked around in time to receive a blow on his head that sent him crashing face down to the ground. The last thing he heard before slipping from consciousness was, "Hit him with a stick! Poke his eye out!"

CHAPTER THIRTY-SEVEN

"OLIVER!" The voice was urgent.

Reluctantly, he opened his eyes. Hannah's face loomed, inches from his. Black marks streaked her forehead. A furious scowl contorted her eyebrows. Her hair, unmoored from its pins, stuck out in disheveled tufts. Runaway locks dangled against her cheek and swept the torn collar at her neck. One sleeve had been partially ripped from its moorings. She didn't look at all like herself. He wondered if he was dreaming.

"Wake up!" She jiggled his shoulder, then pinched it. "Wake up, for heaven's sake!"

"Stop!" He tried to clear his blurry vision. "My head hurts."

She sat back on her heels. "Gator Ned whacked you hard. I feared he'd killed you."

"Gator Ned?" Oliver tried to move. A bolt of white light exploded behind his eyes. He groaned. "Where am I?"

"I'll tell you. We're in deep trouble, Oliver. We're locked up in the engineer's cabin of the *Margie June*."

"*Margie June*?" The name meant nothing.

"Chester Glass's steamboat, named after a streetwalker as most boats are around here."

"Chester Glass, the smuggler?"

"Exactly."

"What time is it? I need to be aboard the *Mermaid* at dawn. I need to be on my way to Baltimore!"

"Too late, Oliver."

"What?"

"Too late." Hannah made an impatient noise. "Haven't you understood anything I've said? We're locked up in the *Margie June*. She's steaming out to sea as we speak."

"What happened?"

"While we were saying our silly goodbyes, mooning about not paying attention as we should, we were attacked by Gator Ned and his crew. They're Glass's men. Glass is part of the smuggling operation I've been investigating. His thugs trussed us up like hogs for slaughter and fetched us here. Oh God-in-heaven, Oliver, wake up and start thinking before we're both tossed overboard, or worse!"

Oliver struggled into a sitting position. "Why would Glass have you kidnapped?"

"We're both here. We're both kidnapped."

"True, but Glass has no reason to want me. I'm here because he wanted you. Isn't that so?"

She was silent.

He pushed himself up another inch or two. "Why, Hannah? You and the Beauchamps were passengers on *Gypsy Dancer*. Why would its captain agree to take the three of you to Key West at the same time he was transporting illegal ordinance to the Cubans?" He thought for a moment. It was hard with a throbbing head. "Did he know you worked for Pinkerton?"

Hannah's gaze dropped. "Not at that time, no. Rosella convinced him we were just three women who needed passage to Key West. She told him we were all that was left of her family and wanted to rejoin relatives in Cuba. He thought we were harmless females in distress. He arranged for us to go to Cuba aboard the *Estrelita*."

"How accommodating of him. Rosella must have been convincing."

"She's very pretty. He was susceptible to her persuasions."

Oliver started to roll his eyes. That hurt, so he closed them and leaned his head against the wall. "I don't doubt that. But the real reason you wanted aboard his vessel was to find out if it was full of weapons."

"That's right."

"And you did find out."

"I did."

"That susceptible captain, who is in league with Glass, knows you found out. He told his partner in crime."

"Apparently." She sounded irritated.

"Perhaps *Gypsy Dancer's* captain became suspicious when you pulled out a gun and started shooting at the wreckers? Possibly he discovered the truth when he observed you didn't board *Estrelita* with your friends. Rosella or her mother may have let the cat out of the bag."

"All are options."

"Hmm, more likely, the captain was suspicious of you from the beginning. After all, you don't resemble Rosella or her mother. Even Rosella would have a hard time convincing me that you were a relative."

"Rosella is young and beautiful, and I'm old and faded. Is that what you're saying?"

"I didn't. . ."

"Oh, pish! It's not important, Oliver. What matters is that we figure a way to escape."

He took a deep breath. "Let's try and do that." With Hannah's help Oliver struggled to his feet. When he was finally upright, he seized a metal support and stood swaying. Beneath his toes he felt the pounding of the boat's engine as it plowed away from the shore.

He looked around, taking stock of his situation. They were in a tiny cabin furnished with a narrow iron cot and a wash bowl. The room was adjacent to the boiler, judging from the noise. Lining the walls he saw buckets heaped with coal, which seemed odd for a bedroom. Perhaps they had been stowed there for lack of space in the coal bunkers. What little light there was in the congested enclosure filtered through a dirty port hole.

He pointed at it. Hannah shook her head. "Doesn't open. Even if it did, it's too small for a human to pass through it."

"How long have we been locked up here?"

"Several hours at the least. You've been out cold all that time. As I said, I worried they had killed you, that you would never wake up."

"I'm awake now."

"Are you? Are you all right, Oliver?" Her voice trembled slightly. An unusual development in Hannah, she of the steely nerves.

"No, but I'm not dead. Not yet. I need to understand our situation better, Hannah. You're here because you meddled in Chester Glass's smuggling operation. I'm here by accident. Where are we going?"

"I can only guess. I think we're following the sharpie."

"Following Jaggard, Spooner and Lexton?"

She nodded.

"Why?

The clang of feet on a metal stair penetrated the rhythmic thump of the steam engine. The door burst open and Gator Ned poked his head in. An evil grin bisected his face. "Well, well, well, little lady, we meet again. How are you and your boyfriend doin'?"

"Poke his eye out," the parrot clinging to his shoulder squawked."

Ned stepped to one side, and Chester Glass followed him in accompanied by two grim-faced men carrying rifles. Oliver barely recognized the man who had called himself Wendell C. Hartley. Their first meeting on the cursed train to Tampa seemed to have happened a million years ago. Billing himself as a business man, he'd worn a sweat-stained suit and an amused expression. The man who stood with feet planted wide on the heaving floor of the *Margie June* was still short, gray haired and barrel-chested. But his round face was set in harsh lines. As he looked his captives up and down, his flat brown eyes lacked any humor.

"You've got yourself in a heap of trouble, my friend," he declared, focusing his harsh gaze on Oliver. "What have you got to say for yourself?"

CHAPTER THIRTY-EIGHT

OLIVER replied, "What am I doing here? I'm supposed to be aboard a ship headed for Baltimore."

Chester Glass exchanged his grim expression for one of faint amusement. "Mister, I knew the first time I saw you that you were trouble. You're here for being in the wrong place, at the wrong time, and in the wrong company. Your lady friend is a pest." He cast a withering glance at Hannah who glared back. Glass scratched his head. "I can't think of a single reason why I should waste time or vittles on either one of you worthless scalawags."

Gator Ned frowned. "You ain't fixin' to toss her overboard! Ah, don't do that! I don't care what happens with the gent, but I wouldn't want the lady to go over the side."

"Why the hell not?"

"Cause I like her, that's why."

"You like her?" Glass scanned Hannah from head to toe. "What's the appeal? She's a nosy, troublesome, lying bitch, skinny and plain-faced. Let the fish make a picnic of her."

"Ah, don't be so mean, boss. I've got a soft spot for this little gal. She minds me of Miss Parsons, my first schoolmarm back when I was a kiddie."

"That's ancient history."

"True, but I've always had my sentimental side." Ned stroked his parrot's bright green head with such delicate affection that the bird began to preen. "I still think of Miss

Parsons. Always did want to get under that gal's skirts." He leered at Hannah. "I ain't particular. Second best will do."

Hannah glowered. She stood ramrod stiff, tight-lipped and white-faced.

Ned hooted. "Just look at her! 'Pears ready to spit. I like a sparky female."

Scowling, Glass turned on Ned. "Shut your fool mouth! You weren't the best glade man I could find, I'd throw you overboard with her. The *Margie June* ain't no floating whore house. We're on a serious mission."

Though half a foot shorter than the gator hunter, Glass's threat startled Ned. Glass's fist shot out to send the man crashing into a metal strut. The parrot abandoned its stumbling master's shoulder and fluttered to the ceiling squawking curses.

"Shut that damned bird up, or I'll shoot it." Glass reached for the pistol holstered on his hip.

Ned pushed himself upright and exclaimed, "Ah boss, have a heart. Piggles won't bother you none. Wait 'til the job is done, then give the gal to me, and you can take ten percent off my cut."

Glass appeared to deliberate. "You're a damned fool, Ned, but I'll consider it so long as she don't make trouble. What about Redcastle, here?"

"Redcastle? Funny kind of name. Toss him to the sharks. I don't care."

Glass gave Oliver a sour smile. "Any last words before you take a long swim?"

"Throw me overboard, and you'll miss a chance to deal with Jake Jaggard."

"How's that?" Glass cocked his head.

"You've been in league with Reuben Spooner so you know he's a fool who won't stand up to you. You probably don't think much of his fancy English partner, either. But Jake Jaggard is another matter. Mess with him, and you'll find you've stirred up a hornet's nest."

"Do tell. Well I can blast that little boat of theirs clear out of the water. I've got me a cannon. Jaggard ain't going to trouble us when he's blown to smithereens."

Ned nudged Glass's shoulder and cleared his throat. "Boss, we can't shoot your cannon at them, not until we've followed them into the glades far enough to figure where they're headed."

The smaller man's eyebrows jumped up. He turned to eye his cohort. "I thought you knew where they're headed. You came to me saying you'd been catching gators in the glades half your life."

"I have. I know every inch."

"You'd better. That's what I'm paying you for. The deal was you're going to lead me to that loot."

"I can, I will. But glades cover a lot of territory. I got to have some clues."

"You're telling me you don't actually know?" Glass stiffened. A scowl darkened his round face. "What have you been feeding me? A fairy story about treasure."

"It ain't no fairy story. Them three wouldn't be headed into the glades if it weren't real. But they're taking a shallow draft boat. They can get themselves far into the glades. This boat won't go anywhere near."

"Shows you are an ignorant fool. I had *Margie June* special built for wrecking. That's near shore work. She'll go in close. It gets too shallow, we have glade skiffs aboard. We can use those. I thought that was the plan."

"The skiffs will work fine, but only if we use them to follow Spooner and his bunch. If you shoot before the time is right, they won't show us where it's hid."

"They'll show us," Glass declared grimly. "We'll skin 'em alive if they don't!"

"It'll be easier if we just stay far enough out, like we are now, so they won't suspect we're trailing. When they pick a spot, we got to lower the skiffs and follow them in."

"*Margie June* don't do so well in rough seas. She's a tender little lady." Glass leered, clearly thinking of the boat's namesake.

Ned cajoled, "Sea ain't rough today. Not much wind. She'll do fine. We can't let those three know we're after them. They're armed to the teeth. They'll put up a fight. There's only four of us, you and me and your crew. Once we know for sure where Jaggard and his pards is headed, we can deal with them."

Glass stood for a moment, fuming in silence. He turned back to Oliver. Well, maybe you've got yourself a bit of a reprieve, Mister Troublemaker. You say you know Jake Jaggard. What kind of a fella' is he?"

"A dangerous one. I should know, we've been friends for years."

"You're a friend of his?"

"We're like that." Oliver held up two entwined fingers. This was not true, of course. He and Jake had never been friends. Indeed, for most of their acquaintance they'd been adversaries. But he wasn't going to inform Glass of that.

"All right. I won't deep six you now. But you better make yourself useful. Otherwise you'll be fish food." Glass shot his prisoners one last threatening glance, then motioned to his followers. Seconds later the door clanged shut. Oliver and Hannah were alone in the shadows.

She muttered, "Since when have you and Jake Jaggard been soul mates?"

"Since never. It was the only thing I could think of that might preserve my hide for a few more hours." He seized her arm and leaned in close. "Now explain to me what's going on."

CHAPTER THIRTY-NINE

Hannah sighed. "I'll tell you what I know after you detach your filthy hands from my arm."

Oliver stepped back. "All right. Stop stalling. We don't have the time."

She made a business of brushing her skin, as if he'd left a residue, then adjusting her disheveled blouse. Finally, she smoothed her hair and said, "You must know that when the Union finally choked off East Coast Confederate ports, blockade runners changed tactics."

He struggled for patience. "They relocated to Havana."

"Exactly. Purchased contraband in Cuba and made for ports in the Gulf."

Oliver nodded. "What you describe happened as the war drew to a close."

"True, but stubborn rebels refused to accept defeat. They, and their partisans, continued investing in the cause."

"Cut to the chase. What's this treasure Glass spoke of?"

Hannah tried to tuck her torn sleeve back into the seam on her shoulder. When this failed to work, she ripped the sleeve off, crumpled it in her fist and used it to dab the grime from her forehead. She stared down at the dirt streaking the cloth and said, "By this time Confederate money was worthless. To purchase supplies—guns, medicine, every sort of necessity the south desperately needed, blockaders had to carry gold. Lots of gold."

Averting his gaze from her bare arm, Oliver asked, "That's the treasure? Gold from the war that went astray somewhere in the Everglades?"

"A ship named *Hedgehog* set off from the Alabama coast headed for Havana. She was loaded with gold loaned by British sympathizers. A tropical storm hit *Hedgehog* and blew her off course. She sank off Cape Sable, Florida."

"End of story?"

"That was the belief. Until lately." Hannah gave up mopping her forehead. She crossed to the porthole and peered out. "I can't see land anymore."

Oliver wondered why Glass had declared her an unappealing female. She didn't have Rosella's flamboyant beauty. But with her neat figure, smooth regular features, intelligence and courage, she seemed appealing to Oliver. Though, he admitted to himself, after his lengthy ordeal, and in his present predicament, almost any semi-presentable female would seem appealing. Looking away from her, he rubbed his temple. Somehow he had to figure a way to get them both out of this mess.

He said, "You can't see land because Glass must be taking Gator Ned's advice . He's heading far enough from shore to stay out of sight of the sharpie."

"How will he keep track of where she's headed?"

"Telescope, perhaps? Finish the story, Hannah. Are we after *Hedgehog's* gold?"

"All I know is there's a report about a skiff belonging to *Hedgehog*. It was located in the Everglades after a storm cleared a waterway that had been impassable for decades. That might indicate some of the crew survived the storm. They saved the gold and rowed it into the glades."

"Even if the report is true, what's to say the same surviving sailors didn't get the gold out long ago?"

"Three skeletons were found near what's left of the skiff."

"But no gold?"

"So they say."

Oliver rubbed his chin. That clarified how Gator Ned became involved. If he was as familiar with the Florida Everglades as he claimed, he must have heard the rumor. He'd reported it to Chester Glass. But he didn't know the exact location. He thought Jaggard, Spooner and Lexton did. Ned might be in cahoots with Glass because he needed the other man's resources to take Jaggard's crew on.

"How did Jaggard and Spooner find out about this, and what's the connection with Lexton?"

Hannah answered, "Spooner's family has an information network that extends to the Keys. Lexton's family financed *Hedgehog* and loaned the gold it carried. That's all I know, Oliver. As I said before, it's mostly speculation and rumor. I wasn't sent here to investigate lost gold. My assignment was to keep an eye on the gun-running."

"Well, we're both here and up to our necks in trouble. If we don't figure out a way to deal with the situation, you'll be entertaining Gator Ned, and I'll be fighting off sharks."

She swung around to face him. "What are we going to do?"

Oliver eyed Hannah's torn costume. "What happened to your gun?"

"It was in my handbag. They took that away from me."

"Your little peashooter was out of bullets. Back in Key West you spent a good bit of time rummaging under your skirt for a reload."

Hannah blinked. "That's true. Turn your back."

"What?"

"I said, turn your back."

Oliver rotated and stood with his arms crossed. He heard the rustle of garments, then a tearing sound."

"What was that?"

"My petticoat. I have a bag of bullets in a pocket sewn to my petticoat. In the dark last night I couldn't find it. You can look now."

When he faced her again, she was holding a black cotton bag bulging with what looked like dozens of bullets."

"What were you planning to do with all those, start a war?"

"I like to be prepared." She handed him the bag. He stood weighing it in one hand while he considered the possibilities.

"We might be able to do something with this."

"Like what? We don't want to blow up the *Margie June* while we're on it."

"No, but…"

The sound of footsteps outside the door made Oliver freeze. Hannah turned pale and whispered. "They're coming this way. Quick, hide the bag."

"Where?"

"Anywhere! Quick! They're about to open the door!"

CHAPTER FORTY

THE footsteps drew closer. The bolt outside the door clicked. Oliver saw the door's handle twist. He thrust the bag of bullets deep into the nearest bucket of coal and straightened as the door flew open.

He had been anticipating another visit from Glass. Instead, the crew, both clad in sooty overalls, strode in. They cast the room's prisoners a disinterested glance, then each grabbed two buckets of coal and departed. They locked the door behind them.

Oliver and Hannah stared at each other. Hannah said, "They took the bucket where you hid my bullets."

"Yes."

"What will happen?"

Oliver took a deep breath. "Either they'll use the coal tonight or they won't. If they use it one of them may notice the bag. If they don't notice the bag, they'll shovel it into the furnace."

"Then what?"

"We may wind up taking a midnight swim after all."

"Or be blown to bits. You could warn Glass."

Oliver shook his head. "I don't think we want to irritate Mr. Glass. I think we'll just have to wait and see what happens.

"Wait and hope for the best?"

"Exactly. That's what a person does in life most of the time. That's what we'll do."

After several wakeful hours that night, Oliver had just drifted into a light doze when he sensed movement nearby. His eyes flew open and he saw Hannah's outline. She stood looking out of the porthole again.

"See anything," he asked.

"Only stars."

Giving up hope of sleep, he got to his feet and joined her. The stars sprinkling the sky outside the porthole winked like a million sparkling fireflies. No land was visible. He said, "*Margie June* must be staying far enough out into deep water so that the sharpie doesn't know she's being followed."

"I suppose." She turned toward him and lay a hand on his forearm. "I keep thinking that the boat might explode if those bullets find their way into the furnace."

"There's nothing we can do about that. Put it out of your mind."

"Easier said than done. Oh Oliver, what will become of us?"

He considered his answer. "I've been in worse scrapes and survived."

She let out something between a sob and a gurgle of laughter. "You have, haven't you? I'm sorry. It's my fault you're in this pickle. It's my fault you had to endure that terrible turpentine camp. I was too stubborn to admit it, but I knew it was true."

"I'll not argue the point. It doesn't matter now. We're in this together. Together we'll find our way out."

"You really think so?" She leaned her forehead against his shoulder. He patted her back in a way that he hoped was comforting. "Hannah, you're trembling."

"I can't help it. I shouldn't say this, but I'm glad you're here with me. If I were alone I would be too terrified to do anything but shiver in a corner."

"You're the bravest woman I've ever met. You never seem to be afraid of anything."

"I'm an actress. The truth is I've been frightened most of my life."

He thought for a moment. "Your life hasn't been easy."

"No, but neither has yours. You know, Oliver, when I first met you I thought I might be in danger of falling in love with you."

"You weren't, though. There was never room in your heart for the likes of me. Your husband deserted you, but you were still in love with him. That's why you tried to shoot him back in Tampa, isn't it."

She nodded. "Yes. It was stupid, but, yes."

He chuckled. "You're a passionate female."

She lifted her head and smiled up at him. "Too passionate. Sometimes I think I belong in a straitjacket."

"Your husband was a fool to run out on you."

"Granted. But he's not the only idiotic man in the world. You're a fool to run out on Marietta. She's still in love with you, Oliver. I know it for a fact. And you're still in love with her."

"We'll agree to disagree."

She sighed. "All right. But in the meantime, put your arms around me, Oliver. I'll feel safe in them, and I need some comfort."

All the rest of that long night the steady thump of the steamboat's engine was like the relentless heartbeat of an animal hunting prey. Despite Oliver's attempt to avoid thinking about the bullets hidden in the coal, he expected an explosion at any moment. There was none.

At dawn they heard feet on the deck above accompanied by excited voices. A few minutes later they were visited by Glass and Gator Ned. One of the soot-covered crew came in with them carrying a tray with a few scraps of bread, two hard-boiled eggs, and a jug of water. He handed the tray to Oliver who set it down on the bed. Despite the meagerness of the repast, he wanted to fall upon it. More then twenty-four hours had passed since he's had either food or water. The same was true for Hannah. Yet she made no move toward the bed. She stood with her hands folded over her flat stomach staring sternly at her captors. Ned's parrot gazed back from his master's shoulder with matching severity.

Glass laughed. "Go ahead, tuck into your breakfast you two. I know you ain't et since I got hold of you. Be my guest."

"Maybe they don't fancy the food," Ned opined. "It ain't good enough for them." The parrot nodded. "Not good enough."

"Well, it's all they're going to get. This ain't no restaurant."

Oliver poured himself some water and took several swallows. He offered a glass to Hannah. She wouldn't look at it. She kept her angry gaze squarely on her captors.

Glass exploded into laughter. "That woman of yours is the stubbornest bitch I ever did see. If I throw her to the sharks, they'll probably spit her right back up—she's that sour."

"Sour," the parrot agreed.

"Now, now," Gator Ned objected, "You leave her to me. I'll sweeten her cup."

"Maybe you will and maybe you won't," Glass retorted. "No time for that now. Guess what, Redcastle. Your pals have slipped into Oyster Bay. They're out of sight so it's by guess and by gosh now."

"No such thing," Ned countered. "I know Oyster like I know my own backside. There's a bunch of little islands in the mouth, and I been on every one of them. No gold there."

Glass faced Ned. "So?"

"So, once past Oyster you get into White Water where's there's more islands and I know all about those, too. A lot of little creeks run into White Water Bay and they're changeable, depending on the water level and whether there's been a storm. Sharpie could be aiming for any one of those."

"So what do you propose?"

"You take me into White Water, staying out of sight between islands. Lower a skiff. I'll follow them to see where they're headed."

"What will I be doing?"

"You can stay hid behind a island. When I figure where they're headed, I'll come back. We'll lower all the skiffs, wait for them to come out with the gold and then take it."

Glass considered this. "Maybe you're a man of your word, and maybe you're not. I got you this far, and I'm expectin' my reward. I don't like the idea of you alone with gold where I can't see what you're getting up to."

Gator Ned threw up his hands in a gesture of bewildered innocence. His parrot readjusted its position. "Boss," Ned said, "Even if I found the gold with nobody to interfere, what would I do with it? Gold is heavy. I got no way to get it out of here without your help."

"Oh, there's ways. You could rebury it, tell me you never found it and come back for it later."

"I wouldn't do no such thing."

"Maybe you wouldn't, but maybe you would. So I'm sending Mr. Redcastle here along with you."

Ned shot Oliver a scornful glance. "What's he going to do?"

"Two things. He knows Jaggard and his crew, so maybe you can use him to bargain if they catch you. But if you've got any brains you won't let them catch you."

"'Course not. What's the other thing?"

"Other thing?" the parrot squawked.

Glass stared hard at Oliver. "Redcastle, you're to keep an eye on our friend, Gator Ned, here. If he double crosses me you're to report the fact."

"Why should he?" Gator Ned objected. "What's to stop him from hitting me on the head and taking the gold himself."

Glass grabbed Hannah's wrist and dragged her to his side. "She's going to stop him. I'm keeping her here by my side. If the two of you don't come back when I think you should, I'm going to feed her to the alligators. When she's et proper, I'll come after the both of you."

CHAPTER FORTY-ONE

Margie June threaded a torturous course through the scattered confetti of islands guarding Oyster Bay. The islands were small, sometimes no more than hillocks of mangrove sprouting from an oyster bed. Flocks of white birds perched in stunted trees, as if the twisted greenery were studded with living balls of cotton. Sometimes the birds rose up in clouds.

Later that afternoon the boat anchored behind one of a chain of similar islands barring the wide neck of White Water Bay. Though expansive, White Water bay was shallow and flecked with shoals. The Margie June had almost gone aground several times trying to shoehorn into it. Even her captain acknowledged she could go no further. "Not even low tide yet," he muttered. "Wouldn't be surprised if we hit bottom when it's out."

Oliver and Hannah stood on the deck alongside their kidnappers. They watched the crew prepare to lower skiffs resting atop the deckhouse. The day was hot and the sun blinding. The air felt thick.

Hannah showed no sign of last night's distress. Now and then a stray breeze lifted strands of hair off her flushed forehead, but she did not deign to brush them aside. Oliver wished he could put his arms around her, as he had the night before. But in this precarious situation there was no comfort to be had for either of them.

Looking down through the water he could see the shallow bay's sandy bottom. Fish, like blades of silver, glided next to the boat. Nearby he saw a tarpon jump.

Egrets waded among the mangroves. Some stood like statues. Others took wing and transmuted into snowy streaks, whirling up into the intense sapphire of the cloudless sky. A dragonfly the size of a hummingbird caught his eye. It hovered over a reed. Its iridescent wings seemed to sizzle with light.

Despite his uneasiness, Oliver couldn't help but be aware of the exotic beauty of his surroundings. Did this primordial water garden really exist? It seemed like a dream. He desperately hoped it wouldn't turn into a nightmare.

"Well, Redcastle," Glass declared, "I hope you and Gator Ned are going to turn out to be a good team. We'll soon find out."

All three of the skiffs had been lowered to the deck. Though they looked more or less the same to Oliver, Gator Ned spent several minutes inspecting them before selecting the one he would take. "This'll do."

"I should smile." Glass rolled his eyes. "You're the one picked all three. I hope you're not takin' that infernal parrot with you."

"Of course I'm takin' Piggles. We ain't been parted since I won him in a card game."

Glass muttered something about who he thought the real winner of that game had been, then pointed. "What's that trash you got with you?" Glass poked at what appeared to be a roll of oil cloth that Ned was stowing in the skiff alongside a knapsack and several canteens of water."

"I guess you don't go into the glades much, boss," Ned retorted. He slipped a cartridge belt over his shoulder, stuck a Colt Army revolver into his belt along with a wicked looking knife, and picked up his Winchester Yellowboy rifle. A machete hung from a loop on his hip. "A man don't survive long in these parts without he's got skeeter bars and a ground cover." He held out his arm. Piggles fluttered from his perch on the ship's rail and settled onto Ned's shoulder.

Glass shot the bird a baleful look. "I thought you weren't planning to be gone long."

"Hard to say. Depends on what we find. Or what finds us," he added with a sly roll of his eyes as he tickled Piggles under his beak. The parrot cooed.

Ned settled a broad brimmed hat on his head and tossed another to Oliver. "Okey, dokie, lower away. Mr. Redcastle, you and I are about to get real friendly." He shot Oliver and evil grin, then winked at Hannah. "Don't you fret, Missy. I'm comin' back for you. When I do you and me are going to be real, real sociable!"

Late that afternoon Ned and Oliver were solitary on a vast sheet of water. It stretched out in the sun like rippled blue silk. Oliver sat at the bow of the skiff rowing according to Ned's directions. Ned lolled at the stern, taking his ease when not issuing commands. He was surprisingly loquacious, imparting information with the enthusiasm of a newly minted travel guide.

"Guess you never seen terrain like this," he remarked as Oliver wrestled the boat through a patch of weed.

"No, I haven't."

Ned chuckled. "First time I seen the glades I was right gob-smacked. So perty what with the birds, and spider lilies, and water so clear you felt you were lookin' through a glass at all them good-eating fish. I thought I'd dropped into heaven. Soon found out it weren't no heaven what with the bloodthirsty skeeters, giant roaches, spiders, deerflies, sand flies, rats, snakes—and I mean poisonous snakes, snakes that'll kill you dead—gators, crocs. You name it, glade's got every kind of pesky critter you can cogitate. Why, it's even got poison trees. Eat an apple off one of them things, and you'll drop dead in your tracks."

A large dark shape rose close to the skiff. Oliver lifted his oar, thinking it might be an alligator. But this looked like something different. Piggles let out a squawk. Oliver pointed and exclaimed, "What's that?"

Ned chuckled. "Sea Cow. Harmless critters, but big. I've known fellers too long at sea who got to thinking they were mermaids. Believe me, they ain't no mermaid. Got a face on 'em would make a mother cry. Rest of 'em shaped like a medicine ball and weigh a ton. Don't want to go roly poly with one of them babies. Do we Piggles?"

"Oh no!" the parrot squawked.

Oliver continued to stare after it as it turned over like an enormous moss-colored boulder and sank out of sight. When it was gone, he flexed his tight shoulders. "I've been rowing in the hot sun for hours. If I don't get another drink of water I'm going to keel over."

"Don't make yourself useless, Redcastle. Around here a useless man might get pushed overboard like rubbish, unless of course you want to have a dance with one of them sea cows." Sputtering hilarity at his witticism, Ned passed up a canteen. Oliver took a long swig from it. The water was hot and tasted of tin.

He screwed the cap back on the container and said, "I don't see any sign of our quarry. If the sharpie came this way, she didn't leave a trail. Do you have an idea where we're going?"

"I do." Ned tapped his head. "I got lots ideas in this old noggin."

"Since I'm the one doing the rowing, are you going to tell me what they are?"

"Maybe yes, maybe no. Haven't made up my mind."

"Haven't made up my mind," the parrot echoed.

Oliver could no longer contain his exasperation. "Look here, Ned, like it or not we're in this together. If I'm to do you any good you shouldn't keep me blind."

"Not likely you'll ever be a blessing to me in this world, but out of the goodness of my heart I'll give you a clue. We're almost there."

"Almost where?"

"See that little poky branch stickin' out on the water over to shore? Looks almost like a snake head rearing up to strike."

Oliver scanned the shoreline. At first it all looked the same —an impenetrable line of green and brown. On closer inspection he made out Ned's branch. It almost touched the water and did resemble a striking snake.

"I see."

"Make for it."

"Why?"

"I'm sittin' back of you with my gun aimed at your head. That's why."

"Very persuasive." Oliver steered the skiff toward shore. As he neared it, a duck disappeared behind the branch."

"Follow that duck," Ned ordered.

"How? It's solid trees."

"You'll see when we get close."

When they were within twenty yards of the tree, Oliver stopped rowing. "I still don't see how we can get in there. It looks dense jungle to me."

"That's because you're half blind, like everybody else. This is what they call *Snake Eye Pass*. Slip under that branch, and you'll see." The parrot took off and flew to the top of the oddly shaped tree.

Oliver paddled up to the clump of trees, then ducked his head to get under the protruding branch. On the other side, a narrow passage opened that had been invisible.

"See that broke stick?" Ned said, pointing at a freshly damaged palmetto frond dangling into the brown water. "Somebody's passed through here. And it happened lately."

CHAPTER FORTY-TWO

"WHAT makes you think the sharpie came this way?"

Ned grimaced. "Just bustin' with questions, ain't you, Redcastle?"

"Anything could have broken that palmetto."

"Something tall did it. Just look up at the top of the palm next to it. It's been scraped raw. "

Oliver shaded his eyes and cocked his head back. Sweat and sun glare fogged his vision, but when he blinked he was able to see the tree in question did show signs of recent damage. "You think it had a run-in with the sharpie's mast?"

"I think they'd be fools not to take the mast down before wigglin' in here. Could be they are fools. All the better for us."

Oliver tried to imagine Jake Jaggard's flat-bottom sailboat pushing into this hidden conduit. It would be a very tight fit. He looked around and saw other signs an awkward ingress had actually happened—a gouged mud bank, dislodged grasses, several other trees with broken branches. "How did you know to direct me to this particular spot?"

Ned wiped his damp forehead. He filled his hat with brackish water and offered it to Piggles, who took a delicate sip. After that Ned dumped the contents of his hat over his head. As the water made cool runnels through the fine layer of dirt and sweat on his mottled cheeks, he declared, "Lookee here, I been gator hunting in these part for years. So has Foxy Pete."

"Who's that?"

"My old injun gator huntin' pard. Me and Foxy been up this creek a hundred times. It's one of his favorite spots 'cause nobody else knows it, and it's full of gator holes. If he found sign of lost gold, he probably found it somewhere near."

"Is this Foxy Pete the Indian guide with Jaggard and his crew?"

"Exactly."

Oliver mulled this over. Foxy Pete was evidently the person who had detected the skiff belonging to the sunken *Hedgehog*. He'd made the mistake of telling Gator Ned about his discovery.

Oliver said, "So he was your partner. He confided in you, and you betrayed him to Glass."

Ned shot Oliver a cold look. "I'd put it different. I'd say that injun' shoulda' kept his mouth shut. If he had, I'd be none the wiser."

"Shoulda' kept his mouth shut," Piggles repeated.

Ignoring the bird, Oliver asked, "How did he connect with Jaggard's bunch?"

"Got no idee. Foxy must have run off at the mouth to somebody else who put them in the know. But from the looks of it, they don't know much. Tell you what, I bet them Yankee fools abandoned that sailboat no more than a couple hundred yards from here. I bet they're on their way into the glades in a skiff. Start working that oar so we can have a look."

At first Oliver was able to paddle. Soon paddling was impossible. Gator Ned instructed him to stand up in the bow and use the other end of the oar to pole. "It's the dry season," he explained. "Low water so you got to pole your way along these muddy bottoms. Actually, I never seen this creek so high this time of year. Think that storm we had a few months back must have mucked the place out."

Poling through the mud, Oliver inched the skiff along the narrow grass-bordered trail of surprisingly clear water. He could see that it was full of tiny fish darting about among the reeds. Myriad other aquatic inhabitants buzzed, fluttered and hopped in the mud bottom . He surmised, this was the bay's nursery.

As he pushed along, he looked around him, marveling at the change in scene. It was another new and extraordinary world. Shallow water spread across what appeared to be endless fields of grass. The pale green and brown of it seemed boundless, like a never ending prairie of water and sawgrass teeming with insect and marine life. Only an occasional bird-infested hillocks of twisted trees interrupted it.

"Oh, lookee there!" Ned hallooed.

Oliver followed the direction of his pointing finger. He saw the tip of a mast poking out of a clump of scraggly trees and bushes.

"So I was right," Ned gloated. They left their damn sailboat here and now we got 'em. Hot damn!"

CHAPTER FORTY-THREE

Ned and Oliver tied up to a mangrove root. They slogged through knee-high water to a teardrop shaped island . The abandoned sharpie was moored behind the tallest of the trees on the island, but that deformed specimen of greenery, with its misshapen branches and load of smallish apples, wasn't tall enough to hide the mast.

Ned chuckled when he saw it. "I wonder if they know they've joined up to a machineel."

"A what?"

Ned pointed. "It's the poison tree I was telling you about. Eat the apples, you're a dead man. Touch the bark, and you'll burn like you've spent a week in hell. Can't figure why Foxy Pete didn't warn them. If anybody knows a machineel, it's him. He once told me he was the only injun he knew who was immune to its sting." Ned pushed his hat up and scratched his greasy head. "Hmmm. I got to think on that."

Oliver studied the tree. With its shiny leaves and pale green fruit it looked innocent. He shifted his attention to the boat. He saw the word, *Stormbird*, printed on its stern. *Stormbird* was larger than he had realized, perhaps thirty feet or more. It had been rigged with two sails, as cat ketches. The hull was exceedingly narrow. Four men aboard would have been cramped in the extreme. After sailing day and night in such conditions, they would have arrived at White Water Bay exhausted and irritable.

Perhaps that accounted for their miscalculation in forcing their boat into the glades. Knowing Spooner's taste for grievance, Oliver could well imagine the level of exasperation among the other members of the party. *Stormbird's* strained passage into the glade must have been harrowing. "Do you think they've gone ahead on foot?"

"Nobody but a bloomin' idiot would do that. Foxy musta' had a skiff hid somewhere nearby."

"Bloomin' idiot, bloomin' idiot!" the bird mimicked. He'd left Ned's shoulder and was hovering above the machineel.

"You stay offa that tree!" Ned shouted. Obediently Piggles flew back. But he eyed the apples on the ground with interest.

Oliver fingered a dangling line on the sharpie. Some of her rigging was broken away, and one of her collapsed sails had a tear that would blow out in any sort of wind.

"Damn fools," Ned muttered, noting the damage.

"Why didn't your friend, Foxy, warn them?"

Ned took on a ruminative expression. "Good question. Why didn't he?"

Oliver lifted an eyebrow. "He doesn't seem to be living up to his name."

"That's where you're wrong. Foxy got that tag for a reason. He's as slick an injun as you'll meet." Ned studied the boat with narrowed eyes, then looked up at the tree. Still gazing at the tree, he opened his pants. As he urinated on its roots, he said, "Tell you what, Redcastle, we're going to make camp at a place I know. We already passed it, but it's real close. We'll wait there until they come back."

"You told Glass you'd return soon as you knew where they'd gone into the glades. He's expecting us to reappear before dark."

"Glass can expect until the cows come home." Ned rebuttoned his pants. "I'm stayin' right here to see what happens, and so are you." He leveled his Colt at Oliver's belly. "Any objections?"

Oliver didn't think Ned would fire the gun. The noise would alert Jaggard and his crew, who couldn't be that far away given the difficulty of traveling in this territory. "What about Hannah? What will Glass do with Hannah if we don't come back?"

"That little lady can take care of her own self. That's what I like about her. Always did admire a lively woman." Ned guffawed then grew serious. "See here, Redcastle, think on this. Glass ain't no friend of yours. He made you come out here with me knowin' I might take it into my head to shoot you dead. But maybe he did you a favor, 'cause you stand a better chance with me than you ever will with him. Did you know he used to run a slave boat? Must have dumped hundreds of them Africans over because they were sick or dyin'. He'd kill you soon as look at you. In fact, he'd kill any man who stood in his path."

Oliver thought the same was probably true of Ned. Aloud, he asked, "What are you proposing?"

"Could you use a pocket full of gold? This might be your opportunity."

"If Jaggard finds this treasure you speak of, he's not going to share. Believe me, he wouldn't be an easy man to take it from. Even if you could take it, Glass is sitting at the mouth of White Water Bay with a cannon."

"That's true, but I know my way around this country better than him. What's more, I ain't so sure he wouldn't put a bullet in me once he got hold of this gold. I'll take my chances waiting here to see what happens next. I'd advise you to do the same. One thing I learned in this life. You never can tell what Lady Luck has in store. "

Oliver knew he had little choice but to fall in with Ned's plan. The man would shoot him otherwise. Perhaps an opportunity would arise when he could escape. Like Ned said, he'd wait and see what happened next.

They returned to the skiff. Ned guided them to another tiny rise of land not far from *Stormbird*. A ring of mangroves sheltered it. Inside the ring they found the remains of a fire. Ned knelt down and smelled it. "They been here all right," he muttered. "I'm not surprised. This is a camp Foxy and I used many a time." He looked up at Oliver. "We got to get a blaze goin' for ourselves if we don't want to be et alive by the skeeters."

An hour later the sun was setting. Ned and Oliver sat in front of a smoldering fire of black mangrove. It did discourage the mosquitoes whining hungrily just above its small cloud of smoke.

The two men made a meal out of some dried meat and a package of dried apricots Ned had packed. After they ate Ned took out a pouch of tobacco and rolled a cigarette for each of them. Oliver accepted gratefully. The smoke from the cigarette helped quiet his still empty belly and keep insects off his face.

He asked, "Any chance that Jaggard and his posse will come back to this camp tonight?"

"Not a chance in the world. No man who knows the glades, and Foxy knows them, would wander after dark. Glades is full of night hunting critters. They can see you when you can't see them."

An eerie call broke the silence. Oliver had heard it before. "That's a panther."

"Yep. Lookin' for his dinner."

"What's to keep the panther or an alligator from coming up here while we're sleeping?"

"Not much. C'ept I'll have one eye open, and so will Piggles. Won't you, Piggles?" He tickled the parrot who made croaking noises that suggested pleasure. Ned shot Oliver a warning look, "So don't you to do anything stupid." He inhaled and savored a long puff of smoke before blowing it out into a languorous cloud.

After several minutes of quiet in which Piggles busied himself pecking up seeds at the edge of the ground cover, Oliver asked, "What sort of man is this Foxy?"

"Oh, he's a quiet sort. Don't say much. Ignorant people think injuns don't have feelings. But they do, just the same as everybody else. Foxy don't say much, but he's deep emotional about some things."

"Such as?"

"Oh, white folks for one. Hates 'em. Hates 'em for what they did to his people. He used to say I was the only decent white man he knew. Guess he don't say that now that I've double crossed him." Ned shook his head. "Greed will make a man do anything—sad but true." He poked at the fire, then glanced up at Oliver. "This isn't the first yarn I've heard about Confederate gold lost at sea. There was a boat I heard about went down with a golden sword full of jewels. Seems like a fairy tale."

"It's true," Oliver said. "It was *Fanny and Jenny*. She carried a jewel-studded sword meant for Robert E Lee, A gift from the British."

In the dim glow of the firelight Ned's expression turned sour. "The much obliged damned British made a fortune on that bloody war of ours. Most of the damned blockade runners who profited were limeys! I know for a fact a steamer loaded with cotton netted about $420,000. No wonder they sided with the south."

Oliver shot him a curious look. He'd begun to wonder about Ned's background. He knew that people were as much a product of their history as anything else. What had formed his character? It must have been something extraordinary.

It was too late to ask. Ned had begun to make himself comfortable. They'd propped a mosquito net over themselves on sticks pounded into the ground and spread an oilcloth on the dirt. As he stretched out, he said, "I'm going to get some snooze time now, Redcastle. Don't think of sneaking off. I'm sleeping with one eye open, my Colt under my head and my finger on the trigger of my Winchester. Piggles will be keeping an eye on you, too. Besides, you'd last ten minutes out here by yourself in the dark. In fact, what with the panthers, gators, crocs, snakes, and spiders running loose, we'll both be lucky to get through the night."

CHAPTER FORTY-FOUR

NIGHT in the Glades was almost as disagreeable as Ned had promised. Oliver woke up to itching mosquito bites, and the sensation of many tiny feet crawling on him. Their makeshift mosquito netting wasn't bug proof. He sat up, brushed a beetle the size of a mouse off his hand, and looked over at his captor to see if he were truly asleep.

Ned was snoring. Piggles was wide awake. At Oliver's movement, his head jerked up from his wing. A faint strip of moonlight gleamed in one of his beady eyes.

Later on, clouds buried the moon, and a cool wind ruffled leaves and grasses. Sleep eluded Oliver. Even in the dark, he could feel the bird's gaze fixed on him. He sighed and rolled over. Not for long. The wind rose in puffs. Fat drops of water spattered the ground. The rain thickened into a soupy downpour. Ned woke up. "Hell's bells!" he muttered, along with a string of more colorful curses. "We got to put the damned ground cloth over our heads. We got to sit in the cussed mud the rest of the cussed night."

Flurries of wind rattled the palm fronds. A downpour of water blew into their faces, leaked into their clothing, trickled down their backs, and drowned their smudge fire. Piggles hid inside Ned's shirt, letting out a miserable squawk from time to time. The wind kept the mosquitoes at bay—Oliver's only silver lining.

He asked, "How do you know so much about the price blockade runners got for southern cotton during the war?"

Ned was silent for a minute. He sighed and said, "I know because I was one of 'em. Well, in a manner of speakin'. I was crew on one of Glass's slave ships. Later I worked under him running supplies from Cuba. I was just a ignorant orphan child back then with no lovin' mammy nor daddy to teach me better. It was Chester Glass educated me in the evil ways of the world.

He paused again. "I seen some awful things when I crewed for Chester Glass. Made me real cynical, he did." Ned hawked and spat. Piggles gave an unhappy squawk. Ned stroked his head to quiet him.

Oliver said, "Yet you went to him with this story about lost gold."

"'Cause I knew he'd bite. And he did."

"Now you plan to double cross him."

"Just the way I know he plans to do me. See here, Redcastle, I don't mind sharing some of the loot with you if you promise to help me take possession. It'll set us both up for life."

Oliver wondered what Ned meant by "help." Did he expect help to take the form of murdering Jake Jaggard, Reuben Spooner, Lexton, and Foxy Pete? Aloud, Oliver asked, "Will you give me one of your guns so I can protect myself?"

"No. I know your rep with firearms. I ain't no fool."

"Neither am I. That gold isn't free for the taking. If it's found it belongs to Sir Harvey Lexton's family."

"So he thinks." Ned laughed and held out his open palm so that it overflowed with raindrops. "I'd say we're in a real fluid situation here. We'll just see what happens next."

When dawn arrived the landscape had transformed once again. Despite the night's rain, much of the water had disappeared and what had been a narrow creek was now mostly mud. Oliver surveyed the grass stretching into the horizon. It looked almost dry.

"Tide's out," Ned said. "Until it comes back, nobody's getting' out of here in a boat."

"If the tide's out, what's happened to the *Margie June*? Among his other concerns, Oliver was deeply worried about Hannah. What might Glass do to her? And what about that bag of bullets in the coal?

Angry voices floated on the humid breeze. Ned stiffened, almost visibly pricking up his ears. "Sounds like we got company."

"What do you want to do about it."

"Nothin' just now. I got some apricots left in my oilskin. We can chow down on them while we wait."

"Wait for what?"

"To see what breeds." Ned began to paw through the last of his provisions.

"But. . ."

"Look around. We can't sneak up on anybody with nary a tree in sight between us and them. We're hid so long as we stay here. They can't leave without their sharpie. They'll have to wait for the tide same as us."

"What do you intend when they come this way?"

"Don't plan invitin' 'em to my birthday party."

"Birthday party," Piggles said in funereal tones. He appeared equally as interested in the provisions as Ned was.

"You plan to shoot them, don't you?"

"Nope." Ned winked. "Never been a marksman. I plan for you to shoot them."

CHAPTER FORTY-FIVE

O LIVER scrambled to his feet and lunged at Ned.
"You lookin' for a gut shot, Redcastle?" Ned's revolver pointed at Oliver's belly

Piggles released a run of high-pitched curses. Ned, his gaze pinned on Oliver, snarled, "Shut up, you consarned bird, or I'll blow your stinkin' feathers off."

The bird was silenced. Ned glared into his captive's eyes, his thin smile dripping icicles. "Don't get flighty, Redcastle. I don't want to kill you, but I'll do it if I have to."

"Shoot me, and you'll alert Jaggard and his crew. Once they know you're trailing them, it'll be a different game. You'll be the one hunted."

"That's why I didn't pull the trigger just now. Simmer down and neither of us will see harm."

"I won't murder those men in cold blood."

"Why not? It's what you did all during the war. Like I said, I know your rep. You was a sharpshooter. Snuffed out people right and left. You got delicate-minded in your old age?"

"I was a kid."

"Me too. I was a mere babe when I did most of the mischief that shames me now. Not all, mind. I've done some bad stuff since."

"Like what, or can I guess? Glass wasn't the one pushing African slaves overboard. He may have given the order, but you did the work."

Ned's expression regained its frosty menace. "If it eases your conscience, you won't have a choice about putting a bullet into them men. When the time comes, I plan to give you the shotgun. But while you have it between your hands, I'll be standing behind you with my colt. You'll be under duress. Can't blame yourself for actin' under duress."

"I was sent here to protect Reuben Spooner, not shoot him."

"Funny how things turn out, ain't it?"

There seemed no good answer to that, nor much to be done about it at the moment. Oliver had no appetite for breakfast, but he forced down the meager bits of dried fruit that Ned allowed him. He would need what strength he could muster to get through the next hours. And it was hours. Occasionally, voices drifted to them on a damp breeze, but there was no other sign that their quarry was nearby. They had been swatting mosquitoes in hostile silence when Ned spoke up.

"I reckon they must have the gold. Otherwise they would still be out of earshot hunting for it."

Oliver answered wearily. "Then why haven't they come this way?"

"'Cause they can't until the water rises and they fix up that boat of theirs. Damn fools don't deserve to live!"

"Is that how you justify yourself? Nobody deserves to live but you?"

"Redcastle, I might pop you just so I don't have to hear your peeving voice."

Oliver surveyed the strange landscape. The water had risen an inch or two above the mud track that would become the exit Ned called *Snake Eye Pass*. But the sharpie would require more water. It would also require a sail that wasn't torn. The boat had been rigged with two working sails, so perhaps they planned to escape White Water Bay with just one. But Glass was waiting there with his cannon.

He thought about Hannah, a prisoner on the *Margie June*. How were Glass and his crew treating her? Would they blame her because he and Ned hadn't returned? The answer to that was probably yes.

Oliver clenched his fists. "Look here, Ned, murdering these men and making off with their gold is impossible. Even if you're successful, you still have to deal with Glass. When he realizes what you're up to, he'll wait for you loaded for bear. You won't stand a chance."

"Maybe yes, maybe no."

"Meaning what?"

"I ain't plannin' to deal with Mr. Chester Glass—leastways not soon."

"You can't get out of here without dealing with that man."

"Oh, I got my ways." Ned whistled softly between his gapped teeth. "There's a route you can get into open water with a skiff."

"How?"

"Wouldn't you like to know?"

"It can't hurt to tell me."

Ned shrugged. "There's a trail down south end of White Water. Takes you through a little bay, then goin' gets tough. Got to wait for high tide, so you can drag your skiff through wet mud. But it's not that far from open water. If I go out that way, Glass'll never know."

Oliver absorbed this information in silence. It hadn't escaped him that Ned had used "I" and not "we." That confirmed what Oliver already knew. Once he'd done Ned's murderous bidding, he'd be rewarded with a bullet in the back of his head. There would be no sharing of gold. Sharing had never been in the plan. Aloud, he said, "Glass will catch up with you eventually."

"Not if I leave these parts, make my way north, change my name and see a barber. You can do a lot to spruce yourself up with a load of gold in your pocket. Think I'll travel, see the world. Glass will never find me."

"The parrot on your shoulder might spoil your disguise."

"There won't be no parrot. One way or another Piggles will stay here."

Oliver glanced up at the mangrove where Piggles perched in resentful silence. A puff of warm wind conducted angry voices into their hiding place. Ned sat up straight.

"That was close. They're comin' this way. Git yourself ready." He pointed at a log positioned so that Oliver could lie on his belly and take aim with a good view of Snake Eye Pass. What had been a thread of muck now held enough water so that Jaggard's crew had started making their way toward the bay.

CHAPTER FORTY-SIX

OLIVER stretched his six foot length out on the ground. Propping himself up on his elbows, he peered through a gap in the mangroves. With one hand, Ned gave him his rifle. With the other, he pressed the barrel of his revolver against Oliver's neck.

"I'll be watchin' close. Make any move to turn that gun on me, and I'll shoot you dead."

"After you've put a bullet in my brain, I can't help you deal with Jaggard's crew."

"That'll be my lookout. Won't matter to you 'cause you'll be dead. Now here's what I want you to do."

Ned laid out his plan. Oliver was to shoot Foxy Pete first. "Cause he's a injun what carries a grudge, and he don't give up until he's got his payback. So I want him gone." Next Oliver was to take down Jake Jaggard and Reuben Spooner. "I'll do the Englishman," Ned hissed. "Never did like them limeys."

Oliver propped the barrel of the Winchester on the log. As he went through the motions of drawing a bead on Ned's quarry, he debated his next move. Why should he murder three men who hadn't done him harm? Ned would shoot him regardless.

What about Hannah and Chloe? Dead, he wouldn't be able to help either one of them. Hannah would be mistreated and possibly killed by Chester Glass. He dismissed a painful image of her starving to death, naked and violated on some lonely mangrove island in the bay. He concentrated his thoughts on his daughter.

Chloe would be orphaned, and Mrs. Milawney would have few resources to help. Perhaps Marietta would come to her rescue. Would Marietta be sorry when she learned of his death? Or would she be as cavalier about that as she'd been about everything else?

A semblance of Chloe's beautiful and seductive mother flitted through Oliver's head. He brushed it away. Whatever happened, he wouldn't be around to see it. Better to die honorably and do no more evil in this world. His death wouldn't make up for men he'd shot during the war. Nothing could make up for the mistakes of his youth. At least he wouldn't have blackened his soul further.

He decided that he'd wait until the last second, hope that his captor would be distracted by the upcoming commotion, then flip over. He'd try to get the drop on him before he could fire his revolver. If Ned killed him first, the others would have a fighting chance. I'm sorry Hannah he said silently. He pictured Chloe and winced. He'd never see her bright hair and blue eyes again.

Jake Jaggard's party of treasure hunters appeared in the distance. Oliver could smell Ned's sour breath and hear him breathing hard. Suddenly, he felt the man's considerable weight on his back. He'd squatted immediately behind Oliver, caging his outstretched legs between his bent knees and pressing the barrel of his gun into the back of Oliver's head. "Don't mind me," his whispered. "I ain't trying to take advantage of you, pretty boy. Just want you to know I'm close by with my piece at the ready."

"If you don't want to rattle my shot, take the damned barrel of your Colt out of my ear."

"I'll pull it back an inch, but only an inch. Will you look at that. At least them idjits got the sense not to try and sail their boat in this place."

Oliver squinted. Two men were in the creek up to their knees dragging the sharpie. As they drew closer, Oliver saw a third man in the boat, Reuben Spooner. Something was peculiar about him. He was draped over the vessel's side as if he were sick, or vomiting or both.

"Something wrong here," Ned muttered. "That ain't Foxy over the side like a dead man. I don't see Foxy Pete. You think they might've done away with him?"

"How should I know?"

"Maybe they saved me the trouble because he ain't there. That boat don't have no cabin where he might hide." Oliver heard what sounded like Ned scratching his head. His knees bit into Oliver's sides. "I don't like it. I don't like it that I don't see that damned injun."

The sharpie was close enough so that Oliver had a clear view of all three of its crew. Reuben Spooner didn't look good. He hadn't moved since they'd first spotted him. Jaggard and Lexton, on the other hand, were making slow but steady progress dragging their sailboat, though Lexton stumbled in the water from time to time.

"That fella in the boat looks half dead. Bet Foxy fed him some of them machineel apples," Ned hissed. "That would be Foxy all over. Pick 'em off one by one."

"You really think the apples would kill a man?"

"If he was greedy and ate more than one. They don't taste bad. It's only after you eat, you realize."

Oliver said, "Jaggard and Lexton only learned about the gold because Foxy came across the *Hedgehog* skiff. Why would Foxy want to poison them now?"

"That's the thing. Foxy didn't appreciate he'd found a clue to a pile of gold. When he told me some English lord was interested in a old wreck he'd uncovered, and willing to pay good for it, I knew what he might be on to." Ned gave a low chuckle. "You see, a unedicated injun wouldn't know about foreign banks not taking Confederate money. But I knew them limey merchants found it best to ship gold uninsured. I didn't tell Foxy his mistake. Kept it to myself while I figured what to do."

"You hooked up with Glass because you knew Jaggard and Lexton were here, and Foxy was leading them to a treasure?"

"Had to think fast and act quick. That's my specialty, Redcastle, think fast and act quick. Now shut up, and look sharp. They're getting close enough to shoot. Don't you forget that I'm right here behind you."

Oliver wasn't about to overlook that Gator Ned sat on top of him with his knees jammed into his sides and his revolver at the ready. He was a big man. It would not be easy to dislodge him before he could get off a fatal shot.

Oliver squinted down the length of the rifle barrel and considered his situation. A few more yards and Jaggard and Lexton would be easy pickings. Back in his sharpshooter days, he would have been pleased to get such targets. But then he'd been a young fool who considered himself a warrior for a righteous cause. Now he'd just be a murderer. Jake Jaggard, for all his failings, had sometimes done him a good turn. Lexton had done nothing to deserve being murdered.

Oliver gathered his waning strength and prepared to try and heave Ned off his back. Piggles let out a warning shriek. Too late. A shot shattered the anxious silence. Ned yelped and toppled to one side. Liberated from his captor's weight, Oliver rolled over, then froze. A muddy figure stood a few feet off aiming a rifle at him.

CHAPTER FORTY-SEVEN

"DROP the gun or I blow your cracker head off!"

Oliver's gun fell, and his assailant walked forward and kicked it away. It landed a couple of yards off in a patch of sawgrass. Oliver noticed the man's feet were shod in what looked like oilskin bags tied at the ankle. Makeshift boots? He glanced at Ned, sprawled and bleeding on the other side of him, apparently unconscious.

He said, "You're Foxy Pete?"

The Indian didn't respond, but Oliver knew the grimy person glowering over him had to be Foxy Pete, Ned's erstwhile Seminole gator hunting partner. He must have stolen up on them through the grasses while the others made a distracting show of hauling their sailboat. So Jaggard and his cohorts hadn't been fooled. They'd known they were being followed.

Oliver spared another glance for Ned, still inert. "Have you killed him, Foxy?"

"Hope so, stinkin' double crossing snake that he is." Pete prodded Ned's side with his foot. When Ned didn't respond, he returned his attention to Oliver. They regarded each other in tense silence. Foxy Pete was a wiry man of indeterminate age. Black hair streaked with gray framed his fleshless dark brown face. Mud daubed his flat cheeks and the deep grooves bracketing his narrow-lipped mouth. His clothing was so caked with slimy muck from the grasses he'd crawled through that it looked as if he was wearing a suit of wet dirt. His trigger finger tightened on his gun. Oliver realized he was about to be shot through the chest.

"I'm not Ned's partner."

"No?"

"I'm his prisoner."

"Prisoners don't tote rifles. You were fixin' to kill us all with that piece."

"I wasn't. Ned was forcing me, but I wasn't going to."

"White men are all damned liars."

Oliver understood it was no use. He was about to be killed and left in this watery wilderness for the alligators to pick over. He steeled himself not to flinch. He wouldn't waste his breath begging to be spared.

The faint bang of an explosion in the distance rippled through the air. Startled by the unexpected noise, Foxy looked away. Anticipating a shot in the back, Oliver scrambled for the Winchester. He heard the crack of a bullet, but felt nothing. Certain the pain of a wound would sting in seconds, he seized the rifle, jumped to his feet and whirled around.

Foxy Pete lay on the ground, struggling to recover his fallen weapon. Blood spouted from his neck. Ned was propped up on one elbow trying to steady his gun. It wavered in his uncertain grip. A stream of his own gore trickled down his shoulder and pooled around his wrist. He had lost more blood than was good for a man and looked it.

"Help me," he muttered. "Help me shoot the son of a bitch!" He fired off another shot at his old partner. The bullet plowed into the trunk of a mangrove tree. Bits of bark went flying. Piggles, squawking indignantly, fluttered to another hiding place.

Ned emitted a squeal of frustration and squeezed off a third bullet. His round whizzed past Oliver's head. Meanwhile, Foxy had managed to retrieve his rifle. He fired. Oliver saw a piece of Ned's skull fly off in the blast. For a split second Ned stared at Foxy in what looked like disbelief. He collapsed on the ground, and his revolver slid out of his lifeless hand.

Oliver had seen many men die violently. Even in war where death was common, it was not a spectacle to which you ever became accustomed. He'd seen sturdy young boys, handsome and eager for life, cut off by a bullet to the brain. It was better that way, better than being gut shot and lying in agony calling for your mother. Oliver had once put such a soldier out of his misery and suffered nightmares about it for years.

That grisly experience flashed through his mind. He wondered if he would have nightmares about Ned. Moments earlier the gator hunter had been a vital, if obnoxious and evil-minded, man. Now he was a lifeless bundle of rags soaked in his own blood. It was the mystery of life and death, the ultimate secret code not to be deciphered until too late in the game.

Piggles, who had been observing this scene from his new hiding place in the mangrove trees, began to screech curses. Oliver was reminded of a Greek chorus of harpies. So was Foxy Pete. He fired a bullet at the bird. Hoping to get Oliver off guard, he spun around. Oliver squeezed off a round from the Winchester and shot the gun out of Foxy's hands. His wasn't the only round fired. Another gun barked. The mud-spattered Seminole dropped to the ground next to Ned.

Oliver faced the new attacker, then froze. Jake Jaggard stood just inside the fringe of mangroves screening the hillock. He wore a straw hat cocked at a jaunty angle, a cynical smile, and carried a Colt Peacemaker pointed at Oliver. "Olly, old man," he drawled. "Fancy meeting you here."

CHAPTER FORTY- EIGHT

"CAN'T say it's a pleasure," Oliver retorted. "Why did you execute Foxy Pete?"

Jake assumed an expression of wounded innocence. "Didn't you just shoot him?"

"You know damn well I didn't! I aimed at his rifle, and I didn't miss. You blasted the man between the eyes."

Jake smiled sweetly. "If that's true, which I by no means concede, you should thank me. I saved your hide."

"Saving my hide has never been your ambition. You deliberately killed the man. Why? He was your partner."

"That Indian was not my partner. The minute we found what we were looking for he plotted to get rid of us. He fed Spooner poison apples and tried to foist them onto me."

"So you found what you were looking for."

"We did."

"I see." Oliver crossed the glade and took a closer look at Foxy and Ned. They both appeared lifeless. He couldn't detect a pulse in either one. Keeping an eye on Jake, he knelt and retrieved Ned's revolver and supply of bullets.

Sir Harvey Lexton stumbled into the clearing. He bore little resemblance to the dashing British aristocrat Oliver had met in Tampa. Inflamed red bumps mottled his face and all other visible parts of his body. His clothing, ragged, mud-spattered and patched with unpleasant stains, clung to his torso.

Lexton started when he saw Ned and Foxy Pete. "Good God! What's happened here?"

"Bit of an accident," Jake drawled. "Apparently, Foxy did away with the fella' on the ground, then tried to do the same for my friend here. Olly's far too quick on the trigger to stand for that."

"It was not by bullet that did him in," Oliver snapped.

Lexton's eyes widened. "Redcastle? Oliver Redcastle? What corner did you pop out of?"

"I didn't pop out of anywhere. I was kidnapped."

"Kidnapped? Good heavens! Kidnapped by the fellow lying next to Foxy?"

"Yes. His name is Gator Ned."

Lexton took off his hat and considered the scene. He shook his head. "Gator Ned? Such colorful names you American have. Well, I suppose he must have deserved what he got. I know Foxy did. The man poisoned our friend, Spooner. He's been sick as a dog." He addressed Jake. "You really must come have a look at him. I'm not at all sure the man's alive. "

Jake waved his Peacemaker at Oliver. "Come along, Olly. Let's see about Spooner."

Oliver hesitated. Finally, he said, "All right, but I'll walk behind you. I'll keep hold of my guns until I understand your intentions."

"My intentions? Good grief, you sound like a threatened virgin." Jake assumed a woebegone expression. "Olly, old friend, and I do mean that. We are very old friends—though not always on the same side of things. Do you really think I would shoot you and leave you in a place like this?"

"You just did it to Foxy over there." Jake and Lexton had started to wade back to their vessel. Oliver followed them warily, keeping a good grip on his newly acquired rifle.

Jake said over his shoulder, "You wound me, Olly. Foxy was trying to poison all of us, and he was threatening your life.

Though I still think it was your bullet and not mine that dispatched him."

"Dammit, it was yours, and you know it."

"Let's not argue about trifles."

"Trifles?" Oliver felt his blood pressure rising. He stood breathing carefully, trying to regain some composure. "The situation we are all in here is no trifle. I don't think you know the half of it. Chester Glass has a steamboat armed with a cannon sitting at the entrance to White Water Bay, and he wants what you've found. I'm sure he's prepared to blow you out of the water for it. Hannah Kinchman, a female who used to work for me, is another of his kidnap victims. I don't know if she's alive or dead. I just heard what sounded like an explosion."

Lexton paused and declared, "We were wondering about that. What's your notion?"

"My notion is that Glass's steamboat has had an accident. He may be immobilized in the mud, mad as hell and ready to blow you to smithereens when you try to exit this place." Oliver decided not to explain that the explosion they'd all heard might be a result of the bag of bullets he had hidden in the *Margie June*'s coal scuttle.

"Good heavens!" Lexton turned to Jake. "You hear what the man says? We do seem to be in a pickle."

"All the more reason to put our heads together and pool our resources," Jake replied.

Moments later they were looking down at the swollen face of Reuben Spooner. He was draped over the sharpie's rail in an attitude of pure misery, and he wasn't breathing.

Lexton shook his head. "Poor blighter! What a way to go."

Jake nudged Spooner, but got no response. He searched for a pulse, then stood back and shook his head. "He would eat every damned one of those apples Foxy kept pushing."

Deeply dissatisfied, Oliver took a long inhale trying to calm himself. "But you didn't eat them?"

"Pretended to, old man. But no, I didn't. I know about the machineel. Heard stories about men who clung to it during hurricanes and were nearly burned alive."

"Why didn't you warn him?"

"Warn him that Foxy was trying to kill us all when he was standing there with his gun at the ready. I've no ambitions for sainthood, Olly. I wasn't about to risk my life for Reuben Spooner who, I must say, was one of the most annoying sons of bitches I've yet to meet. And I've met and dealt with a lot of annoying sons of bitches!"

Oliver looked at Lexton. "Did you know the apples were poisonous?"

Lexton shrugged. "No, but I've never been inclined to consume the local fruit. And foxy seemed just a bit too eager to foist those apples on us."

"Lucky for you."

"Yes," Lexton agreed, "it was lucky." He shot a troubled glance at Jake. "Though now I wonder why you didn't warn me."

"No reason to, old man. You refused them all on your own."

Oliver surveyed the two adventurers. Was Jake to be taken at his word? It had never been safe to take him at his word before, not when there was money involved. On the other hand, Lexton was a rich man with powerful connections. Killing him would be unwise. Nevertheless, Oliver resolved to watch his back, to keep his gun close, and to be very careful.

CHAPTER FORTY-NINE

OLIVER and Sir Harvey both insisted the dead be "decently" buried. After some objection from Jake, followed by his signature offhand shrug, they spent the rest of that afternoon digging shallow graves in a corner of the hillock that served as a campsite.

That is, Sir Harvey and Oliver dug. Jake spent most of his time dozing against a mangrove. At one point Piggles reappeared to rain down more curses on them. When Jake fired off a careless shot, he disappeared.

"A waste of time and effort," Jake remarked when, hours later, they stood over the graves. "Come night the critters around this place would have picked them clean."

Oliver retorted, "Bugs will pick us clean if we don't get a smudge fire going."

An hour later they sat in front of the fire, breathing smoke, and watching a brilliant tropical sunset. "Beautiful," Sir Harvey commented. "Not so bad to be buried with a view of this sunset."

Oliver mused, "I saw deputies drag a man off the train to Tampa. Spooner told me he'd tried to escape the turpentine camp but failed. I wonder if he was the man on the train."

"He was," Jake said. "He told us about it."

"Why was he going back to Tampa of all places?"

"To meet us. We were waiting for him there."

Oliver glanced back at the spot where they'd buried Spooner and shivered. He turned in time to see the last light of the sinking sun spray pink and orange threads into the haze.

Lexton remarked, "We don't see sunsets like this in my part of the world."

Jake drawled, "You don't see anything like this in England because there is nothing like this in your part of the world."

"Very true and just as well. I'd trade a sunset like the one we're admiring for a pint and a nice hot pork pie in front of my home fire any day."

Oliver said, "I gather, Sir Harvey, you're anxious to get out of here and back home to England. You found what you came looking for."

"Yes," Lexton agreed, "with my friend Jaggard's help. I couldn't have done it without you, Jake."

"My pleasure," Jake replied modestly. "Glad to assist."

"You'll be well rewarded once we're back in England."

"Nothing against rewards, but I did it to help a friend and not for the reward."

"But you'll accept?"

"Wouldn't dream of insulting you by refusing, old man. Never look a gift horse in the mouth, I say."

Oliver listened to this exchange in amazement. Jake and Sir Harvey were talking of dividing up their spoils as if already safely back in merrie olde England. He pointed out that far from warming cups of ale in front of a roaring fire in an English pub, they were squatting on a dirt hillock in the wilds of Florida. Many dangers surrounded them, and Chester Glass blocked their exit.

Jake replied, "I see your point, Ollie. Time we put our heads together."

Through the smoky glow of the fire, both men turned expectant looks on Oliver. He stared back. "You want me to tell you how to get out of here?"

Jake said, "You always were a prince at squirming your way from sticky situations. When last we met the Tampa bigwigs were railroading you into that turpentine camp. A fate worse than death. Yet here you are."

"No thanks to you. As I recall you said you'd help me out of that snag."

"And so I would have, as soon as I'd completed the mission here. But you beat me to it." He winked at Sir Harvey. "See what I mean, Lexton. The man is a genius when it comes to wriggling out of adversities." He turned back to Oliver. "So, what do you suggest?"

Oliver gazed back at Jake, still uncertain of what lay behind his persuasive smile. "I might have an idea or two. I'll have to sleep on it," Oliver said demurely.

"You mean to keep us in suspense all night? Is that kind?"

"I'll be kind when I'm home in one piece. I mean to stay alive all night and get some sleep as well. If you want to leave here without chancing Glass's cannon, talk to me in the morning."

CHAPTER FIFTY

IF Jake planned to exterminate his fellow travelers and steal the spoils, he showed no sign of it. Oliver told himself to stay awake and keep guard, but that proved impossible. He collapsed into a deep sleep.

At dawn he found, to his surprise, that he was still alive. After breakfast on a tin of cold beans, the campers scattered the ashes of their smudge fire, cast a last glance at the fresh graves, and returned to the sharpie.

Stormbird rode gently in two feet of water, enough for the flat bottomed boat to be hauled out of the sawgrass meadow in which she floated— if they made a quick start.

Sir Harvey climbed aboard, lifted a piece of torn sail, and pointed at a rusted metal chest stowed amidships. "This is what we found buried under a rotted log in your godforsaken Florida swamp." Sir Harvey brushed moss off the lid. "We think the crew of the *Hedgehog* must have buried the gold with the idea of retrieving it later."

"But they never did?"

"No, and having spent time in this wretched place, I can see why they never made it back to civilization. No decent boat, no food or clean water. We'd never have uncovered this chest but some of the mud on top had been washed away. When I saw the sun strike a spark off the metal corner, I knew what it had to be. Want to have a look?"

Oliver shook his head and kept a tight grip on his gun. "No thanks. I've seen gold before." Too many men had already lost their lives in the quest for this treasure. He didn't care to add to their number.

"This is a lot of gold," Jake said in his most persuasive tone. "A king's ransom, in fact."

"You're welcome to it."

Sir Harvey lifted an eyebrow. "Oh, but if you can tell us how to get out of here safely, you deserve a share."

"Thanks. When you're both home in England you can mail my share. I'll be most grateful."

Jake cocked his head. "Olly, this distrust of yours breaks my heart. On my honor, I don't plan to do you harm. Sir Harvey is a man of principle."

"Glad to hear it, Jake. I've learned an ounce of caution means keeping your distance and your gun at the ready. Doing exactly that, Oliver explained the southern route out of White Water Bay that Gator Ned had described.

Jake frowned. "You're sure this will work? If we have to waste our strength dragging *Stormbird* over an endless plain of grass we'll perish the way *Hedgehog's* crew did."

"I'm only relaying what Gator Ned told me before Foxy Pete shot him. He seemed confident of it at the time. You can take your chances with Chester Glass if you prefer."

"We only have your word for it that Glass and his cannon are waiting for us."

"That's true. It's a free country, Jake. Do what you please."

"Oh, I will. I always do. What about you? You're going with us, aren't you?"

Oliver shook his head. "I'm staying here."

"Why?"

"Because I have to find out what happened to Hannah Kinchman. I can't leave this place without her."

Jake rolled his eyes. "You're serious?"

"Yes."

"You realize that if Glass is waiting for us, he's also waiting for you. Be sensible. The woman is probably dead by now?"

"I don't know that for sure, and I can't leave until I do."

Jake looked amused. He shot a mischievous wink at Sir Harvey. "Why Olly, have you fallen in love with the Kinchman female?"

Oliver tightened his grip on his rifle, refusing to be distracted by Jake's mockery. He said, "Hannah and I are fellow travelers, which is a kind of love, I think. I can't leave her behind."

CHAPTER FIFTY-ONE

JAKE and Sir Harvey campaigned to change Oliver's mind. They argued that if they tried the southern route he had described, they would need his help to drag the boat across the stretch of sawgrass blocking the open water of the Gulf.

Oliver refused. "If Ned thought he could do it alone, surely the two of you can accomplish it."

Perhaps Jake would have forced the issue if Oliver hadn't been armed. At any rate, there wasn't time to keep up the dispute as the tide was beginning to wane. Naming him "mulish," and threatening "hell to pay" if his proposed route proved false, Jake and Lexton departed without him.

Left alone, he waded back to the graves they'd dug the night before and stood for several long minutes gazing at them. When he was young he had taken death for granted. He had expected to die young himself, so he had dismissed the shadow of the grave with a shrug. That was when he was little more than a child. Now he was mature, with many years and many deaths behind him. Now, once again, the inscrutability of the human condition seized him.

He heard a forlorn squawk, a flurry of wings. Claws dug into his shoulder and a weight settled. He jerked his head around and came face to face with Piggles. The green bird had dropped onto his shoulder. Its yellow beak was inches from his nose. If a bird's eyes can have expression, Piggles' were doleful. "Gone," he droned.

"Gone," Oliver repeated. He raised a hand to brush the bird off his shoulder, but Piggles clung, drawing blood as he dug his talons deeply into Oliver's tattered shirt. Piggles would not be dislodged. Oliver considered shooting him. Perhaps that would be a kindness as there was little chance a bird like Piggles could survive in this wilderness. In the end, Oliver let the pitiful creature stay fixed to his shoulder.

He stowed the last canteen of water he possessed in the skiff he and Ned had hidden in the grass two days earlier and climbed aboard. Other than his two guns and Ned's oilcloth and mosquito bar, he had no more supplies.

Except for the glitter of dragonfly wings, and the occasional splash of a jumping fish, the Florida morning was hot and still. Long legged white birds fished for their breakfasts at the edge of the reeds. They stiffened and stared as Oliver's skiff floated past, but they didn't fly away. He guessed they hadn't seen enough men to be frightened of them yet.

He slipped from *Snake Eye Pass* and into White Water Bay. As he turned the skiff north, he was glad of his hat. Piggles found a scant patch of shade under the triangular brace at the bow of the boat and settled there with his wing covering his head

Oliver saw no sign of Jake and Sir Harvey. He wondered what route they had decided to take. They had been suspicious of Ned's southern route. Perhaps they were ahead of him and planning to take on Chester Glass. If so, they hadn't yet encountered Glass. If they had, he would be hearing the sound of cannon fire. Only bird calls and the rhythmic plash of his oars interrupted the dreaming serenity.

And what of Hannah? Was she still alive? Did he stand any chance of finding her? Why was he risking his life again this way? Wasn't his first obligation to his daughter? Shouldn't he be trying to get back to Chloe before all else?

When he thought of turning away and giving up, he couldn't. He had to make some attempt, however hopeless, to rescue

Hannah. So he kept rowing , ignoring the hunger pangs in his empty stomach, the pain in his aching muscles, and the doubts besetting his brain.

CHAPTER FIFTY-TWO

O LIVER steered a zig-zag route between the tiny dots of land peppering the inlet. Mindful that Chester Glass might be scanning the bay through his telescope, Oliver hoped to hide his passage, at least partially. His indirect course lengthened the journey, but it also gave him the opportunity to see the islands of White Water Bay at close quarters.

They were similar to all the others he'd investigated—thick growths of mangrove laced with palmetto, sea grape and other tropical invaders. Yet they each had their own character. Several had little shell beaches. On one islet agitated birds circled what looked like a dirty gray towel spread on the sand. For a terrible moment Oliver feared it might be Hannah's body they were pecking. When he drew close, he saw it was a dead stingray that had washed up.

Several islands were rookeries. Oliver saw a pair of pelicans skim low over the blue water. Except for their massive beaks, they looked like swans. A moment later they resembled nothing he'd ever seen as they ascended almost straight up and then dropped like arrows to spear a fish. One failed to bring up a catch. The other, successful, flew back to the trees bearing its wriggling prize.

Piggles came out from under his hiding place and watched with interest. "Hungry," he muttered.

"Me too," Oliver agreed. He squinted at the island. White and gray birds occupied most of the mangroves. Where there were birds there were nests. Where there were nests, there might be eggs. He wondered what a raw pelican egg would taste like. Then he wondered how he would fare if a flock of angry pelicans attacked him with their enormous beaks. He rowed past the rookery island.

Keeping to his meandering course, he worked the oars of the skiff until he felt as if his arms might fall off. He was just rounding a largish island when he spotted a dot in the distance. It had to be the *Margie June*. If he could see her with his naked eye, Glass with his telescope would certainly be able to see him. He maneuvered the skiff close to the shoreline where it would be sheltered from view. He decided to wait for nightfall to row any closer. In the meantime he would fish for his supper.

White Water Bay was an angler's paradise. Catching spotted sea trout in its brackish water proved easy, even with a makeshift rod. The hard part was figuring out how to cook them without attracting attention. In the end Oliver cleaned his catch and ate them raw. Piggles accepted a fish filet for himself, then flew off, presumably to vary his diet with seeds. He returned at dusk as Oliver was preparing to make a run to another island close to the *Margie June*. From there he would have to devise a plan for recuing Hannah—if she was still alive to be saved.

With the silver beams of the moon lighting his way, Oliver set off at nightfall. Ahead, he could make out the dark mound of the land mass he aimed for. After landing the skiff, he dragged it into the greenery. Then he waded around to the other side of the island to see what he could of the *Margie June*.

When he arrived at the other side of the island lights from the Margie June glimmered on the water. The crew was awake. The lights flickered at an odd angle. He squinted, trying to make out the condition of the distant vessel. It was only a dark outline against the moonlit sky. It seemed to be listing to one side. Was it aground? Had the explosion he'd heard done it serious damage?

He was mulling this over when he felt a tingling sensation in the back of his neck. He wasn't alone. He whirled just in time to dodge being clubbed. When he wrestled his assailant to the ground, he found himself staring down at Hannah

CHAPTER FIFTY-THREE

A T least, he thought it was Hanna. The mud coated woman beneath him appeared to be wearing nothing but her undergarments. "Hannah?"

"It's me, Oliver. I'm sorry. I didn't know it was you. Oh, I'm so glad to see you. You really are a sight for sore eyes!"

Several seconds ticked past while Oliver struggled with astonishment. He stared at Hannah's muddy face, then he lowered his gaze to her torso. Her formerly white camisole and bloomers were as sheathed in muck as the rest of her. He said, "What happened to you?"

"After you left? Oh, it was horrible. They kept threatening me with unspeakable things. Then the explosion came."

Hannah explained that while she was held captive on Chester Glass's steamship, she had been anticipating an eruption from the bullets hidden in the coal scuttle. She had been laying schemes for what she might do when it finally happened. "Of course, I had no idea what the result of a blast might be, or even if there was going to be one. So I made several plans of action."

Glass and his crew, on the other hand, had been caught totally off guard. The discharge had disabled the steamboat's boiler and driven the ship into a mud bank. They were still working to free her. Distracted by *Margie June's* distress, Hannah's captors paid no attention when she picked the lock on her door, tore of her encumbering skirts and jumped overboard to swim to the nearest island.

"You swam here with no clothes on?"

"Of course. I couldn't swim in a long skirt, and it was my only chance of escape. Besides" she added, flushing slightly, "I do have some clothes on."

"Not many. You're lucky you weren't eaten by an alligator."

"I did worry about that. It's one reason why I haven't tried to leave here."

"What's your other reason."

"I don't have a boat. Are you going to let me up, or are you going to keep me flat on the ground like this?"

Oliver rocked back on his heels while Hannah pushed herself into a sitting position. She made a motion to brush herself off, then grimaced. "Not much point in that when I'm already muddy, is there?"

"I was about to ask you about that. You look as if you've taken a dirt bath."

"I have. It's the only thing that keeps the mosquitoes off. You should try it. They're already feasting on you."

He swiped an insect off his arm and said, "If you swam here immediately after the explosion, you've been here a day and a night. Have you had anything to eat?"

"No. I caught a fish but couldn't bring myself to eat it uncooked. I was tempted to eat one of those apples over there, but there was a dead lizard under the tree. It gave me a bad feeling."

Oliver glanced at the tree she indicated. "You're lucky to didn't eat an apple. That's a machineel. Its fruit is poisonous. Remember Reuben Spooner, the man I came to Tampa to find?"

She nodded and, after giving her a drink from his canteen, Oliver told her what had happened since the last time he'd seen her. She listened with widening eyes. "So Gator Ned, his partner and Reuben Spooner are all dead now?"

"Dead and buried. If I ever get back to Baltimore I'll have some explaining to do."

"What about the treasure?"

"That's gone, too. At least I believe so. Jake and Sir Harvey haven't passed this way, have they?"

Hannah shook her head. "I would have seen them."

"That means they must have taken the southern route out of here."

Hannah threw up her hands. "Oh Oliver, what are we to do? Glass and his crew are bound to come here eventually. When they realize the treasure is gone they'll kill us both. Even if they don't come we'll starve to death."

Oliver squinted at the distant dot on the water that was Glass's grounded steamship. "There's only one thing we can do, Hannah. We'll have to try and slip past them, and we'll have to do it tonight before we're both too weak to do anything but roll over and die."

"I have another question."

"What's that?"

"Where's the parrot you talked about?"

Oliver looked around. Piggles was nowhere in sight.

Chapter Fifty-Four

TWENTY minutes later Oliver showed Hannah the skiff. She looked dubious. "If Glass sees us he'll have no trouble shooting this little thing out of the water. We'll be finished."

"We'll be finished if we stay here. We have to try."

"Even if we manage to get past the *Margie June*," Hannah pointed out, "we'll still be in trouble. We have no food, and we'll need to be out of sight by dawn. Can you manage an ordeal like that, Oliver? When was the last time you had a decent meal?"

He stared at the skiff and then at the distant spot on the water that was Glass's grounded steamship. He came to a reluctant decision. "You're right," he said. "Without food and water we'll never survive. I doubt we can be out of sight by dawn. Glass and his crew can hunt us down. Here's what I think we have to do."

As he laid out his plan, Hannah's eyes widened. "You want us to board *Margie June* tonight, spike her cannon, put holes in her remaining skiffs, and steal food and water? Oh Oliver, how can we do all that without being discovered?"

"We can't. We'll have to hope that they're sleeping when we board. I have a firearm for each of us. If they're asleep we can overcome them, lock them up, do what we need to, and get away."

An owl hooted in the distance, almost as if questioning the sanity of their plan. They both turned their heads to listen for it, then looked back at each other. Slowly, Hannah nodded. "All right, How do you spike a gun?"

Oliver had never spiked cannon such as Glass was using. However, he knew that rendering the weapon useless meant choking up its vent. The best way to do this was to hammer a spike into the vent, then fill the bottom with clay or a plug of wood. Oliver had no spikes or wood plugs, nor a hammer, either.

His gaze dropped to Hannah's shapely legs. They were bare. "What happened to your stockings?"

"One fell away when I swam here. The other was so grubby I took it off."

"Do you still have it?"

She reached into a pocket, pulled out a dirty tube of damp cotton and dangled it in front of Oliver's face. "Why do you care about what's left of my stockings?"

While Hannah watched in bafflement, Oliver stretched the stocking out on the sand and checked it for holes. There were two small ones at the heel. These could be sealed by tying a knot. Otherwise the garment was intact. He looked up at her. "If you'll let me have it, I'd like to fill it with sand."

"With sand? Whatever for?"

"To gum up a cannon."

Hours later, Hannah and Oliver approached the *Margie June*. They had set off in the skiff when lanterns were glowing from several locations on the steamer. By the time they got close only one light flickered on the foredeck. The tide was out. Less than a foot of water covered the mud bank on which *Margie June* was stranded. The ship lay almost on her side.

"So they haven't been able to free her yet," Hannah whispered.

Oliver nodded. "Good news for us. Only one light showing, so probably only one watch posted. If we're lucky he'll be drunk."

"I know they had a good supply of rum aboard," Hannah said.

Oliver stopped rowing. While the skiff bobbed gently in the shallow water he studied the situation. Even if Glass and his two crew members were asleep, it wouldn't be easy to climb aboard *Margie June* undetected. He didn't ask himself if he was even capable of making the climb. Given that he'd had little rest and almost no food, such an athletic endeavor was uncertain. But if he and Hannah were to survive, it had to be done. He speculated that if he went around to the stern of the ship where it listed close to the water, he might be able to haul himself up onto her.

"All right," he said in a low voice. "I'm going to row us close. When we're within twenty yards or so, I'm going to get out and walk to the *Margie June*. With the tide out, I can do that."

"What am I supposed to do?" she whispered back.

"Wait with the skiff until I return."

"What if you don't return?"

"If you see any sign of trouble, start rowing north as fast as possible."

"Don't be ridiculous, Oliver. I'm coming with you."

"I'm not the ridiculous one here. This could go very badly."

"All the more reason I should come with you. I can help you get onto the boat."

"You can't lift me."

"Perhaps not, though I'm stronger than I look. You can lift me. Once I'm aboard I can help you get up. There's a length of rope in this skiff. I can use that to help you once I'm aboard."

Oliver considered her suggestion. A rope secured to the deck might make all the difference. He sighed. "All right. I suppose neither of us is likely to survive anyway." He laid out a plan in which he would silence the ship's night watch and lock up Chester Glass and the other crew member aboard the boat. Once that was done, Hannah would locate food and water while he disabled the cannon and *Margie June's* remaining skiffs."

Nodding, Hannah agreed to the scheme. "We're in this together, Oliver."

"Let's do it, then. From now on, no talking. We're lucky Piggles left us. Sound travels over water, and he's a very talkative bird."

CHAPTER FIFTY-FIVE

CAUTIOUSLY, Oliver rowed toward *Margie June's* stern. Close by, he and Hannah beached the skiff on the mud bank where the steamboat lay on her side. Trying not to slip and slide, they made their way through the sticky mud to the ship's lowest point. *Margie June's* deck was still a good ten feet off the ground. Oliver knelt and motioned for Hannah to settle herself on his shoulders. Since she had long ago discarded her skirts and now wore only pantaloons, this was fairly easy.

She arranged herself on his neck, her arms grasping his ears as if they were reins on a horse. Her legs dangled down his chest, her bare toes just touching the mud. When she settled, he took a deep breath and endeavored to get to his feet. This proved to be quite an awkward operation. Hannah was not a large woman, but Oliver was lightheaded from hunger and thirst.

The stink of the mud and the dead and dying shellfish attached to the ship's hull threatened to turn his stomach. Bracing himself against the ship and ignoring the razor cuts to his hands from barnacles coating its bottom, he took a deep breath and slowly rose to his feet. When he was upright, Hannah demonstrated that she really was stronger than she looked.

Grasping the edge of the deck rail, she hauled herself to a standing position on his shoulders. As her feet dug into his neck muscles, he fought not to collapse beneath her. A moment later he was released from her weight. She had scrambled over the side.

After saluting to indicate she was all right, she disappeared from view. He leaned against the hull, breathing hard. A few minutes later, a rope dropped down. He tied his rifle to it and Hannah pulled it up. Next he passed the r evolver. When that was done, she signed indicating she had secured the rope. He saw her grasp it with both hands as she prepared to help haul him up.

He had doubted she could do it. Once again, Hannah proved herself. While he battled to climb the rope, she strove to pull it up. Between the two of them, Oliver was able to join her aboard *Margie June*.

Walking upright on the ship's tipped deck was impossible. After taking a moment to recover, Oliver passed Hannah the revolver. He took the rifle and the rope. With Hannah following behind, he crawled on his hands and knees toward the bow of the ship. He had hoped to find the night watch asleep. Luck was with him. The glow of the lantern still burning on the foredeck showed both of Glass's crew members snoring unconscious. An uncorked jug of rum was conveniently positioned between them.

Hannah held up a hand to caution Oliver against any sudden move. Then she unhooked what remained of her camisole and slipped it off. Naked from the waist up, she stuffed the tattered garment into the slack mouth of the unshaven drunk nearest her.

He opened bleary eyes and goggled up at her, his gaze widening as he took note of her bare breasts and the gun she pointed at him. Clearly, he thought he must be dreaming. Despite the dangerous situation, Oliver couldn't help but be amused. Nor could he help but admire Hannah's body. She looked attractive in clothing. Without it she was beautiful.

While the gagged mariner lay blinking in stupefaction, Oliver followed Hannah's lead. He removed his shirt and stuffed the sleeve into the other unconscious seaman's open mouth. Before he could react, Oliver rolled him over, planted a knee in his back to control his struggles, and tied his hands to his ankles. That done, he yanked Hannah's captive to his feet and hissed, "Where's Glass?"

They found Chester Glass asleep in the cabin where Oliver and Hannah had been imprisoned. It turned out he was a light sleeper and kept a pistol under his pillow. Unlike his crew, he was not drunk.

While Hannah held a gun to the back of their captive seaman's head, Oliver yanked open the door to the cabin. It screeched against the floor. Glass leapt out of his bed, gun in hand and fired off a shot. A split second later he caught sight of Hannah's bare breasts and hesitated. "God almighty!"

Hannah took advantage of his momentary fluster and fired her pistol. The bullet struck his arm above the elbow. His gun crashed to the floor. Before he could retrieve it, Oliver rushed into the room and hit him over the head with his rifle butt. Glass slid to the floor next to his weapon.

"I haven't killed him, have I?" Hannah asked. She had her weapon jammed into the befuddled crewman's neck.

"No. Just a flesh wound. He'll wake up soon. We need to take his weapon and lock the two of them up in here."

"What about the man on the foredeck?"

"We can leave him lie. He's tied up good and tight."

Oliver seized Glass's gun. While he did a quick sweep of the room looking for any other weapons, Hannah forced her seaman to remove his shirt and pants.

"What do you want those filthy things for?" Oliver asked after they had locked the two men inside the room.

Hannah was already pulling on the shirt. "Really, Oliver, I can't go out to sea in a skiff half naked."

He couldn't stop himself from saying, "You can if you wish. I wouldn't mind."

As she pulled the seaman's pants up to her waist, she glared at him. "I don't wish. Stop being ridiculous, and get on with it!

CHAPTER FIFTY-SIX

WHILE Hannah rummaged for food and water, Oliver poured sand into the cannon. He had just finished knocking holes in the bottoms of *Margie June's* two skiffs when she reappeared. She carried four canteens of water and an oilskin bag of food. She also had a shirt for Oliver.

Forty-five minutes later, they had returned to their skiff. *Margie June* was disappearing into the distance behind them. Oliver worked the oars while Hannah sorted through their supplies. "We have cheese, dried meat and half a loaf of stale bread," she said.

"Feed yourself, then give me something to eat before I pass out."

"I stuffed myself while I was foraging." She handed him a canteen and a square of cheese."

While he ate and drank she took the oars. "Oliver, what if those men die?"

"Why should they?" He pulled on the shirt she'd found for him.

"They're locked in a room, and Glass has a bullet in his arm."

"You got out of that room. If you can do it, so can he."

"I suppose. But what about the man on the deck. You left him hog-tied."

"He'll wiggle loose eventually. I just hope it's not too soon."

No sooner were these words out of his mouth than bullets began to pop. At the same time, wings fluttered over Oliver's head. Piggles settled on his shoulder. Hannah let out a little shriek of dismay.

Oliver said, "I knew it was too good to be true. He's back."

Hannah exclaimed, "Never mind the bird. What about the bullets?"

"I think we're out of range."

"Are we out of range of the cannon?"

"It'll be a while before they get the cannon going."

"That last bullet seemed close."

Oliver returned to the oars. He gave a strong pull and the skiff shot forward. He said, "They have only moonlight to see by. There's no chance they'll hit us. We've gone too far."

Nevertheless, Glass and his men kept shooting. An hour later, as Oliver guided the skiff past a cluster of islands guarding Oyster Bay from the Gulf of Mexico, sporadic gunfire still reverberated faintly over the water.

For the next three days Oliver and Hannah rowed the skiff only at night. They stayed close to the shore and took shelter on shady Mangrove hammocks during the day. He was glad that he'd stowed Ned's "skeeter bar" in the skiff. The screening allowed them to get some rest protected from the clouds of insects infesting the Everglades. Occasionally Hannah rolled close to him, and he put his arms around her. It was a comfort. At her insistence, he kept his rifle close in case a wandering alligator visited. Fortunately, none did.

At first food was not a problem. Hannah had secured the bag full of edibles and Oliver was able to do some hunting and fishing. They joked about eating Piggles, but it was only a joke. The bird kept them amused.

At the end of the third day, they sat eating a mullet baked in the coals of a small fire and the last of the cheese. Oliver offered the third of their four canteens to Hannah.

She took a delicate sip and handed it back. "I know we don't have much water left."

"We don't. It's a problem."

"What's Piggles drinking? I haven't seen you give him water."

"He seems to be taking care of himself."

Hannah sighed, "It's ridiculous to run out of water when we're surrounded by so much of it." She swept a hand indicating the liquid expanse lapping at their hammock. Only grasses poked up from the drowned land they could see nearby.

Oliver finished the last of his fish. Brushing crumbs from his hands, he said, "True, but we can't drink it."

"It looks so clear."

"It's too brackish." He smiled at her. He couldn't help it. Hannah had made herself a hat from the broad green leaves of a plant growing nearby. It made her look like a female leprechaun. A very appealing leprechaun.

"What are you grinning about?"

"You. I never thought I'd find a woman wearing torn pants and a dirty shirt attractive. It must be the hat. With those leaves flopping over your forehead you look as if you just popped out of a lily pad."

She frowned. "Don't be silly. Only frogs pop out of lily pads. We were talking about water."

Oliver shrugged. "I've been hoping for a fresh water creek, but so far no luck. Tomorrow we'll have to stay out on the Gulf after daybreak."

"What if Glass has got his steamer going? What if he's out there looking for us?"

"We'll have to risk it. Staying close to shore in daylight is our only hope of finding a creek with drinkable water."

"What if we don't find one?"

Hannah was right to worry. They might find what they needed. But in all this lonely territory, they might not. He shrugged. "Tomorrow we'll stay close to shore and keep our eyes open. Maybe Piggles will lead us to fresh water."

"I doubt it. So far he's just made a nuisance of himself." She shot him a solemn look. "Do you think we have much chance of making it out of this wild place alive?"

"We've made it so far when the odds were against us."

She chuckled. "That's true. We're a good team."

"We are." He took her hand. It felt small but strong in his. "I'm glad you're with me."

She smiled. "I can't say I wouldn't prefer to be safe at home. But if I have to be here, I'm grateful you're here with me."

Impulsively, he said, "If we do make it home, is there any chance we could still be a team?"

She gazed at him in silence for what seemed like a long time. "Oliver, there's something I haven't told you."

"What's that?"

"Do you remember back in Key West you asked if my misadventure in Tampa had turned out well? I said it had."

"I remember. I thought you were joking."

"I wasn't. After you were sent off to that dreadful turpentine camp, Gilbert came to see me."

"Gilbert, your runaway husband?"

"Yes."

Oliver sat up straight. "What did he have to say for himself?"

She cleared her throat and went on resolutely. "He apologized to me for all our lost years."

"As well he should. The man treated you shamefully."

"He did. But we're both older and wiser. He said he still loved me. He begged me to come back to him, to renew our vows and resume married life together."

"Surely you didn't believe him!"

Hannah eyes looked wet and anxious. Uncharacteristically, her gaze dropped from his. "Oliver, I know you won't understand. I'm getting on. I don't want to spend the rest of my life alone."

LOUISE TITCHENER

"You're not alone now."

"No, we're together, and I'm grateful. But we were forced into this situation. We both know that Marietta is the woman you really want."

"What makes you think you know better what I want than I do?"

"Because I do. Because you're as stubborn as a mule and won't admit the truth. Be honest. Have you ever dreamed about me?"

"I don't remember my dreams."

"Do you remember dreaming of Marietta? I ask because you dreamt of her last night. You said her name."

He opened his mouth to protest, but she cut him off.

"You've never got over Marietta. And the truth is, Oliver, I've never got over Gilbert."

He gazed at her, trying to sort it all out. "That's why you tried to shoot him?"

She nodded. "Yes, I suppose it is. Anyhow, I agreed to his proposition. I told him that after I finished this assignment, I'd resign from Pinkerton and join him in New Orleans. He's there now. He's making plans to open his own theater. If he's successful, we could have a good life together. At least, that's my hope."

Oliver was silent, digesting this news. Finally, he said, "First we have to get out of here alive."

Hannah nodded. "Yes, first we have to do that."

As the sun slipped down, Oliver and Hannah set off in the skiff. They took turns rowing north. It was a warm, calm night, so they stayed far enough out in the Gulf to avoid going aground in the shallows near the shore. Oliver was at the oars when the sun rose. Hannah was asleep, her head cushioned on the bag that held what was left of their food.

Oliver hated to wake her. But when pink light brightened the sky he leaned forward and tapped her shoulder. "It's sunrise, Hannah. We need to row closer to shore and start looking for fresh water."

"Speaking of water," she said, sitting up and reaching for the last remaining canteen. "I think we should both take a sip. I know you've been holding back, but if you don't drink you'll collapse."

He nodded and accepted the container from her hand. After they'd both slaked their thirst and breakfasted on a stale biscuit, leaving a few crumbs for Piggles, Oliver headed the skiff toward land.

Hannah said, "Let me row, Oliver. You look exhausted."

"All right."

She started to move forward so they could change places. Then, abruptly, she sat back down and shaded her eyes. "What's that?"

"What's what?" He turned his head and saw the object in the distance that Hannah had noted. For an instant he feared it might be *Margie June*. Then he realized that wasn't possible. The ship in the distance was sailing. An hour later, as it closed in on them, he recognized the vessel. It was the *Estrelita*. He turned to Hannah and smiled. "I think we might be saved."

EPILOGUE

Four weeks later Oliver paused on the steps of his town-house in Baltimore. He wanted to open the door, but hesitated. Though he owned the house, though his daughter and everything else he held dear was inside, he felt like an intruder. Yet, he knew he was lucky to be here at all.

A merciful fate had blown the *Estrelita* to Hannah and Oliver at the right time and place. The Cuban fishermen sailing her had rescued them. They had provided food, water and clean clothing. Fernando had even given Oliver the welcome news that Pansy and Antonio were happily married. As a crowning blessing, Piggles had taken to one of the sailors and abandoned Oliver.

Fernando was very amused by this. The kindly old man arranged to drop Oliver and Hannah off at a citrus grove south of Sarasota. The owner, who was preparing to ship oranges to New Orleans on his small schooner, agreed to take them along as crew.

In New Orleans, Hannah and Oliver parted—she to report to Pinkerton, then join her actor husband, he to find his way home. Oliver worked on the docks for room and board. He wired William Walters asking for money to pay his passage back to Baltimore and to purchase a decent suit of clothes. While he waited for Walters' response, he visited the theater where Hannah and Gilbert Kinchman were mounting their first show.

He watched the pair perform together and found himself caught in a jumble of mixed emotions. Hannah looked happy, and he was glad. In his own way, he loved her. Fortunately, it was the kind of love that allowed him to applaud the satisfaction she appeared to have found with her husband. He left the theater wishing her well and admitting to himself that she was right. His feelings for Hannah were not the same as the emotions he still harbored for Marietta.

Eventually, Walters sent Oliver the funds he required for the long trip back to the East Coast. When he finally arrived in Baltimore, he reported to his employer. Walters accepted his account of the trouble in Tampa and of Reuben Spooner's demise.

Then, to Oliver's astonishment, Walters presented him with an envelope postmarked London, England. It contained a large check from Sir Harvey Lexton. Jake Jaggard and his aristocratic partner had got safely out of the Everglades with their treasure. The Englishman was making good on his promise of a reward. It was a substantial reward. Gazing at the numbers on the check, Oliver realized that now, for the sake of his daughter's health, he really could afford to relocate out west.

At last, Oliver was home. Taking a deep breath, he walked up his front steps and lifted the knocker. The door opened, and Mrs. Milawney stood gawking at him. As recognition dawned, a sudden smile wreathed her round face. "Oh Lordy, it's you. It's Mister Oliver come home at last!"

She threw her plump arms around him and hugged him so tight that she left him breathless. She stepped back, coloring at her audacity and laughing up at him at the same time. "I hope you don't mind me taking liberties, sir. It's that good to see you, I couldn't help myself," she explained with a wink. "We've been so worried. So worried!"

Oliver took her hand and kissed her cheek. "It's wonderful to see you, Mrs. Milawney. It felt good to be hugged. It feels wonderful to be home." He stepped inside the door and shut it behind him. He looked around, taking in the familiar details of his entrance and hallway. He could smell the fragrance of fresh baked cookies wafting up from the kitchen downstairs. "Where's Chloe? Is she well?"

"Oh she's very well. Very well indeed, sir."

Oliver detected an odd note in Mrs. Milawney's voice. He looked at her closely. She avoided his gaze. "Is something wrong? Are you sure that Chloe's all right?"

"Oh yes, sir. She's fine. It's just that since you've been gone there's been changes."

"Changes?"

The sound of female laughter floated to his ears from the kitchen stairs. He lifted his head in time to see Chloe emerge from the back of the house. She caught sight of him, gave a little shriek and ran toward him. She stopped short, gazing up at him shyly. She clutched a cookie. Her white pinafore had a chocolate stain. She looked like an angel. Dropping to his knees, he called her name and held out his arms. She came to him. "Daddy," she murmured in his ear. For Oliver, it was a moment of pure happiness.

As he breathed in her warm, childish scent and lay his cheek against her silky hair, he became aware of a figure behind her. He looked up and saw a beautiful woman standing with her hands clenched at her sides. Even in the dim hallway her green eyes glinted. Her auburn hair was touched with fiery light.

"Marietta?"

"Hello Oliver. Surprised to see me?"

Taking Chloe's hand in his, he stood up. "Very."

"Mrs. Milawney wrote to me. She said that you had disappeared on an assignment to Florida. I came to take care of Chloe."

Oliver looked at his housekeeper who nodded her agreement. "Oh sir, I was that worried. I didn't know what to do, so I wrote to Chloe's mama. She came right away, and Chloe was so happy to see her."

"How did you know where to contact her?"

Marietta stepped forward and put a hand on his. "Mrs. Milawney knew because I've kept in touch with her. I've wanted to know anything she could tell me about Chloe. Did you ever believe I didn't care about our daughter? I've missed her, Oliver. It's been wonderful being here with her these past few weeks."

"It has?"

"Yes. It has. And I'm going to tell you something." She drew herself up to her full height and looked him in the eye. "I'm staying. I'm not leaving Chloe again. Not ever!"

Oliver was silent, trying to take it all in. The three women gazed expectantly at him. Mrs. Milawney had her hands pressed together as if in prayer. Marietta and Chloe stared at him with anxious eyes. With their bright hair and beautiful faces, they both looked so much alike. Whether Chloe was his biological child or not, she was his daughter. He loved her. And, despite everything that had happened between them, he still loved Marietta. Hannah had made him see that. He could no longer deny the truth.

He shook his head and shot Marietta a wry smile. "If that's the way you want it, Marietta, we'll work something out."

She smiled back. "That's the way I want it, Oliver. That's the way I'll always want it."

ABOUT THE AUTHOR

Louise Titchener is the author of over forty published novels in a variety of genres. Her other Oliver Redcastle novels include: GUNSHY, MALPRACTICE, and HARD WATER. Her Toni Credella series is: HOMEBODY, BURIED IN BALTIMORE, BURNED IN BALTIMORE, and BUMPED OFF IN BALTIMORE. Her paranormal thriller, AGELESS, is about a woman who moves through time without aging and is available as a Kindle ebook on Amazon.